J.R. GRAY

Evernight Publishing

www.evernightpublishing.com

J.R. GRAY

DEDICATION

Patty, Loyalty is everything. I'm one lucky fuck.

ACKNOWLEDGEMENTS

Sal, Thanks for your lists and charts and pages and pages of notes. This book would not have gotten here without you.
Karen, for always helping me make something one hundred times better than it started.
Kerry, this never would have been published had it not been for you helping me get it there a year after I wrote it.
Patty, for picking me up in the aftermath.
Nathan, for always being there.

J.R. GRAY

EVER SO MADLY

J.R. Gray

Copyright © 2016

Chapter One

Madden

"Just fucking do it, you coward." I ground my teeth together. "Jump," I said with force, like the word could hurtle me over the edge. It was long after the last bell, and the mines were deserted. I was alone, utterly alone, and I wanted to jump.

I stood on the edge of one of the countless pits carved into the surface of Harden. The holes spanned a third of the way to the planet's core and stretched as far the eye could see. Ore was the most precious metal in the known galaxy, and it was only found here.

The drop would be a few kilometers, and the chances were good my body would explode on impact.

I could taste oblivion, but it was still too far out of reach.

My hands shook. One step forward was all it would take to end it all. Years of battling with my mind could be ended that easily. I leaned forward, looking down at the blackness. Bile rose from my stomach, and my ears rang. The hard life on Harden had beaten most of the fear out of me, but heights still made me dizzy.

I closed my eyes, inhaling the stifling air which persisted even into the dead of night. I forced my foot up off the dusty ground and pushed it out to hover over the hole.

"Madden!"

Hearing my name startled me. I pulled my foot back quickly, turning around to face the only person I still cared about, Colton.

"The fuck are you doing, man?" Colton's once dirty blond hair was nearly bleached from all the time he'd spent as a diver in the mines. His sunken eyes had bags under them, causing him to look about ten years older than he was, from the neck up. From the shoulders down he was sculpted, pure muscle. He had one of the most dangerous jobs on the planet, and his body showed it.

"Dicking around." I stepped toward him, taking myself further away from the ledge. Like a switch, as soon as I was away from the drop, my breathing returned to normal, and the tightness in my chest loosened.

"You've got issues, Madden." He took a tentative step closer, and I felt like he was appraising me.

"They don't call me mad for nothing." I grinned, putting on a mask. I had no desire to talk about the weight I carried.

Colton was a great guy, but he saw nothing beyond Harden. None of us were ever getting off of this hellhole, and no one seemed to care. I'd seen the rest of the universe. I knew what was out there. But I was pretty sure I'd botched my one chance for escape, hence the stronger-than-usual overwhelming urge to quit breathing.

"Got a race for me?" I prompted when he didn't say more. I was short on credits, but sometimes he could swing something.

"Nah, I got news."

My gut flipped, and I kicked at the dust. "I don't want to know."

"You're gonna want to hear this." There was disappointment in his voice.

A part of me knew why he was sad, but I couldn't believe it. "Don't fuck with me, Colt." I searched his face, but he wouldn't meet my eyes.

"Are you really sure you want to leave?" He lifted his gaze to mine. "Well not that you have much choice now, I guess."

All the nerves I'd felt this morning came rushing back, and my breathing was choked off. "Colton."

"Yeah, you got it, man." I could see the misery written in his features. He'd told me more than once what he thought about what I was doing.

I pushed a hand into my sternum. "Fuck."

"Why do you want to leave? Shit, you could have any job you want here." He shook his head. "You know how they'll treat you when you come back. Is it really worth it?"

He would never understand. He was content, so my boredom with the mind-numbing tasks of digging this forsaken planet went over his head.

"I'll be back."

"Yeah, probably, but as a jumper." The disappointment dripped from him. "You know it won't be the same."

I rubbed a hand over the back of my neck. "It doesn't change anything."

"A'right, if you say so." He turned, shoulders hunched forward. "You got to go, man. They've been looking for ya for hours."

Hours? The test shouldn't have been scored that fast. Days was the usual.

"No one could find ya." He paused. "But I knew where you'd be."

"You always do."

"I'm shocked you're not out racing and trying to kill yourself." He looked over his shoulder as I followed after him.

It hit me in the gut. We both liked to race, but I never knew he'd noticed.

"I'm outta credits after last weekend." I shrugged. No "buy in" cash meant no one would race you. Colton sometimes hooked me up, but this was the first he'd spoken to me since I'd signed up for the damn test.

"If you'd hold down a steady job then you'd have plenty." He swung a leg over his bike and put his foot on one pedal, helmet dangling from his fingertips.

"Looks like a job won't matter for a while."

He stared at the low lights of the city off in the distance. "You really gotta get back, man. You're the first in over a century."

"Has it really been that long?" I'd never heard of anyone who'd passed the test, but there had to be more.

"It's been all over the vids for hours. You're only the second person ever, bro. Big shit. It's going to draw all sorts of attention." With that he gripped his clutch and hit the starter, bringing his bike to a roaring start. "Unwanted attention." He left the rest to me unsaid, but I knew what he meant. He'd used the cover of racing to conduct meetings or some sort for a long time. The engine would prevent anyone from listening so I could answer freely.

"It looks like I won't be your problem now."

"Don't say it like that." He sighed.

"I have my path, and you have yours." It was harsh, but I couldn't stay on this planet another fucking day.

"We could be on the same path. There are things I haven't told you."

"What?" He'd got my attention, even if I didn't want to give it to him.

"Just don't go, I didn't want to tell you until I was sure."

"It's too late. I'm leaving." I picked up my green helmet and shoved it down on my head. Getting on my bike, I quickly started her up, heading towards the start of a new life.

Chapter Two

Jocelynn

Jacob dragged me under broken boards and around barrels of what could only be toxic waste by the smell of it. I'd never been to this side of the city. Our destination was hidden in the ruins of the former grand palace. The floor beneath our feet was rotted, looking like it would give way under the slightest weight, but the tracks in the dirt told me we were not the first to traverse this path tonight.

"Are you sure this is safe?" I asked, sidestepping a sinkhole blocking most of the street. Looking down as we passed, I saw hundreds of tiny eyes staring back up at us. A shiver ran down my spine, and I moved closer to my brother.

"Not even remotely sure, and that's half the fun, Jocelynn." His blue eyes glistened with amusement in the low light. "But you said you wanted to get out and live a little while the Baron and Baroness were distracted."

"Living, in case you are unclear, is the opposite of dying. More so, death by toxic chemicals left over from before the peace, is not an ideal way to go." I shoved my shoulder into him, knocking him off balance.

He stumbled into a tower made of the rusted-out barrels, causing the ones toward the top of the stack to groan and wobble.

Jacob looked at me with the crooked half smile he wore when he knew he was in trouble.

"Oops." He grabbed my hand, squeezing it before he took off running.

I was forced after him as the containers started to crash down in our wake. With every turn he whipped us around, the tide of debris we had disrupted came closer. We were both heavily trained, and I had no trouble keeping up. The only thing holding me back was the damn boots I'd chosen to wear for their style. They wouldn't quit rubbing the back of my heels raw with every step.

Thundering crashes drove me forward, and I kept my gaze on the ground, avoiding the worst of the decaying floor. Jacob gasped, and I looked up to see the containers were starting to tip ahead of us. We were trapped. I froze as ice ran through my veins, rooting my feet to the floor. His name choked up in my throat as my stomach tried to claw its way out of my body. I tasted bile as Jacob yanked at my arm.

"Move your feet!" he barked.

My breathing came in heavy gasps as the first cylinder smashed to the floor a meter in front of us. "No."

Everything slowed, and I saw a door half hidden by scrap. Jacob stood a foot taller than me and outweighed me by quite a bit, but I shoved at his larger body to get him moving. I got him to stumble in the right direction. I darted ahead of him, shoving years of disintegrated garbage out of the way, before we were swallowed in metal and chemicals. Understanding dawned in his eyes, and he kicked the larger pieces from our path. He wrenched the door open before diving through it, rolling to land gracefully on his feet like a cat, while I half cartwheeled in, ending up in a heap.

"Well, we'll have to find a different way back home," Jacob mused when we slowed to a stop, dust billowing up behind up as the avalanche settled.

He kicked the door closed and pushed his fingers into his hair, tousling it as he looked back at me.

"But it looks like we are right on time. I have some … er … people to talk to." He flashed a grin and ducked into the crowd, which appeared not at all disturbed by the din we had kicked up. Talking was probably the last thing on his mind.

I looked down at my muck-covered fingers, sludge caked under my freshly painted nails and sighed. I would have to be up hours early to take care of all this before the Baron saw the state I was in. "Remember why you're here," I said to myself. This should be fun. I turned in a circle looking for a place to clean up before deciding I was going to wipe my hands on my leathers.

I stayed in the shadows, not ready to venture into the light like my brother. He did this a lot, and it showed in the familiar way he greeted the group, but this was my first time sneaking out of the palace grounds. A flash of red caught my eyes. The group Jacob stood with all bore red stars, stapled into place on their jackets. Most were tattered and faded, but the color was unmistakable. I found it odd as it was the exact color of the Baron's house color.

As I lowered my hands to my thighs to wipe them clean, a figure stepped in front of me, blocking off my view of the group. I paused, looking into his well-worn face. He couldn't have been more than three or four years older than I was, but he had the look of one of the desert people. The pigment was rubbed from his skin, a trait only obtained by working in a mine or growing up on one of the outlying planets where the thermal wind whipped the dust into the air, clouding out the sun and bleaching the people. He had to be a member of one of delegations here for the Worlds' Fair. It would be the only reason a miner would come to Trenton.

His chin length dark hair was faded at the ends, the same bleached look as his skin, which told me I had been right about his age. The longer one lived on such a planet, the more bleached the hair and skin became, made worse by the mines. He wore what looked like two days of stubble on his jaw. The color had hints of red, and I wondered if it extended into his hair in the sunlight. He had the build of a man who'd earned every muscle with tireless hours of work. I knew he wasn't an elite. People on this planet were soft. Most didn't even bother with the health facilities, unless they had an obligation to the guard, like my brother and I did. But even with years of combat training, we didn't look like this man did. There was something about back-breaking labor that changed a body. Realizing I was staring, I looked up into his eyes, large and nearly silver, all kindness there, which shocked me more than the rest of him. His eyes convinced me I wanted to know more.

"Let me," he said, pulling a bandana from the pocket of his jeans. He grabbed my wrist, not unkindly, and cleaned off each of my fingers. It was an odd sensation to have someone not indebted to me like a servant was, perform the menial task. He moved to the second hand, taking care to get as much of the dirt off my nails as he could. When he was finished, he didn't drop my hand. Instead he lifted it to his lips and brushed them over the back.

My mouth fell open. I was used to being treated with the utmost respect. Men weren't allowed to touch me. A strange sensation came over me, and my chest grew tight with nervous energy. Hard life equaled hard attitude in my experience, but he was quite the opposite.

"Thank you," I murmured, not really sure how I should react to him.

"I'm Mad, and your name is?"

He didn't release my hand, and I scrambled for a name, as mine could give away too much.

"Or shall I just call you m'lady?" He leaned in before releasing my hand. "As that is clearly what you are."

Was he mocking me? I looked down at myself. Even in plain clothes, he saw right through me. There was no hiding from him, that I was certain of. Another sensation I was not used to. I'd never had anyone look through the mask I wore—even my brother was easy to fool with a fake smile.

"Jocelynn," I said before he could assume anything else about who I was. "I'm bad at this cloak and dagger shit."

"Then how about Jo while you're here?" His lips broke out into a knowing smile.

Where the hell had Jacob gone off to? I could strangle him for leaving me alone.

I wrinkled my nose and shook my head. "No. Do I look like a Jo to you?"

"That bad?" he asked.

"Names bring about a certain image in your head, and I don't want mine to be Jo." I grimaced. I'd never had a nickname. Everyone called me Jocelynn. In fact, those around me got yelled at for calling me anything else.

He stuck his tongue out, an entirely childish gesture, but it made his roguish charm rather cute.

"I am a lot of things, and Jo is not one of them." I gave him a harsh look like I had been trained to give servants who did something unpleasant. I cringed inwardly. It was distasteful behavior, even if it was expected at home. I couldn't treat real people like that, but the look had a whole different effect on him.

He grinned back at me, taking a step closer. "Fine, how about Lynn then?" The corners of his mouth turned up.

Now I knew he was mocking me.

"It's like you insist on labeling me something so awful so no one else will give me a second look all night. Is that your design?"

"No, but damn good point. Shall we stick with Jo then?"

My attitude had the reverse effect on him, like he thought I was flirting.

"There is so much in a name, Mad. I can tell a lot about you just in your choice." And I could.

"I think I am starting to get it. Your wit far exceeds Lynn. I see my dontopedalogy has addled me again." He offered a wink with the sentiment.

I studied him, not answering. He couldn't be a miner, or from out of the outlying worlds for that matter. It was impossible to expect this cultured intelligence of vocabulary from an uneducated world, yet his look said otherwise. He was a puzzle, one I wanted an answer to.

"You don't know what it means?" he challenged my silence.

"I am quite aware of the meaning of dontopedalogy, and have witnessed your propensity to put your foot in your mouth." I folded my hands, unable to keep a smirk from forming on my face.

He gave a low whistle. "And here I thought the only people who frequented underground parties were sex-crazed, drugged out delinquents."

"You assumed you were the single individual here with an impressive vocabulary? That may be the case out on the rim planets, but here a good portion of the young are educated." My mind filled with guesses. Maybe he was the son of a dignitary, forced to one of the rim planets to govern. The Baron usually reserved those positions for men he trusted as they were hard but sensitive tasks.

His intense eyes searched mine as he took the dig appropriately. "I've encountered quite a few on this planet with an affluent upbringing who can't string a sentence together."

"Touché, as I have myself." I paused a second for effect. "It is I who should be shocked, as you come from the outlying worlds. Your accent and vocabulary are refined."

He gave me a slow clap. "Nice save. I almost wrote you off as a bitch."

My lips twitched up again. "I prefer assy."

He made as if glancing around me. "I think I'm going to enjoy your assy."

I burst out laughing in spite of myself.

He waited a moment before replying, "I thought these fringe things were avoided by the likes of you. You know since they are quite often put on by the Reds."

I kept my face blank. Jacob hadn't mentioned them, but I was smart enough to keep my annoyance off my face. Now the red made sense. "I followed my brother here for a promised good time. I stay out of politics." I wanted to stay out of them at least until they were thrust upon me.

"And I followed some from my planet here for the same, but I educated myself a bit before I did." The air between us was thick. "Now, are you going to give me something to call you? I wouldn't want to give those around us the wrong impression of your character, whatever Jo might portray."

I hesitated for a moment. "J, if you must."

He stepped into my personal space, tilting his head to whisper in my ear. "I must."

I shouldn't have liked the feel of his hot breath trailing down my neck, but I did.

He pulled back, all charm once again. "My apologies, J. Can I buy you a drink to make up for the confusion with your name?"

Smooth. "I have no objections to a drink with an entertaining stranger."

He linked his arm through mine and led me toward the shady-looking lean-to bar, staffed by people I wouldn't have trusted with dishes, let alone something I would consume.

"What do you want?" He flipped his comm around so it could be scanned by the crude reader, which was at least three generations out of date.

What had Jacob said about the drinks? It had flown right out of my head. "Er…"

He chuckled and turned to the man waiting for our orders and mumbled something. My eyes scanned the room for my twin. I wanted to kick his ass right about now. He'd always had more freedom than I did, and he readily indulged. I spotted him surrounded by a group of half-naked and sweaty men. I blew out a breath. It wasn't shocking. His secret was well kept from the Baron, but common knowledge among the lower classes.

Mad turned back around with two fizzy, neon blue drinks. There were small tabs in the bottom releasing bubbles that swirled around the liquid, creating a tornado-like effect in the glass.

"Thank you." I took the drink but didn't bring it to my lips, staring right at my brother.

"If you think I'm going to drug you and or try to poison you, you're quite wrong. I prefer your dry wit to unconsciousness." He took a long pull from his glass, and when he lowered it, his lips were stained blue at the seam. "I'm not attracted to unconscious."

His tongue licked over them, which caused my hands to sweat, and I absentmindedly brought my drink up, taking a small sip. It was like a sunburst in a glass. A cosmic explosion bottled and subtly sweetened to perfection. I took another drink, holding the liquid in my mouth, letting the bubbles pop over my tongue.

"Good, eh?" I looked up at him, and he wore a coy smile.

It was nothing, and yet it was everything.

Chapter Three

Madden

"Finish and we'll go dance." It may have sounded too eager, but I'd never been good at concealing my feelings. I wore my heart on my sleeve.

Obliging me, she brought the plastic cup to her lips and pressed her eyes closed as she took another swallow of the intoxicating liquid. When she closed her eyes, her light brown lashes lay against her cheek. She wore a touch of face paint and a hint of glitter on her lids, above a thin professionally applied black liner around her almond-shaped eyes. Her red lips shimmered when they caught the light, and I hoped I'd put the blush on her cheeks. She had long blonde hair tied up in a twist at the back of her neck, and her blue eyes were lively from the ruckus she and her companion had made at their entrance, which had drawn my attention immediately.

"You might have to buy me another drink to get me out there." She wrinkled her nose at the idea.

I had long since learned looks rarely held me to a person. At first glance, I'd expected to find her as shallow as every other pretty face on this planet. She was everything, but I had been here less than a week, and Trenton had already put a bad taste in my mouth. It was fake and cold. I missed the empathy even if it came with the heat and labor of the mines.

Strangely, she hadn't fawned all over me like other girls here had. Her poise never faltered as she threw my jibes back. Her wit was more intoxicating than the drink, and I doubt she knew it. When she opened her eyes again, I could see her pupils reacting slower, as the drink took hold.

"It would be—" But I was cut off by the striking boy she had come in with.

"J, what are you drinking?" He grabbed the glass from her delicate fingers and downed the contents, shooting a hard look in my direction. "Didn't I warn you?"

"If you hadn't left me to fend for myself, maybe I'd know what I was drinking." She reached for my arm, linking hers through it to pull me along as he dragged her off the dance floor.

I knew she was only dancing with me to irritate her companion, but I willingly followed her to where the bodies writhed in the center of the large warehouse. She wasn't intoxicated. Even with low tolerance, the drink shouldn't have given her more than a warm tingly feeling. I had chosen it for a reason. I could feel the young man's eyes on me, and I looked up to find him back with his friends on the edge of the mass of people, staring me down. Their appearances were similar, and I guessed he was her brother, not a suitor. She started to sway to the music, and everything else in the room faded. I was drawn into her, moving in to her personal space to mimic her movements. Song after song we stayed like this, not quite touching but rhythmically reacting to one another on a purely biological level.

We were both sweaty by the time the music slowed. I leaned in to offer her another drink, but she cut me off, sliding her fingers around the back of my neck, drawing me in to close the last bit of space remaining between us. We fell in sync, and I rested my chin against her temple, feeling as if all the blood in my body had drained from my head, pooling below my belt. If she noticed, she didn't care. Forward as it was, I slid my arms around the small of her back, solidifying the connection so we could absorb the feel of one another.

She pulled back, and I tightened my grasp on her, not wanting to let her go just yet—or ever. She kept me close, tilting her head up to look into my eyes. Hers were deep swirls of blue, a raging storm of crashing hues. Before I could stop myself, I leaned down and brushed my lips over hers. I froze when they didn't immediately mold to mine. Lingering there, I was relieved when she parted them and ran her tongue over the seam of mine. I opened my mouth to allow her entrance. My heart picked up speed, and the tips of my fingers tingled as I wrapped my hand around the back of her neck. She gripped me by the ear, moaning softly and rubbing up against me, deepening the kiss. The taste of her frayed my nerves, leaving me desperate like an Ore junkie.

She was yanked out of my grasp. My eyes snapped open, and I growled, seeing the boy.

"What the hell?" he asked.

She looked between us and then focused in on the boy. "Jacob?" The words were calmer than I felt.

I knew it was stupid and forward of me to feel this way over someone I'd just met, but she had been the first girl I'd ever felt a connection with. I didn't want to let it go.

"Keep your fucking hands off, Scab." He shot me a look. "We've got to get going, Jocelynn."

That got me hot in the ears, and I knew I could take the skinny prick. I took a step toward him, but her eyes met mine, and she frowned.

"Why do we have to go?" she asked. "You are never home this early."

"I got a call asking where you were," Jacob replied, keeping his eyes on me.

I could tell he was lying. His eyes darted around seeming to keep track of the Red Stars in the room. I watched him. He had gone from cool and collected to jittery. Something had to have happened. It was the only explanation. She sensed it, too, because she nodded without further questioning, something which seemed to go against her personality.

Her whole face fell, and she turned to me. "I have to go." She didn't wait for a reply, letting Jacob lead her away.

I reached a hand out for her, but I didn't follow. I knew I wasn't near her league. The mirage was a punishment sent by the universe for my past transgressions. The room moved around me, but I stood still, watching how meaningless this all was.

My chest ached, and I craved the idea of her. Intelligent and unobstructed by class, she wasn't worried about saying the wrong thing. On a planet with four million people, a million of them in this city, could I have any hope of finding her again?

Chapter Four

Jocelynn

"I feel like a pincushion," I groaned in frustration.

A sharp pin stabbed my side. I grunted, certain the tailor stuck me on purpose.

"But you look so lovely." Jacob leaned against the doorframe, sinking his teeth into an abba fruit and letting the juice run down his neck, not bothering to wipe it.

I held up my middle finger and smiled sardonically.

"One of these days you're going to have to learn how to be a lady. Half the known universe depends on it." He licked at his lips.

"Sometimes I wish you were born first."

"And I thank all the great powers of the universe I wasn't, so I'm free to fuck off," he shot back.

We both knew with his "defective" attributes, as the Baron saw them, it was better for him not to be required in the spotlight.

"Clean yourself up. You have juice running to your collar." I pursed my lips. "Just because you are second doesn't mean you won't be subjected to as much prodding as I am." I growled and shot another look at the little man fixing my clothes who'd stuck me again. I tried to be nice to every last person who worked for us, but because of all the tight clothes the tailor was on my last nerve. He didn't so much like my unladylike behavior.

The tailor muttered apologetically and shrugged, but I saw his smirk.

"Be happy you didn't smell my breath before the fruit." He took a step closer to me, grinning wickedly, as he wiped his fingers on a bolt of expensive fabric behind the tailor's back.

I laughed in spite of myself. "Gross, I didn't need to know about your early morning activities." We both knew I was curious.

"Don't be jealous. I saw how you looked at that scab last night." He played it off as he smoothed his fingers over the day of stubble around his mouth, wicking away what was left of the juice, but there was a hint of something there.

"Says the boy who undoubtedly sucked a slave's cock this morning?"

There was a moment of thick tension, and the tailor looked between us. I didn't back down.

He pushed his tongue into the side of his cheek, grinning coyly. "I've never agreed with the separation of classes as such."

I rolled my eyes. "Then why did you take issue with the scab?"

I knew he had as many friends and lovers among the slaves and scabs as he did inside our own sect.

"Because he wanted to fuck my sister."

"I've never thought of you as the possessive type," I said.

The tailor finished with me and nodded, helping me out of the uncomfortable heap of fabric before gesturing for Jacob to take my place on the pedestal.

"Don't use that fabric." He waved at the one he had smeared juice on and glanced at my dress. "The Barron wishes for us to complement each other while he stands alone in the house red."

The tailor barked at him in common, so fast I had a hard time following.

"Yes, yes, I know he originally wanted me in the red, but we are to be presented at the aging ceremony, and he wants us to look striking together." He winked at me. "The white and purple like my sister's gown will look better with my alabaster skin tone, don't you agree?"

The only reason I wasn't wearing it was because the Baron had forbidden it until I was named as his successor.

The tailor said something about having said so in the first place and went about his work.

"You are so bad," I said when the man stepped away.

"But at least I won't be washed out in red." He shrugged coyly. "We have the worst house colors for our complexion."

I tried to resist the smile spreading over my lips.

"See, you know how the Baron looks on the vids!" He bounced his brows. "Looks like a Scilian fruit." He held his arms out in front of his stomach and puffed out his cheeks.

I repressed a laugh. "Hurry up. We have orientation to get to." I ducked out of the room to pull on a large cotton shirt with sleeves that passed below the tips of my fingers and a pair of wool pants that tapered down my legs, hugging them to my ankles.

When I walked back in the room, Jacob was back in his clothes and waiting.

"Damn, boys get off easy."

He offered his arm, and I took it. We didn't have far to go as the palace was placed across the great square from the Imperial Institute. I pulled my jacket tighter around me and left my shirt hanging around the tips of my fingers. I would have caught hell for going dressed this way to an official event, but the last thing I wanted was to stand out in a place I'd been attending for years. I already had to be a public face for the House of Akillie. There were some places I tried to hide in plain sight.

The sun shone through the thin layer of clouds that lingered high up in the atmosphere, causing the bright red glow of the sun to turn the skin an amber hue in the full light. The star above Trenton was dying. Black cracks spidered over the surface, and it cooled by the year, but the home world was such a pride to the Akillie house they refused to abandon it. My boots clicked over the large gray stones that made up the square. They were mined from Becca, one of the hot planets, at the rim of known space and brought in as a sign of wealth. It was one of the planets in Akillie rule and possibly where Mad had come from. I wondered if I would see him again.

He had to be here to work the Worlds' Fair. It was unlikely I would cross his path again. But I wanted to.

He felt so familiar, while at the same time exciting and exotic. Behind my closed eyes, I could see the way he looked at me before he touched our lips together. My lips burned in memory. I licked over them, inhaling, almost thinking I could bring back his scent. Instead I inhaled the clean ocean air I breathed in and out every day.

"Come on, we are going to be late." Jacob dragged me up the large stone stairs, out of my fantasy.

We took seats toward the back, with some of our friends. My brother liked to sit here so we could make an easy escape when the time came, or leave early if he got bored. I tended to zone out during these things so it never bothered me. It was more a formality I attend than anything. My whole existence was tailored to this life. If I didn't know it at this point, I wouldn't.

I stirred, feeling eyes on me, and I scanned the coliseum-shaped room to see if someone had turned in their seat to stare at me. It wasn't until my eyes reached the edge of the aisle we sat in that I saw him.

Chapter Five

Madden

My mind hadn't left her in two nights. I ran through our conversation over and over in my head. Why hadn't I asked for her scan? Why hadn't I gone with her? I tried not to live in past actions, but I found it impossible not to run through every scenario that would have left me with a way to contact her. I had myself so turned around and distracted, I almost missed my first lecture. The morning bells rang, and I had minutes to get in and take a seat. I slipped into a row near the back to avoid unwanted attention. Already out of place with these people, the last thing I wanted was to be anything but background noise.

I scanned the row to see what I'd gotten myself into. There wasn't a single face like mine. Deep down I'd known it would be the case, but it was harder in person. Like a moth to the flame, my eyes fell on her. Not four seats down, she sat with Jacob. She looked up at the same moment.

"J…" I didn't know what to say to her. I'd run through a million things from that night, but not one plan of attack for this occurrence.

She looked down at herself for a moment like she was nervous, but she replaced the mask over her emotions and looked me in the eyes. I moved closer.

"You're a jumper. Interesting." She stood and took a step toward me like I was a game that became much more intriguing.

Her brother laid a hand on her shoulder. They exchanged something in a look.

"You worry too much. Let's go sit with him." She turned to me. "If that's okay, Mad?"

I was stunned, but I did my best to keep my guard up as well. "Please do."

They followed me back to my seat, and we blended into the crowd as the spaces around us filled in.

"More than a scab, I see," Jacob said. "And here I thought you were only here for the fair."

"Some people are more than they seem," I commented looking at J, holding my hand out to her. "I'm Madden, and since we'll be seeing more of each other, it might be better to be on a first name basis."

She placed her hand in mine, but she had changed. As if dictated by protocol, she slipped into an almost regal figure. She must have been the daughter of some dignitary or adviser to the House of Akillie. The breeding seemed so ingrained it had to be instilled with generations of snobbery.

"J. Let's stick with J."

I hadn't noticed it before, but her voice was articulate. It spoke of her birthright. She wasn't a jumper. She wasn't here because she had earned her place like I had. She was here because her place was garnered at conception, but it hadn't changed her. She treated me like anyone else from the moment I met her, while her brother seemed to hold some air of pretension. It was a puzzle I turned over in my mind. I wanted to figure her out as much as she did me.

I brought her hand to my lips and kissed it. Her cheeks pinked a little, and I had to wonder if the reaction was also training.

"You forget I already know what to call you, but if you prefer J." I half shrugged, wondering what the big deal was.

"Today I want to be just J. It's easier."

My mind spun. Jacob rolled his eyes. J's lip curled up, and she scowled at him.

"What does your name matter?" I released her hand, drawing her attention back to me.

She scooted to the edge of her seat, bringing her face closer to mine. I was suddenly hot, remembering how she tasted. "Because we are no more than equals sitting here, and I don't want to change your perception of me."

Usually the class division stuck, even at university. But then Jacob had seemed to know all the "scabs" as he had put it the other night, and was more than friendly with a few I knew resided in my building. It struck me his bias wasn't against me, or my kind, but against anyone talking to her. It was the only fitting explanation.

"I knew you were of noble birth the moment you spoke. You play the part well, but you have tells." It was a white lie, but I'd figured her out. I turned into her a little, inhaling her scent, stifling the moan threatening to leave my lips.

"Can you be sure it's not the other way around? I could be of low birth with years of training." She cocked her head to the side.

I leaned even closer, taking a chance in the packed room and trailed my fingers down her spine. "I don't think anything less than a century of pure bloodlines and rigorous poise could have produced a more perfect act. It's impossible." I met her gaze.

"Then why didn't you dismiss me when you saw through my mask?"

Because I'm wearing one myself.

"Because I've seen what's hiding inside, and it's not the usual elitist crap. You fascinate me." I dropped my voice to a whisper. "You're not like them." I nodded at the rest of the room.

She turned into me, her lips nearly touching my ear. "How do you know?"

"Because I've worn a mask my whole life, so I can see right through yours."

Her soft cheek touched mine. As she pulled back, my stubble caught on her skin, causing a slight burn between us. There was so much in a glance, and then it was gone. She smiled and nodded. It was all the conformation I needed.

My gaze barely strayed from her for the next hour. She would look over, and I wouldn't look away. We held a silent conversation with our eyes, and I wanted to get lost with her. She couldn't possibly feel what I was. But it was hard to imagine something so intense being one sided.

She trailed her fingers up my thigh, and I dropped my eyes from her face for the first time, shocked at how close her hand was to my groin.

"What are you doing?" I hissed under my breath.

She used her left hand to scribble out a message on the screen her scan bracelet projected onto her arm. It was barely legible. *I have to combat your staring somehow.*

I swiped my hand over her arm to erase the screen then wrote with a finger, *So, you decide to arouse me?*

She grinned coyly, turning her arm to tease with her fingers again. I narrowed my eyes and growled. She retracted her hand and skimmed over the image of my words, touching them, before she erased them.

She wrote, *Something tells me you're not used to someone who can match you at your game.*

She was right. I'd experienced two types of women: those who dropped their clothes instantly and those searching for husbands. Those kinds were all about the hook. Neither had held my interest. A beautiful body was nice to look at, and I had given in to many, men and women, but I'd learned none of them held my attention, so I stopped trying.

I grabbed her hand as it moved to my hip, pulling it to my lips so I could kiss her palm. Strands of blonde hair fell in her face as she smiled, and I used my other hand to tuck them behind her ear.

Pulling her hand down from my lips, I used the screen on her arm again. *Spend the day with me?*

She looked from the words to me and back. I could hear Jacob sigh from the other side of her. I wanted to snarl at him to stay out of it.

I placed my hand over the screen holding her arm. My skin prickled. We weren't two people meeting for the first time. Whatever she was, our souls were the same. I had known her before, and I couldn't let it go.

She dropped her blue eyes to my hand and tapped it. I moved it and she wrote...

Chapter Six

Jocelynn

I can't... I could feel Jacob's eyes burning into me.

Later then? Give me your scan? He reached down to dig in his bag, pulling out an old beat up communicator. Not like the one I wore. His looked like he had dropped it off a bike on a high speed chase.

The lecture ended, and the people around us started getting to their feet.

I looked at Jacob then shook my head. I knew what he was thinking with a single look. "I'm sure I'll see you around," I said to Madden.

His face fell, and it hit me in the chest like the hilt of a blade. The sensation was unnerving. Men never affected me.

"I'm sorry," I said as Jacob urged me to my feet with a hand on my shoulder.

"When will I see you again?" He stood in our way.

I looked at Jacob then back to him. "If it's meant to be, we'll see each other." I would never say it out loud, but it would be. Never before had a stranger captivated me like this. My heart picked up with one scowl from him, and he'd had an intense effect on my mood. I was instantly elated.

"Playing hard to get." He took a step after me as Jacob urged me back.

"No games. I'm leaving it to fate." I had to keep face in front of my brother. I could tell he was already disapproving of the relationship. Had my brother not been there I might have ditched my afternoon meetings and spent the day with him. I would put myself in his path at some point now that I knew he was here. I could risk it. Jacob was allowed to have fun as long as he wasn't attached. I could do the same. I tried to convey this with my gaze, but he didn't know me well enough to pick up on the cues.

He narrowed his eyes. "I'll find you again, and I'll figure you out, J."

I was sure he would—with my help.

"Good luck. I'll be rooting for you," I teased as Jacob dragged me off. We walked out of the bowl-shaped room heading toward the top, mingling with the crowd.

Chapter Seven

Madden

I watched her walk away, knowing there wasn't a damn thing I could do about it. I started up after her, determined to think of something before I caught her. Students closed in around us, and I tried to push my way through them, but it grew impossible as she faded into the distance. I wanted to chase after her, and I lifted a foot to do just that when I was grabbed from behind. It was enough to jerk me off balance. I whipped around, only to see a flash of red parting the sea of people. I pushed a hand into my hair.

"Fuck." Day one and I was already distracted from what I came here to do. There was no point in forming an attachment to anyone when I needed to spend three years here and get out. The color wasn't going to leave my mind, and neither were the reason I had to get off Harden.

There was no way I was staying here or going back for that matter. I dug out my ancient comm and checked the time. My next lecture would be trade, and I had less than an hour to find the place I needed to be. If I got high marks I hoped they would let me transfer from the program to something more beneficial. I didn't care about trade or the internal or external politics of House Akillie.

And yet, I still wandered around the streets, hoping I would run into her again before I slipped into the next lecture ten minutes before the class was slated to begin. I didn't bother getting out my tablet or any note taking utensil. I had learned more about trade than I would ever need from my parents.

The rest of the students looked about as awake as the great sleeping dragon and as lively as a stuffed cat. It was warm, and a middle-aged man took a space in the middle of the room and unloaded his equipment. He wore tweed slacks and a clashing jacket of the same material. The colors gave me a headache. He slipped on a pair of glasses and touched the side, instantly projecting a class overview in the center of the room above his head. As he spoke, the image changed, reflecting his words.

I would put hard earned money on the fact that he'd been in his position for a long time, and his speech was well rehearsed and hadn't changed one syllable in a decade. I had already started plotting the questions with which I would throw off his perfect lecture. I had to get good marks, but there was no rule against having fun while doing it.

Lifting my hand in the air to start the fun, I paused, distracted by a cloaked figure who sat beside me. I lowered my hand before the teacher saw and turned to look at the man who sat directly next to me when more than two dozen seats were open around the hall.

The man didn't turn toward me, and he didn't lower his hood. I stared for a moment but then refocused on the lecture. I had to pay attention to absorb the material as well as time questions to baffle the unknown professor.

"How do you ever expect to find me again, when you are so unobservant?"

I gasped and turned in my seat. A few students turned to look at me, but I ignored them. "What are you doing here?"

"I figured I'd slum it and see how the beginner lectures are." She lowered her hood and turned to look at me with a devious grin across her red-stained lips.

"I should be situationally aware when my stalker is sneaking around with a giant black cloak on?" I raised my brows at her, hiding my smile.

"You should be situationally aware at all times." She drew one knee in to her body and turned toward me in her seat. "Isn't the cloak a nice touch? I stole it from my brother."

"And where is the killjoy?"

"I'm assuming swindling an unknowing man into bed with him, but he could already be in bed. My brother is quite good at these types of activities." She was so blunt about her brother's exploits. It intrigued me.

"And yet he's so protective over your company." I took a chance and brushed my fingers down her arm.

She dropped her gaze to where I touched her, but didn't pull away. "Ironic, isn't it?"

"A bit hypocritical, but I'm sure it's because he cares about your wellbeing, as I am a lowly scab." I waited for her reaction.

She gasped, looking me right in the eyes. "Then I shouldn't be here, or..."

The sarcasm dripped from her words.

"Maybe not if you'll get in trouble." The banter was more of a turn-on than even the first night.

She started to get to her feet. I didn't know what to do. I couldn't let her leave. She turned, picking up her bag, and I made a rash decision, grabbing her by the arm.

"Don't go," I hissed.

She wore a smirk when she sat back. "If you insist."

She'd called my bluff like a pro.

"You are infuriating."

"Act like you don't love every minute of it." She leaned in closer to me, and I realized my hand was still on her arm. She hadn't moved to shrug me off.

I brushed my fingers against her ribs. "I do. Now tell me when I can see you again?" I wanted to get to her before the class ended and she vanished.

She dragged her teeth over her lip.

The muffled background noise of the professor suddenly stopped, and my gaze flickered to the center of the hall where he stood. There was a question posed to the class on his projector, and he turned a slow circle waiting for an answer. I could feel Jocelynn's eyes on me.

I closed my eyes and raised my hand. I assumed she got hit on regularly by the cookie cutter elitists. I never wanted her to see me that way.

"Yes, you there." The professor pointed at me.

I swallowed past the lump in my throat. "I know your question is on the trade route structure and the economic threats the terrorist organizations pose to it, but I think I have a more insightful point than the purely economic risks and the stress to the House's resources to protect the routes." I took a deep breath. He meant the Reds and the other fringe groups like them. I glanced down at J, and she waited expectantly. "I think it's more than the structure of the trade routes causing the issue. I think the fringe groups are growing because of unrest, and they've found the structure of the routes gives them easy access for exploiting the House of Akillie and the Emperor. If we could allow for varied routes and allow for a daily randomized flight paths this would minimize the risk."

Both of the professor's brows shot up. "But then how is smuggling controlled? Without the established trade routes, ships can avoid check stations, and we lose all control of tax."

He thought he had me, but people like him never thought outside the box. "I disagree. I think with varied trade routes only known by the House Guard and the captains the day of the mission we can maximize policing and free up Guard ships to watch for smugglers. There is new tech being tested for inventory scans and doc downloads from Time2."

"I've heard of no such tech." He tried to call my bluff just as J had done, but I had him.

"I do believe it is slated to be presented at the Worlds' Fair tomorrow morning. If I may?" I pulled a microchip from my pocket and held it out to him. "They haven't thought of using the tech for trade but…" I shrugged.

He waved me down, and I placed it on his tablet. I flipped through the preliminary reports filed in the House library before the Fair started. When I found the one I wanted I opened it up, highlighted the section I meant, and projected it to the class.

The bells chimed, and he turned to the class. "Think on it until next week."

As the room started to clear, the professor gave a low whistle and turned to me. "Why are you in my class?" He turned to me.

"Because new students start at the bottom." I flashed him a smile.

He looked me over for a long moment. "I want you moved to my five hundred level class." He picked up his tablet and handed the microchip back to me. He hit a few keys. "What's your name, kid?"

"Madden."

"You're moved. I'm sending you the meeting times." He hit another few keys. "You've got me impressed."

I looked back to where J sat, and she was gone.

Chapter Eight

Jocelynn

I hated leaving him, but his point was too perfect. The Baron would be sitting in on a security meeting I had ditched to find Madden, and if I presented it there before the conference tomorrow I would blow them all away. We had been discussing the very same trade issue for more than six months as the raids continued to grow weekly. I didn't have time to waste, but I would make sure he got all the credit.

My mind was spinning as I burst into the meeting, finding it drawing to a close. I straightened up, staying by the door as all the eyes in the room lifted to my disturbance. The Baron was the last to look up after he finished reading something on the projected screen in front of his seat.

"And what do we owe the pleasure, Jocelynn?" His gaze was harsh, but after eighteen years of such looks they didn't faze me like they did his underlings.

"I did not expect the meeting to be wrapped up this soon." I stalled, meeting my brother's eyes.

He shook his head at me.

"Well, when there hasn't been a solution to the issue in some odd months you can expect meetings to be short, but clearly you have other more important things to attend to, so you are excused." It was a harsh dismissal even from him.

"I figured finding a solution to the issue at hand was better than listening to an update stating nothing has changed, as you said yourself. But if you don't think it to be a good enough excuse then I shall go." I inclined my head slightly and turned, counting back from five in my head.

Before I got to zero he spoke. "Do enlighten us."

It was wrong of me to embarrass him, but I was not about to take an ounce of shit for missing one meeting when Jacob did it weekly. I crossed to the large holographic table and took my seat. Tapping the screen to bring up my keyboard, I navigated through the presentations on the fair tomorrow.

"Why is she wasting our time with the Worlds' Fair?" one of the men commented, clearly annoyed I had spoken to the Baron like I had.

"Give her a minute," Jacob snapped.

I found what I was looking for and flicked it up on to the projector to display in the middle of the room for all to see.

"I found this."

The room was silent while everyone read the brief description of the presentation for tomorrow.

"Jocelynn, my temper is getting short," the Baron said.

"It is the ability to transfer data at Time2. It makes weigh stations and check points void." I waited and let it dawn on him.

"Now, if we use it with this—" I flipped another new tech to the screen about encoding data with tracing flags for unique identity. "If we combine these two, then we can put more of our House Guard resources toward holding off raids, but the beauty of randomized trade routes is the fringe groups won't know where to attack."

No one spoke. All eyes were on me. I sat with my back stiff from all the years of stringent training.

"I want all the science officers there in the morning. No exceptions." The Baron tapped the table and stood.

The room clambered to their feet, bowing their heads as he turned and left. I sat back and breathed. Jacob sat on the table in front of me and waited until the room cleared.

When the room was empty he spoke. "You ditched the meeting to chase down errant tech you heard about where?" He curled his tongue over his teeth.

"I think I proved my point to everyone else here. Why do you doubt me, brother?"

"Because you never miss these things, and this is the first I'm hearing of it. You don't pre-read all the presentations like you used to for the fair..." I could see it dawn on him, and I looked away. "It was that scab?"

"What was?"

"He put this in your head. You are taking a big fucking risk listening to an untested."

I held up my hand to silence him. "I don't want to hear it. I looked into it myself. If it backfires it is because the tech is not as good as claimed, not because he planted ideas."

Jacob looked around the room, and he looked off balance, flustered almost. "And if he works for a fringe group and is filling your head with these ideas to help someone else?"

"It wasn't like that." I knew it wasn't. He'd said it to impress the people in the room, and he didn't know about the other tech, I was certain.

"You have to keep them at a distance, Jocelynn."

I sighed, knowing he was right.

The next morning I was up before the sun, researching my points and making notes in my comm. My head was spinning when I was through, and I was only more convinced this would work. It could be the end to our supply chain loss and a crushing blow to the fringe groups all in one go. I pushed my fingers through my hair, looking out the window. The suns had risen, and I realized I'd been working longer than I'd thought. I needed to get myself put together and hurry to the fair.

I took my seat on the Baron's right-hand side, with time to spare, not even breathing hard from the run over here, which was quite unladylike, but I doubt anyone took notice. I crossed my ankles and folded my hands in my lap, waiting for the start. We sat in his private booth surrounded by the ministers of science, each of them with a tablet ready to inscribe the notes or to read them close at hand as they were put out by the presenters.

I looked around the room. It was barely half filled and only filled as much as it was, I assumed, because the Baron was here. An official visit was a big deal. His tour of the fair was usually set months in advance when the most important new tech was submitted for consideration.

They started on time, and it was a tsunami of information. If I hadn't done the research this morning I would have been lost. I could see a stupor take over most of the group, and only those who I knew to be genuine geniuses seemed to follow.

I leaned closer to the Baron to explain the more difficult parts.

He nodded, glancing over at me. "I knew I made the right choice."

I sat back, and Jacob murmured, "Fucking know-it-all."

I flashed him a smile. "Put in a little effort and you'd get the praise." Easier too I imagined because expectations for him were so low.

"Not worth the wasted energy, and I still don't believe you had anything to do with this." He narrowed his eyes. "I'll figure you out."

I scanned the crowd, feeling a little smug even if I wasn't solely responsible for it. I wondered if there was a way I could give Madden the credit. I would figure it out. There was nothing like an accommodation from the Baron to raise a scab's worth. My gaze landed on him, in the front row, directly across from me.

His professor, Hornsbee, sat with him, and they chatted back and forth. He might have thought he was pretending, but I could see the ease in which he made friends and was becoming a part of things here. It would be best to make my escape. If he saw me with the Baron, he would put the pieces together.

But I didn't want to leave. I wanted to assimilate myself into his world and live there. I already felt too much. I had to lock down my feelings. He couldn't know. It would make this too hard. I could only imagine things were easier without the pressure I had on me. He laughed, and I could almost hear it from here. It couldn't be wrong to enjoy him for a little while. I knew it lasting wasn't possible, but I could pretend.

I almost hoped he would look up. Then he'd know and I wouldn't have to hide it anymore. If wishing made it so. It would save me from imagining what was possible. I wanted to be saved from my own mind tonight.

"Let's have a look shall we?" The Baron broke my concentration.

"Go down, sir?"

He nodded, getting to his feet. His entourage followed, and I had no choice but to bring myself closer to the fire. We descended to the floor of the large auditorium, and the Baron stood in his circle until the presentation ended and his advisers could take over the question session. I knew he had already made up his mind. After years of being on his advisory council, I could read him well. He would have left by now if he thought it was a waste of time. Politeness had never been one of his attributes.

I backed away, making a rash choice to slip back into the crowd when Madden looked up. Our eyes met, and his lips curled into a smile. He turned back to Hornsbee, and I could tell he excused himself. I had to put more distance between myself and the Baron. I weaved through the crowd, getting closer to him. I realized as I did I could have escaped, but I didn't want to. I wanted to see him again.

"Hey there." He wore a smirk.

"Good morning, I see you've made quite the impression on your professor."

He half shrugged and stuck his hands into his pocket. "I did at the expense of scaring you away."

"You didn't scare me away."

"You missed my big moment." He was faux offended.

"I saw enough."

"How do I know?" His lips twitched, and I knew he was hiding a smile.

"I'm here, aren't I?" I didn't back down.

"I guess I'll concede as much." He chuckled.

"I win!"

"I didn't say that." A smile spread over his lips. "Why did you leave? I was hoping for…" He trailed off.

"I had something to take care of. You were hoping for?" I cocked my head to the side, wondering if he was shy or smooth. Either way he had me curious.

"To have you to myself." He stepped closer.

"And if you had me to yourself what would you do with me?"

His lips twisted into a smirk, and there was a wicked gleam in his eyes. "I don't think you really want to know."

"Try me," I whispered.

He didn't speak for a few moments, and my heart picked up speed waiting for his reply.

"Come spend the day with me," he said at last.

"You didn't answer my question." I crossed my arms over my chest.

"I know. Maybe you need to get it out of me."

I growled under my breath, and he smiled roguishly.

He held out his hand. "Are you coming?"

Chapter Nine

Madden

My heart raced, and my stomach dropped when she didn't take my hand right way. I wasn't this smug. Maybe she could see through my act.

"Where are we going?" She set her smaller hand in mine, and I closed my fingers around it.

"You'll see." I chuckled, turning to leave when a hand touched my shoulder from behind. I turned to find Hornsbee, my professor, standing there.

"Leaving so soon?"

"I didn't have any questions," I lied. I had many, but as this tech and project had nothing to do with me, it would do no more than show my intelligence to Hornsbee, and spending the day with Jocelynn sounded more appealing.

"That shocks me." Hornsbee turned his gaze to J, looking her up and down. "Interesting companion you have here." He reached out for her hand. "Jocelynn, isn't it?"

She smiled, taking his hand, and something unreadable passed between them. "It is. Nice to see you again, Sir Hornsbee."

They didn't shake. He took just her fingers, gently, in his and inclined his head in respect. "It's a pleasure to see you again. I thought I saw you in my class briefly yesterday. You should have stayed and added to the fun this one provided." He gestured at me as he released her hand.

He looked at her like a piece of meat, ripe for the taking, and she drank in all the flattery but stayed poised. If I hadn't figured out she was noble before, this was confirmation.

"I had another engagement, forgive me."

Hornsbee narrowed his eyes as he dropped her hand. "This genius a friend of yours?"

"Newly yes, he's quite a surprise, isn't he?" she replied, displaying nothing on her face.

"Indeed. He has high potential, makes me want to learn more about him."

Their entire exchange set my nerves on edge.

"As do I. Beg your pardon, but we do have a previous commitment." She gave us the perfect opening for an exit.

"Carry on then. Tell your brother it was good to see him." He pressed a finger to his lip, looking between us. "Madden, if you will, I have some friends I'd like to introduce you to after lecture tomorrow. Small gathering, if you're not already engaged."

I looked over at her, then back to him. "Sure, see you then."

The exchange left my head spinning. I could write off Hornsbee knowing her easily as she'd been in training here for years, but the way he treated her, and his shock at our acquaintance, but more than anything else the way he spoke of her brother left an uneasy feeling in my gut. I hated feeling like I was missing something, and here, without the previous knowledge of social construct, I was left feeling as such more than I liked. I tried to push it out of my mind as we walked down the narrow stone street.

Architecture on Trenton was nothing like Harden. Buildings here were made to be beautiful and prestigious, whereas they were built to withstand the intense heat and sandstorms on my home world. What a difference money made.

When we entered the Grand Square, Jocelynn stiffened. Turning to look at her I knew something was wrong.

"J?"

"Where are we headed?" Her line of sight tracked a crowd on the other side of the square.

"To the grand library."

She pursed her lips and nodded. "Let's go then." She dropped my hand and strolled forward.

I jogged a few steps to catch up. "You're so hard to read sometimes."

She shrugged one shoulder, and I stepped in front of her to hold open the large door.

"You like a challenge. I'm sure of it." She sauntered into the heart of the library and looked up at the domed ceiling.

I growled playfully. "You shouldn't be able to read me so well." I nudged her toward the place I'd found the other night, and she followed.

"You're easy to read."

I ran my fingers over the books before we stopped in a secluded seating area. I'd spent a few nights here and had never been disturbed, so I figured we'd be safe.

"I am not easy to read." The book I'd been reading the night before was still on the table. She sat on the loveseat, and I decided to go for a bold gesture sitting right beside her.

She turned to look at me but didn't complain. "As easy as that book." She took a glance around and then stood to shed her cloak before sitting back. "Let me see if I can show you how easy you are to read," she smirked.

"Go ahead."

She held my gaze. "You brought me here to show me something and because no one comes to this part of the library. It's where all the research the Baron funds is stored, and even the graduate students don't bother with most of it as they can pull it on the nets."

"Well I've always preferred a book I can hold in my hand. Something about it." I laughed and nodded.

"But that too was easy for you to devise, all obvious details."

"I'm not done." She looked me up and down.

The room grew warm, and I shifted under her intense gaze.

"Because this place is rarely visited I'm sure you intend to use it to get to know me better."

I swallowed hard. I hadn't realized how transparent I'd been. "I didn't mean to…" I sighed. I'd blown it already.

"If I had an objection I wouldn't have come." She turned into me so our thighs pressed together. "Now, what did you plan on showing me?"

My gut stirred with arousal, and I wanted to push her against one of the stacks and have my way. I restrained my desire, turning up my charm.

"This." I picked up the thick tome and laid it over our legs. I flipped through the pages until about halfway, where I'd stopped.

"Here is all the practical data they'd need to implement it, and I think it would even work on Time4, which I suspect the Emperor's trade ships use."

She picked up the book and scanned the page. "Yes, I used this."

"Used it?"

She chewed on her lip and sat silent.

"What is it?" I pressed.

"I used what you said, and…" She took a breath. "Took it … had someone take it to the Baron. You could have all the credit for figuring it out. It's your research and your mind. It's only fair, plus it will put you in his favor."

Bile rose in my throat, and my chest constricted. I shook my head slowly. "I wasn't looking for credit for anything, and I am not privileged to information I'm sure you are. It was just an issue Hornsbee brought up, and I knew I could impress you with it."

A wave of emotions washed over her face. And I couldn't read any of them until disappointment settled there. "It would help with the politics and standing out in your program."

I shook my head again, and she trailed off.

"I'm sure Hornsbee will take care of it. This is a minor thing." I didn't want to be in the Baron's world. I didn't want the pressure and politics. I was here to get the schooling I needed to get off Harden and into a new life.

A tiny crease formed in her brow, making her even cuter than she already was, sitting there with the huge book in her hands.

She checked her comm, and I knew she'd say our time was up. I stood when she did, and she pressed her teeth into her lip.

"I get it; you have to go."

She nodded. "I'm sorry."

I leaned down to brush my lips over hers. "Can I see you tomorrow?"

She parted her lips over my upper lip as I sucked her lower into my mouth. I would never get enough of her taste. I grabbed at her waist when she pulled back.

She laughed. "I really have to go, Madden."

"Tomorrow then?" I pressed. "I'll give you my scan."

She shook her head without breaking contact with me. "I have a full day ahead and presentations to attend for the next several mornings."

"Is that so?" I grinned. At least I knew whereabouts to find her.

She narrowed her eyes. "Shall I call you my stalker?"

"Maybe, but I wouldn't have to take such measures if you'd give me your scan."

She detangled our bodies, and I reached for my bag. She gave me one last look. "I can't." And she was gone.

Chapter Ten

Jocelynn

The next morning's presentations were uneventful, and Jacob kept falling asleep with his head on my shoulder. How very noble of him. When the last one of the morning ended, I shoved him off playfully. He startled awake and nearly lost his seat. I lifted a hand to my mouth to cover my laugh.

He glared back at me and whispered, "Arse."

I smiled sweetly. "Methinks you should stay awake next time."

He rolled his eyes and stood. "Lunch, yeah?"

"I'm down. What are we getting?" I followed him out of the stuffy hall, suppressing a yawn.

"No idea." He scanned the rows of buildings across the street from the large auditorium through the large glass windows.

"Nothing heavy, or I'll be asleep in the next." I lifted my arms to stretch my back after sitting in the uncomfortable seat for hours.

"Wouldn't that be a sight. Miss Perfect asleep in a meeting." He laughed. "Dockeian?"

I groaned but followed as he started off toward the place. Rain fell lightly as we stepped outside, and I pulled my cloak tighter around me. "I think you'd eat there every day if you could."

"I can and don't!" He jogged to catch up, slugging me in the shoulder as he passed, his boots stomping through the rain.

"Only because I don't let you!" I picked up my pace, hitching my negative-space bag higher on my shoulder as I ran.

Jacob glanced back at me and rolled his eyes, body stiffening. "He's following us."

I fought the urge to look back. "Who?"

"That scab. How did he even know where you were?" Jacob muttered under his breath.

I couldn't help the smile spreading over my face.

"Seven bolts of Docle. You love the attention, don't you?"

We slowed as we approached the entrance, ducking into the dim place. The attendant snapped to and walked us to a table, letting us bypass the clear line before us. I hated the attention. I'd tried to argue and wait, but it only resulted in a scene. I'd grown accustomed to giving in. Jacob enjoyed the perks of his position, but I hated the looks we got. As we took our seats, the door opened letting in a cool draft. I glanced at the door seeing Madden slip inside. It took effort to keep my expression stoic as Jacob rambled on about a new fling he had.

Gradually the tables around us were filled, and I scanned them as the guests took their seats. At last, my eyes landed on Mad at a table behind Jacob. I pushed my food around my plate sneaking glances at him. He smiled at me, eyes unwavering, even when he placed an order. I wasn't close enough to hear him speak to the server, which made me wonder what he had ordered. I laughed out of turn imagining him trying Dockeian blindly. The cuisine was an acquired taste for most who had not been raised on Trenton or of course Docke.

I watched him, half listening to my brother as he rambled on. He was as intent on keeping his eyes on me for as long as possible as well. Servers came and went from his table, and he, while polite, never looked them in the eyes. He dug into his food, bringing the first bite to his mouth. I sat up straighter, excitement building. He'd ordered an over spiced dish that would water the eyes of the most hardened Dockeian fan. For a moment there was no reaction, but then his body shook in a violent shudder, and tears brimmed at the corners of his eyes. His nostrils flared, but then the sweetness of the nut oil and the infused rich flavors of the cooked pasta took over and he calmed.

He laughed at himself. I was sure it was for my behalf as he met my gaze. He brought his glass to his lips and took a pull of the water. When I glanced back at my brother he had stopped talking and was glaring at me. He followed the direction of my gaze and scowled.

"Have you heard a word I've said?"

"Maybe two or three, but it's doubtful I got more or even the gist of what you were saying." I smiled sweetly at him.

He scoffed and turned in his seat. "Get your arse over here. If you two are going to make eyes at one another you might as well sit here so we can have a discussion." He waved at the place next to him.

Mad picked up his plate and drink, taking the seat next to me in the bench, instead of the one next to my brother. His fingers brushed over my thigh, and I assumed it was on purpose. I turned in the bench, drawing my knee up to my chest so I could half face him.

"Looks like you took chance into your own hands."

His expression was smug. "I would rather take charge of my destiny than leave it up to the powers of the universe."

"No one cares. How's the Dockeian?" Jacob asked.

Mad stabbed another forkful of the pasta and placed it in his mouth. "Spicy, but I was raised on heat. It covers the taste of the Ore."

"Harden?" I held in my gasp. Harden was the only place in the universe Ore existed. I calmed my voice. "And here my guess had been Becca."

"I would have put him on Dolton or any rim planet after seeing him at the orientation," Jacob said. He leaned in as if suddenly more interested.

"Good point." We both turned to him.

"I'm rare, I know. I'm not a highborn, and I'm not from a rim planet. I earned my place with the stupid test." He shrugged one shoulder waving it off. But it was not some meaningless achievement like he treated it. "But I guess the lady is correct as I was born on Becca and spent a lot of time on the rim planets."

"You know you're the first in…"

He blew out a breath. "Do we have to talk about it? Yeah, I know, a century. Since it was instituted I'm the second."

"Did you have help?" Jacob's words were loaded.

He and Madden stared each other down. "None, and you can't look at me any worse than how they do at home." He dropped his gaze to his dish.

Jacob pursed his lips, his gaze unwavering. It was almost like he didn't believe something Madden was saying.

"You're treated poorly for your genius?" I frowned.

He gave a quick glance to my brother before answering. "No one understands it. You're expected to go work in the mines. They take pride in belonging there." He shrugged. "It's not like here where the opposite is expected, more so with you highborns."

"You know half of us couldn't pass the test they give you," Jacob added giving a low whistle.

"I've been told, and it's glaringly obvious after coming here." He kept his eyes down. I couldn't tell if he was ashamed or angry.

"Do you like it?" I brushed my fingers over his arm trying to… I didn't know what I was trying to do. Give him comfort maybe.

"The cool climate is my favorite part thus far. You don't know how lucky you are to have this year round." He met my eyes again and smiled, returning the gesture.

A shiver ran up my arm at his touch. He heated the skin under his fingers infusing a warm glow into my flesh. "What? No way, I hate the cold. I would much rather have the warmth."

I dropped my hand as he played over my arm, and he lowered his to skim the tips of his fingers over my palm before lacing our fingers together.

"Because you could afford a coolant unit. Try sleeping when it's 48 degrees Celsius."

I squeezed his hand in mine. "I'll give you that."

"Have I earned permission to have your scan yet?" He didn't miss a beat.

I pushed my plate back and pressed the bottom of my wrist comm so it projected my unique code on my arm so his reader could scan it.

"Jocelynn." My brother's voice had a warning tone as he stood, placing his hand over the code.

I looked at him, setting my jaw before I leaned in to press a kiss under Mad's ear. The gesture disguised my purpose. "Meet me at midnight under the Akillie statue," I whispered and then pulled back to speak in my normal tone. "I'm sure you'll find me again." I had the presentation dinner tonight, but I could cut out early and have enough time to meet him while everyone else was busy. Jacob would have his pants down and a servant pressed into a wall as well, leaving me free for a few hours.

He said yes with his eyes, but shot a glaring look at Jacob. "I will make it happen."

"None of us doubt you." Jacob threw down a handful of credits, more than covering ours and Mad's food, and when Mad tried to object my brother waved him off. "It's not my money, and you may as well take it. This place will cost you a week's worth of the pension they put you on, I'm sure."

Mad got to his feet, allowing me to get up. I brushed my shoulder against his chest as I passed.

Tonight couldn't come fast enough.

Chapter Eleven

Madden

My last class was intergalactic trade, and ten minutes in I wanted to scream. Not because I didn't understand the material, but because it was elitist, skewed, and downright false in most parts. The professor wore a tweed jacket with patches on the elbows. He looked like a relic out of a twentieth-century book. He wore glasses that projected images to the large screen as he talked.

Hornsbee explained trade only from an Akillie point of view. I was sure the other large faction, the Jok House, would have a much different story about it. But on Harden we saw it from the outside. Our planet was fought over for its valuable resources putting us at odds with both houses. But the Emperor controlled all and had put us in the protection of Akillie, making everyone in need of Ore beholden to them. Some, myself included, felt the Emperor played favorites to increase conflict between the great houses. If they were at odds with each other, they would never rise up against him.

I was pulled out of my musing by a nudge to my shoulder. My gut filled with nervous excitement. Had she followed me? I'd taken my seat in the back row having had a feeling this class would infuriate me. But when I looked behind me a figure stood in the shadows. No one else seemed to have noticed. He was too large to be Jocelynn. I started to turn back, but the figure held out a micro disk to me. I frowned and took the thing from him. He stepped further back into the shadows, backing toward the door. I watched him slip out and looked around again. Not a single person had even turned.

Glancing down at the silver disk in my hand, I wondered if it was a message from J. I slid it into my comm, and the screen glowed dimly, blades flying in from the edges to form a red star in the center. My eyes went wide, but the image faded leaving a scrawling message in a handwritten script.

Madden,

Changes start with individuals standing opposed to tyranny. It takes bright minds infused in all levels of government. We stand against the Emperor and his cruel division of power. As a Harden you know of the oppression we face. But even inside the bleakest oppression, at the darkest hour, dawn draws near. Come see the light we have to offer with the Red Stars

Intidafa.

I reread the message three times. *Why me?* The question settled in my mind. I was smart, but would I ever be in a position to effect real change like they talked about? I had to have a skill they desired. There had always been whispers of them on my home planet, but they only recruited people they could use. Holding this disk could get me bounced back to Harden. Going to this meeting could be seen as treason to the House of Akillie. But I knew from rumor alone a Red Star invitation was a one-time thing. It was a band of honor on Harden to be invited into their ranks. If turned down once they wouldn't ask again. Collecting masses of supporters was never their means. They didn't instill hate or act as terrorists. The whispers said they had real plans to take down the Emperor.

But no one knew enough about them to be sure. For all I knew it could be a completely different tactic. I wanted to go. I wanted to know what all of the hush was about. When the map flashed on the screen I committed it to memory and shut off my comm. I had no doubt if they could get something like this into my hands it would be wiped remotely from afar. I shoved it in my bag and sat at the edge of my seat waiting for the lecture to finish. I needed to get a wrist comm, like the locals used. It would go a long way to me not losing it.

I shot up the moment it was done, heading back to my room to change. I felt like an idiot as I stared at the few things hanging in my closet, mostly old tees with metal tech logos. I pulled on a black one and some jeans. Sneaking around was not my strong suit. At six foot three, I couldn't hide anywhere. Besides, people stared at me anyway because of my otherworldly features.

I left my room and took off toward the less traveled parts of the city where the map began. I followed the imprint in my mind, knowing it was the long way around to a building in the heart of the abandoned city. I could have taken a more direct route from memory alone, but I figured this was some sort of test. If I really thought about it the route was probably meant to suss out any tail I might have. There was none. I was too boring to draw the attention of anyone past the excitement of my proclaimed genius the first few days. I was old news. I guessed they wanted me to come alone, not that I had anyone to tell. Colton would have been the only one, and well, he was light years away and wasn't speaking to me.

The sun was low in the horizon when I had left, and by the time I neared the meeting place all trace of natural light had vanished. The worn streets glowed with the illuminating bricks used on all public streets here, giving me enough light to find my way and see the aging structures around me.

I couldn't shake the feeling there were eyes on me. I scanned the buildings, but there was no one. It felt like I was walking into a trap.

It looked like I was in a warehouse district, long abandoned. I took the final turn into a dead-end and frowned. *What the hell?*

Walking to the end of the street I searched the buildings on both sides, finding no doors or even a window. It hit me—most people don't look up when searching, so I scanned the walls. They stretched five or six stories into the sky, windowless, and without a means of entrance into the buildings.

Fear cut through me. I could be executed from a rooftop. This could have been a set-up.

I slid my communicator from my pocket and checked it. Five minutes until meeting time. I spun in a slow circle again looking for anything I might have missed. It had to be a false trail or a decoy because there was nothing here.

The full circle brought me back to the brick wall at the end of the alley, and where the bottom once met the ground now stood a staircase down.

I took a tentative step toward it, and there, imprinted on each was a tiny red star. My stomach flipped as I stepped down onto the first one then the next. An iron door stood at the end, and I knocked, unsure what to do next. The door swung open instantly, and I was swept into blackness.

Chapter Twelve

Jocelynn

"Jocelynn." The Baron's voice rang out, drawing me from my thoughts.

"Yes, sir?" I straightened in my chair, keeping my hands folded in my lap as I looked over at him. Etiquette dictated all my actions at such events, but the gestures and movements were so ingrained it was harder for me to break protocol at this point than to abide by its strict rules.

"Wasn't it lovely to have the daughter of Lord Arbor here for the opening ceremony?" He fixed me in a hard stare. His eyes were the color of mine, deep blue, but his hair was black. Gray streaked away from his temples, and down into his full beard. It was impossible to deny the Akillie blood held strong genes. He would have been a handsome man, except for his harsh eyes, which instilled fear in most of his subjects as well as advisers. Some argued a good ruler needed such things to impose order. I knew I lacked such hardness.

"Yes, Aubrey has been all kindness and pleasantries." I nodded at the girl sitting next to my brother.

She smiled over at me. "I look forward to the weeks we will spend at your winter palace, Baron." She inclined her head at him.

The Baron cast a look at my brother sitting between Aubrey and me. Jacob leaned back in his chair with his arms thrown over the sides, defying protocol. He held a large glass of fire whiskey, and I knew he was on his way to getting drunk. He'd hardly spoken two words to her all night, despite her constant chattering to us both, and I'd been forced to pick up the slack. I knew why he did it, and my heart went out to him, but I felt bad for her.

She seemed a bit dense and airheaded, but she was nice enough and beautiful. She stood five feet ten inches tall, towering over me, and her dark tendrils of curls fell to her butt. She was rail thin and the perfect arm piece for the younger son of the Baron, plus her father ruled over a planet currently in Jok control.

Angling to get it out from under the House of Jok's thumb and into Akillie hands would mean more wealth and power. Their main export was liquid crystal. They had perfected a technique to make it into display screens on large space craft.

We might have had control over Ore, the most valuable element in the universe, but they had the tech for time-folding giving them better access to trade and exploration. The marriage would bind the planet to Akillie, thus gaining us substantial resources and of course, pissing off Jok.

"We look forward to the official visit from your father." The Baron turned back to a conversation happening on the other side of the large table.

"So, Jacob, I've been told you play quite the game of Quad."

He grunted.

I blew out a breath and wiped my fingers on my napkin, glancing over at the clock. We'd had six courses. Dessert was being served. Before long Jacob would excuse himself and then soon after, I could do the same, feigning exhaustion. But the key was him leaving.

"He is getting fat from all the whiskey, and I doubt he could hope to keep up anymore." I shot him a look, getting my point across.

He set down his tumbler and straightened in his seat. "I still attend all the same training sessions you do."

"You've been slacking." I shrugged.

"A wager then?" he snapped.

"Are you challenging me?" I smiled at Aubrey and nearly squealed in delight at Jacob's sudden turnaround.

"I am." He made eyes at her then looked back at me. It was one of his biggest talents. He could make anyone fall at his feet with his charm. I'd never possessed the particular skill.

"Can I come?" Aubrey looked giddy.

Jacob shrugged one shoulder. "If you would like."

"Then it's settled, you two must compete when we are all at your winter palace."

I was pretty sure she bounced in her chair.

Jacob shot me a look. I cracked a smile. Poor girl was way too simple to hold his attention even if she'd had the parts between her thighs he preferred. Servants came around carrying trays of dessert, which Jacob and I both waved off. He narrowed his eyes at me, refilling his glass of whiskey.

"New diet?"

"Whatever would I need a diet for, brother mine?"

He looked me over before pushing back from the table. "I must beg your leave, Aubrey, I think the fowl isn't sitting right."

She clambered to her feet in a ladylike manner which impressed me. "Are you ill?"

"Maybe." He put on the most faux frown I think I've ever seen him wear before going on. "Maybe I should beg off our breakfast engagement."

I scoffed, and he growled under his breath. Sick was code for he didn't want to leave his bed for breakfast as there would be better company between his sheets.

She set her hand on his shoulder. "Let me bring breakfast to you. I would feel better if I could check on you in the morning."

I could feel the internal groan radiating off my brother. "That would be lovely." He patted her hand on his arm then broke away, making a hasty exit.

My gaze flickered to the communicator on my wrist, twenty minutes until I had to meet Madden. It would take me at least that long to change and get out to the square. I grabbed a slice of pie from a passing tray and set it in front of me, because I needed a distraction. There was a chance he wouldn't wait for me. The minutes ticked by and at five minutes to, after making polite conversation with Aubrey for the longest fifteen minutes of my life, I rose to my feet.

"Sir, I have an early morning training course. Please excuse me."

The Baron studied me. "And your brother, where did he pinch off to?"

I swallowed. "He was ill, sir."

"Code for he went to find more amusing debauchery than the striking female I have placed before him." He scoffed, stroking his fingers over his graying beard.

I remained silent. It was better not to lie to the Baron's face, nor would I admit the truth of where I knew my brother had gone. If he was caught in bed with a man, the Baron would have to do something about it. Right now it was ignored for the most part, which I think suited everyone.

"Go if you must. I have no further need for you here."

It was the kindest dismissal I was going to get. I gave a slight bow and forced myself to walk calmly out of the place. I broke into a run when I reached the hall, skidding around the corners in heels.

I slipped into my room and yanked off my dress, tossing it into a pile in the corner.

I dug through the clothes on the floor, picking up a pair of leathers before pulling them on.

A skin tight green tank went over the corset I didn't have time to try to get myself out of. The top of the black lace corset peeked out over the top of the tank, creating a nice image. I looked at my hair in the glass, and it was still beautifully sculpted and pinned up from dinner. It wasn't worth fussing over either.

Late by a few minutes, I ran from my room heading out the back way, toward the fountain in the square. The outside air was cold as we were heading into fall. Brisk wind pulled at my cloak as I wrapped it tighter around myself. I had grabbed the red one, the house color, and wished I'd commissioned a black one like my brother had. Another thing to put on the list if I was determined to keep up this sneaking around.

The sky was covered in a low cloud layer, blocking out the six moons usually illuminating the night. I could make out the shade of the fountain from far off as I approached the abandoned square, but there was no figure in sight. I checked my comm again. It was ten past. Maybe he'd left.

I couldn't stay out here long. The color of my cloak would draw unwanted attention.

Chapter Thirteen

Madden

"Shit." The city around me had turned black, boasting even less life than it had a few hours ago. The cool air soothed my nerves as I walked toward where I hoped she would be.

It was after the last bell when I walked out of the abandoned building, and my head was spinning with information and the familiar faces I'd seen. Most of which some parts of me had known, without fully putting it together, and others, while well proven, seemed impossible. I couldn't wrap my head around the atrocity hidden in plain sight. In a hierarchy which had stood for centuries, how could it go unnoticed for this long? I had a lot to think about, too much. I wasn't the right person for this, not by a long stretch. I'd come out with more questions than answers, and I hated feeling like I was behind the curve. I had to put it out of my mind until the next meeting if I was going to focus on Jocelynn at all.

The square where we'd agreed to meet was around one more corner. She wouldn't still be there. I was so late. The night was bitter cold, and it was wrong of me to leave her waiting. I took a step into the expansive square, scanning it for any sign of life, but there was none. It would be impossible to find her again since we were in different levels and different course studies. They didn't put off-worlders in the kinds of strategy classes she would be in with her higher ranking bloodline.

She wasn't there.

I crossed the empty space, skirting the fountain at a distance toward the direction of my building. There had to be a way to find out who she was and "accidentally" on purpose run in to her. I was determined not to let her slip through my fingers. I knew I would never meet anyone like her again.

A flicker of red caught my eye as I neared the mouth of the street leading away from the square. *Would one of the Red Stars have followed me?* I stopped in place and turned. But it was all wrong. Instead of a hint of red on the jacket this figure wore a full red cloak. It brought a distant image to my mind, but I couldn't place the significance of it. I watched as they approached, sliding my cold hands into my pocket where I kept the weapon I'd been given.

When the person was a few feet from me she used both hands to lower the hood. There wasn't enough light to make out her features, but I knew it was Jocelynn. I closed the distance between us and hesitated. She reached out for my arm and stepped into my body.

"I was about to leave."

"I'm so sorry. I was held up." I slid my arms around her waist feeling how the cold had seeped into her clothes.

She leaned into my warmth. "Any glancing eye can see us from a window. Let's get off the street."

"Where do you want to go? There's got to be a tea shop still open." I looked around, having a good grasp of my bearings in the city now.

"They will close soon. Your room?"

I stifled my surprise. "Sure…" Heat stirred in my gut.

She looked up at me, blue eyes gleaming. "Lead the way."

Chapter Fourteen

Jocelynn

"Where were you last night?"

The words pulled me from the illusion of his arms. I clung to the warmth of his memory, as the hangings around my bed were thrown open, spilling bright light into my dark cavern.

"Fuck," I groaned. "What are you doing up so early."

"It's after first bell."

I bolted up. "What?" I rolled out of bed nearly taking Jacob out.

"Yeah." Jacob brought a mug to his lips. "I was up before you were with that horrid female you helped the Baron push on me while you lay abed."

I stared at him for a moment before ducking behind the screen to change. I threw on my guard uniform and stepped back out.

"She is sweet, just not the correct gender." I tucked my sword under my arm and glanced at the mirror. I had no time to apply makeup before the conference. I would have to leave it until they did me up for the opening ceremony. I hooked the formal sword to my belt and pushed my hair up into a tie.

"Where did you go last night?"

I looked back at him, scrabbling. "I was at dinner while you ditched out."

"See there is the flaw in your plan. Dear Aubrey told me how you had an early morning, so how shocked would I be to find you here, still abed, after the first bell?" He gripped his bicep with his opposite hand.

We never lied to each other. "I went out." I gave up on my hair and stood before him.

"With the scab?"

"Jacob!"

"What do you want me to call him?" He set his cup down and pushed both hands into his hair.

"Call him by his name."

"That was a test. This is becoming a thing, isn't it?" His eyes searched mine.

I looked at my feet. "It's not a thing. It's me enjoying something that is just mine. It's nothing more." It *was* a thing. I was scared to admit it out loud, but I could think of nothing else. I wanted Jacob to leave so I could check to see if he'd messaged me this morning.

"Why do you insist on lying to me?"

I wouldn't look at him as I scoured the room for my cloak. I couldn't find where I had tossed it. "Because you're disapproving."

He sighed. "I don't want to see you hurt, and attachment can only lead to that. You know what your fate will be as well as I know mine."

I still avoided his eyes. "I know, and I don't want to think about it."

"Why?" I could feel his eyes on me.

"Because with him I don't feel like I have to put on a face. I am cherishing it until he decides I'm not worth the effort." I saw my cloak behind him. I reached for it, but he wouldn't move.

He cupped my face and tilted my gaze up to meet his. "Enjoy it. Escape reality for a while if it's what you need. You've put on a better face your whole life than I have, but know this won't go past your coronation. It will come out." He paused, and I could see how sad he was for me. "Treasure his admiration in your limited number of days."

I nodded, dropping my head to his shoulder. "We should like this status. It's an honor to be given this place in life by the universe. But yet we are ungrateful like scabs."

He wrapped his arms tightly around me. "At least scabs don't have pressure to put their penis in a vagina they have no interest in for the good of the Akillie name."

I shuddered. "Don't ever speak in those terms to me again."

"Want to hear me say cock and pussy?"

I pulled away from him, winkling my nose. "Jacob."

When Jacob finally left I checked my messages, finding one from Madden.

M: **Is it later yet, do you want to meet me?**

I laughed. He must have sent it as soon as he'd woken up.

J: **You know I have a full day.**

Before I could even turn my screen off he replied.

M: **Lunch?**

J: **Tonight. I have other engagements for the day.**

M: **Can I keep you all night this time?**

It was a loaded question.

J: **Maybe.**

I wanted this. Even with the reservations from Jacob I had to chase it.

J: **If you come to my suite.**

A low burning heat formed in my gut, and I knew it was going to be hard to think of anything else until then.

＊＊＊＊

After hours of strategy meetings, which I was scolded by the Baron for being late to, I was shoved into a room with three maids to fuss over me. I sat and closed my eyes while my hair was washed and dried. I tried to visualize myself back in his arms. I hadn't slept so well in years. I, for the most part, had given up on sleeping more than an hour or two. My lips curled into a smile, and I hardly noticed when they started painting my nails and shining my skin. Not a single blemish could show on the giant vid screens while I was part of the opening ceremonies.

My dress was brought in. It was a work of art. Commissioned months ago, it was handmade and hand embroidered. First I was bound by two women into the dress's corset. The black lace peeked out over the top of the dress, which cut low on my chest, creating a layer of lace covering most of my breasts. The overall illusion was stunning, and I felt it made me look like a different person, which at this moment I was thankful for.

If Madden showed up at the ceremony, there was a good chance he wouldn't recognize me like this. When I was dressed, I looked in the mirror. The only part of *me* left was my eyes. I put on a smile before heading out to the carriage. The Baron was already sitting in the coach when I climbed in. He nodded at me, and we took off around the park toward the capital building. The Worlds' Fair was the kick off to the large science conference among all the prominent worlds under the Akillie's rule. New graduates from the institute were drafted into their chosen fields, and additionally, research was proposed, planned, and funded at the institute. I would sit in with the Baron on the important meetings, on top of my classes and course work. I was exhausted thinking about it.

I wanted to be anywhere else. I might have even taken a role as a salver across the seven dunes over being pinned into a dress that felt three sizes too small and painted like an expensive doll, which was really all I was. I was to look pretty, say my lines, and wave to the crowds who came to see the House of Akillie. I tried to draw in a breath to calm my nerves, but even that was impossible with the binding around my chest. Hadn't this shit gone out of style five centuries ago? But silly fashion always sprang back into popularity. Nothing was ever new.

I paced the room we waited in, my nerves worse than normal. I didn't think I'd ever get used to the public speaking.

"Jocelynn," Jacob called to me through the din. Had our positions been reversed he would be standing up here. But four and a half minutes had given him a free pass.

My eyes scanned the faces for one closely resembling my own.

"Jacob," I hissed, beckoning him over. Dressed in a light gray suit with a double-breasted jacket and four bottom trousers, all complemented by the purple button down and tie that matched my dress, he looked striking, even more so than I did.

He wore a coy grin, and I could see through the bodies milling about that he had another hand clasped in his own. I scowled at him, and he shrugged, not apologetically but remorsefully. He knew as much as I did the burden I carried being firstborn. I didn't hold it against him. I held it against my mother. He darted away without a backward glance towing a man behind him. Jacob's companion wasn't a noble either. He looked like he was from one of the hard labor worlds. I shook my head and laughed. It was his favorite time of the year. All the delegates brought crews with them, giving my brother a wide variety to work his charm on.

Too soon I stood on stage to the right of the Baron. He gave the welcoming speech, going on for far too long about the prosperity of the House of Akillie. He boasted of their wealth, and how new tech meant bright futures for all their worlds.

"And your pockets," I said under my breath. It was all a show. A show of Akillie's wealth. How many planets were entrusted by the Emperor to his care, and that he was the most prosperous Barony in the known universes. There were six other Houses which the Emperor entrusted the running of the known galaxy to. The two wealthiest were my house, Akillie, and Jok, who of course was our biggest rival.

The Emperor ruled over all, and for very little work took an exorbitant amount in taxes as well as tech and men for his personal guard. The scheme was brilliant in my mind. He got Akillie and Jok to hate each other by dividing the best planets between them and then shifted the more valuable ones back and forth depending on what he was given each year.

The Jok's higher math capabilities had made such a thing possible, along with countless other things we Akillies and our science founded society had no hopes of mastering without outside assistance. We worked our asses off for tech to be handed over to him, and he had the best of both houses. I was the only one who seemed to notice, and I never brought it up to the Baron. Such talk would be treasonous. I did my part and smiled as I would replace him when he was surely killed off by one of the other Barons. As many people stood around us as allies, there were many who hated us.

My eyes landed on Madden. He was standing there, in the crowd, staring at me. The hurt showed in his posture. How long had he been there while my mind wandered? No one but the dignitaries came to these things. He was a student, and while he had full access there was no requirement to be here.

He knew who I was. There was no easing him into it. No turning back now.

Chapter Fifteen

Madden

Jocelynn wasn't *a* noble. She was *the* noble, the heir. Arguably there wasn't anyone set to inherit more status except the Emperor's son. I stared, mouth agape. This was who I'd had in my bed the night before. My legs wouldn't move from the spot. They were rooted in place as I watched her give the opening speech. It didn't look like her, not entirely. It was her, but the face paint and stiff posture made it clear she wore a mask, giving her an almost detached appearance.

Now I knew the reason she hadn't told me her full name and why she was reluctant to give me her scan. My stomach fell to mingle among my intestines, feeling like I had been sucker punched. I wasn't sure if I should feel betrayed, lied to, or relieved she wasn't the daughter of the ender. The thought had crossed my mind. I knew there had to be a reason she would only see me on her terms. I puffed out my cheeks as I blew out a breath, refocusing on her.

She spoke eloquently. It was a side of her I hadn't seen before, poised and stunning. I fixed my gaze on her while she spoke, my eyes never leaving hers. Sadness settled over me as realization struck.

We couldn't ever be together.

She was having fun, flirting and messing around with a scab, but the Baron would never let us be more, even if Jocelynn really wanted it. I repeated those words to myself over and over. I was nothing more than a rebellious streak for her. I had to grind it into my head, or there was no way I could do what I needed to.

Her eyes met mine, and I saw the hint of worry on her face as her voice pitched, before she replaced her mask. She knew I knew. I set my mouth in a line, holding my feelings back. I put on my own mask and turned away from her. Her words faltered as I walked out of the crowded hall.

I was swimming against the current as I bumped and jostled my way through the sea of people. Maybe I was imagining it, but I thought I could hear a difference in her voice as I got further away. She was hurrying through the last. It was slight, but in the few days we had spent together I could already read her mood, which she hated.

I found a place in the back, out of her direct line of sight. I took a seat, listening to her musical tone and resting my head back against the wall. She finished her speech, and I realized I hadn't really absorbed a word of it. Her father welcomed us and started his own drone, going on about duty and privilege and honor. I closed my eyes, the heat in the room getting to me. Honor to bring in all the tech and research developed over the last year and share it because we were all his minions. She was, too, or at least his blood.

A fist hit my shoulder, and I jerked out of thoughts. My head snapped around, finding Jacob standing over me.

"Get up. She wants to see you."

I opened my mouth to speak, but he roughly grabbed my arm, cutting me off.

"I don't care what excuse you have not to. She wants you, and I'm here to get you." He dragged me toward one of the back exits.

I planted my feet using my larger size to stop our movement.

His lips pulled back in a snarl when he turned back around. "Don't cause a scene. It wouldn't be good for you or for her." There was a sharp look to his eyes Jocelynn never had. His kind was all the same—killer instinct, and they weren't afraid to use it to get what they wanted. It was best to keep a distance. When he pulled me again, I went. Jacob slid his arm through mine, keeping them locked together so all but a knowing observer would think we were strolling and chatting.

He led me through a set of doors, typing in codes as we went. We weaved through a maze of corridors until he set his hand on a scanner, causing a door to appear in the wall where there wasn't one before. We slipped through the slim space in the door, and I looked back, feeling the rush of air pass my cheek as it slammed closed in the space we had occupied moments before.

"Madden." Her voice drew me in.

Our eyes met, and her makeup was marred. She'd been crying. I was weak for another set of reasons. It ate at me to see her like that. I wanted to make it better. I wanted to take away her pain, even at the expense of mine.

"Jocelynn."

She nodded and dropped her eyes, curling her shoulders in, looking defeated. "For what it's worth, I'm sorry." Her voice exuded more confidence than her body language.

"Are you sorry you were caught, or sorry you lied to me?" I couldn't let my feelings enter my tone. I would lose it. If I was just a toy she was stringing along I had to run. There were cracks forming in my soul, and I couldn't take it.

"I didn't want to lie to you. I should have stayed away from you." Her words hurt. "But I couldn't. I've never felt this way about anyone before. I know you won't forgive me, but I'm sorry."

"What? Couldn't resist a plaything? Well there are tons of men who would be that for you, knowing full well what you are. As your brother does himself. You didn't have to do this. There was no reason to lead me on."

"The last thing I wanted was to cause you pain or ruin things for you here. I was selfish for wanting it." She lifted a hand to her eye, but dropped it before she touched her face. She took three or four shallow breaths, like she was trying to maintain her composure. I wanted her to show me some real emotion. Something more than the poised falsity she presented to the worlds.

"Wanting it?" The ache in my chest spread. She was full of mixed messages, and I wasn't sure I could blame her. Look at who she was. Who she was raised to be. I was nothing to her.

"Yes." There was hesitation in her answer. I wanted to shake her. I wanted her to speak openly. "For wanting you."

"Feelings are pain. To not feel them is to be dead." The chasm in my chest widened. There had been a spark between us, but now it felt as if it was a figment of my imagination. She was cold and closed off.

"That's not what I meant." She took a step toward me. "Don't go."

I had to look away to hold my ground. "I get it. You got it out of your system. You don't have to keep this up. You don't have to worry. I won't do anything to embarrass you if that's why you called me back here." My walls were in place for good reason, and I had to reaffirm it to myself.

She stepped into me before I finished, taking my hands in hers. "Is that how you feel?"

Refusing to meet her eyes, I nodded.

She sank to her knees. "I feel more for you than I should. I couldn't lose you. I think I'm falling for you." Her ears went pink, and she brought her hand up to cover her mouth. "Am I right to believe you feel nothing then?"

Her composure wavered for just a second, but I saw it.
"*I* feel nothing? You stand here, as the ice queen—
Baroness, whatever the fuck you are, stringing me along,
and now you're telling me *I* feel nothing? You have a lot
of nerve, J. I don't care who you were, and I probably
wouldn't have even if you had told me, but you shouldn't
have strung me along."

"I wasn't." Her words were barely audible, but
they drew both her brother and my attention.

"Then what do you want, Jocelynn?" The anger I
felt fled, and a spark of hope took its place.

She shook her head and turned away from me. "I
can't."

"It's not that you can't. You won't. I'm not
stupid. You had your fun, so can I go?"

Chapter Sixteen

Jocelynn

"If one of you opens the damn door I'll show myself out," Madden growled when neither of us moved.

Jacob burst out laughing. I would have if I wasn't so irritated and hurt.

"This place is set up like a maze. They give us sheets to memorize with our numbers as preschoolers. You'd have a better chance of surviving space without a suit than getting out of here by yourself."

He scowled, clearly not keen on being the butt of the joke. "Let me the fuck out. Getting lost and starving to death in a maze would be better than being ridiculed by you two for my ignorance."

"Who do you think is ridiculing you?"

"Your quips are all the same." He crossed his large, tattooed arms over his chest.

"Has your opinion of me degraded so quickly?" I crossed the room to stand in front of him. My heart ached, and all the blood had drained from my face. He had been a bright spot in the dull life I was bound to in servitude. "I'm trying to let you go." It took all energy I had let to keep the emotion from my voice. I had to push him away for his own good.

"What did you expect?" His words were void of the musical tone they once held. "You lied to me and used me."

"I expected you to be upset for withholding the information, but you knew I was Trenton blood." My heart was being ripped from my chest. He had no idea of my feelings for him, and it was entirely my fault. "It went too far…"

"You're not just Trenton blood. You're the direct ruling fucking line. Akillie is different, even for your brother." He scoffed.

"I wanted for something I wasn't allowed. I can't say I'm sorry enough." Years of training and here I was about to let tears fall. I not only felt like I'd failed him, but my entire line. So many of my house before me where strong, and here I was weak and in love with someone I could never have. Why couldn't I push past it?

"Are you blind? A normal Trenton I could be with given my new status. I bet you will marry a first of one of the lesser houses to form a trade alliance. You have no choice in the matter." He clenched his fists. "And you know it. So, I couldn't be more than a toy. You knew there was an expiration date when you started this. You kept it from me."

The words whipped across the room like daggers, hitting harder as he went. I could see the pain behind his eyes. What made it worse was I'd put it there. I took a tentative step toward him. He backed off until his back was against the door. I closed the distance, and he growled, keeping his arms between us.

"You're right. You started off as a toy." I laid my hands over his chest, looking up at him. "If you ever felt anything for me, please at least listen before you write me off as evil."

"You have me trapped. So get to talking." His demeanor dripped scorn.

"You're not trapped. If you wish you leave and never see me again, Jacob will show you out." My feelings aside, I couldn't blame him. I was shocked he even let me touch him.

He looked to Jacob.

"No skin off my back," my brother replied. "But you should listen to her. I've never seen her like this about anyone, let alone a toy. You're more than that."

"I never expected to see you again after the club, and then I couldn't stop thinking about you…" A lump formed in my throat, and I couldn't get the words out. I dropped my head to his chest. After only a few days the movement had become so familiar. As my forehead touched his soft shirt, I jerked back muttering, "I'm sorry. So sorry."

His hard demeanor didn't change.

"Jacob, just let him go." My voice broke, and I felt the red in my cheeks deepen. "We owe him that much at least." I wanted to get away. I needed to hide my shame. Jacob was right about attachment. Our kind wasn't allowed it. I pulled back, trying to hide my face long enough to wipe the tears away. "I'm sorry. I won't bother you again."

"You couldn't stop thinking about me?"

I nodded. "I didn't know I was missing a piece of myself until I met you."

Warm arms wrapped around me, forcing my face back into Madden's chest. I breathed him in and shook.

He kissed under my ear, then whispered, "This isn't a game for you?"

I shook my head. "No, not at all. I swear to you."

"Me either," he said.

"I should have stopped it. This is my fault." I fisted my hands in his shirt. "I shouldn't have let it get this far knowing it wasn't possible."

He cupped both sides of my face and tilted it up, forcing me to look at him. "I doubted you felt the same way for a moment. A day with my other half is better than a lifetime of meaningless encounters." Our mouths met, and he stroked his tongue over the seam of my lips. I parted them, allowing him access to my mouth.

"Fuck, do you two really have to do that here? Straight sex is so boring." Jacob scoffed from the place he'd sat.

We ignored him.

"I want this," he said, smiling into my lips. "For as long as we're allowed."

"I do, too." For the first time since I'd put on the corset, I could breathe, and I hadn't even taken it off yet.

Jacob was at my side yanking me out of the moment. "We've got to get him out of here. The Baron is coming down the hall."

Chapter Seventeen

Madden

I looked between the pair of them. "The Baron, as in your father?"

"We don't call him father." Jacob wrinkled his nose. "He's not very fatherly. He's much more Baronly."

I looked at Jocelynn. She was trying to compose herself, wiping at the smeared kohl under her eyes.

"The translation is, he's an over controlling bastard who treats even his children like subjects. Bad for you if you don't have a reason to be here." She looked at Jacob.

"There is no other way out of here." He shoved us apart and Jocelynn toward the sofa, before turning into me. He stepped into my personal space and had a wicked look in his eyes. "You're both lucky I love my sister more than my own arse."

A moment later the door slid open, and the beast of a man who stood behind it was yelling before he fit through it. The suit he wore looked like two hundred years of breeding wouldn't have been enough preparation for a peasant to pull it off. He oozed all the poise and prestige of a king. The clothes were tailored to perfection, and for his age he was shockingly attractive. Not a day under sixty, distinguished gray crept from his temples back through his black hair, but it made him that much more handsome. He was trim and fit, cut from a cloth I'd never hoped to obtain. I could see the staunch resemblance to his children now. Both of the twins carried his strong jawline, high cheekbones, as well as full lips. I assumed the light hair and eyes were their mother's genetic contribution. Other than that, they likely bore little resemblance to her.

Jacob grabbed me and touched his lips to mine. I was in such shock I couldn't push him off before he shoved me away.

"What is the meaning of this?" The Baron looked down his nose at me, pulling his lips back to expose the points of gleaming white teeth.

Jacob donned what is best described as a sheepish look, masked with shock. I knew then he was an extraordinary actor, and nothing from his lips could be trusted at face value. J had slipped back into the depths of the room in the commotion as if she hadn't been involved with us. She penciled on kohl. As flagrantly as Jacob put on a mask, she, too, wore one.

Jacob drew into himself, hunching his shoulders forward as he looked at his feet. "Sorry," he muttered under his breath. "I know he shouldn't be back here."

I tried to follow his lead, taking a step back to stand half behind him.

"Why would you bring a scab back here?" The Baron snarled. "And…" He trailed off. He was clearly off put by the kiss.

"He is a friend. We were about to leave…" Jacob chewed his lip in a way I'd never seen him do. It was pure production for the Baron's benefit. He was an artful deceiver with years of experience playing his father. I felt like I was watching from the outside as he skillfully guided his father's attention away from Jocelynn.

The Baron scowled. "You know how I feel about such things being out of place, as this one is."

The Baron treated me sub-humanly. To him I was no more worth a glance than even recognition of my ability to breathe.

"It won't happen again."

"See to it you don't happen into its presence again." He turned to me, his hard gaze appearing to memorize my features in case I made a further offense.

A man like him could change my destiny. The look solidified the necessity to never come eye to eye with him again. I'd been judged and proven unworthy to keep the company of the lord and lady in waiting. It confirmed everything I had felt but half an hour before. I pressed my palm into my chest when he turned away, stalking off toward the exit. Jocelynn's gaze called to me, and I looked back over my shoulder to meet her eyes. There was everything and nothing in one glance. Nothing the Baron had said mattered after one look. She rushed to me before the door was shut behind him, collecting my hands in hers. Her forehead met my shoulder, and I enveloped her in my arms.

"I'm sorry," she whispered into my arm.

I stroked my fingers down her back, all the anger I had felt bleeding out of me. "My mind hasn't changed. Even a few days with you is better than a lifetime of regret."

"Not many people would feel that way after one encounter with him." Her voice was hardly audible.

"None of that matters. Let's get out of here before it happens again." I cupped her cheeks, bringing her face away from my shoulder so I could look into the deep blue of her eyes I had become intimately familiar with. "Once was more than enough."

"You both are so welcome for taking all the heat, which I am sure will come with some sort of wildly fun punishment."

I had forgotten Jacob was in the room, and we both turned to look at him.

"Thank you, brother mine." She pulled out of my grasp to wrap her arms around his neck. "I owe you more than one, and I admit you always save my arse."

He rolled his eyes and smacked her cheek. "I know where your attention is at. We need to get him out of here and you changed before we blow this place."

"All I heard was blow," she countered.

He raised both brows and shook his head. "There are some things you need to keep to yourself. Isn't that what they teach you in all those godawful etiquette classes I always ditch?"

"If you ditch them so often it's a wonder you can correct her," I said pulling her back to me by the loose ribbon of her undone corset. She spun into my arms, wrapping her own around my neck. I lowered my head to whisper over her lips. "Can we find some place to be alone tonight?"

She looked at her brother out of the corner of her eyes, and he sighed. "I will do my best to cover both your asses, but if you get caught it's on you. I plan on having my own much needed stress release tonight."

I lowered my mouth to hers, stroking my tongue over the seam of her lips until she parted them, allowing me access. I tilted my head to the side, deepening the kiss as energy danced between us, causing my heart to pick up speed and my blood to boil in my veins. She had an electrifying effect on me I couldn't ignore. It took hold in my mind, giving me the high of an addiction.

All too soon she was yanked out of my arms. Our outstretched arms reached for one another, fingertips grazing as Jacob dragged her backward.

"Say good-bye." He stepped between us before looking at her. "I'll take him out. You go clean yourself up."

The ceremonial paint she wore was smudged in places where our faces had rubbed together. It would be evident to anyone who looked at her what she'd done.

Chapter Eighteen

Jocelynn

"Wipe that shit off your face, and let's go." Jacob burst into my room as I was reaching around my back to try to get my dress the rest of the way off. I had gotten to my room mere moments before he appeared, ready to leave.

It had been a long two days, and I was ready to be done with the Worlds' Fair and back to my semi private life. At least until I was married off, but I had a few years before that would happen. I planned on enjoying it while getting to know Madden.

"Good for you that you can be the utter disappointment everyone expects you to be wearing that." I gestured to the ill-fitting pants he wore and the partly unbuttoned shirt. "But not all of us have the luxury. They preened me for hours before it took three servants to bind me into this thing."

"Keep opening your mouth and I'm going to stand here and laugh while you try to get yourself out of that Antion Eliese death trap." He crossed his arms over his chest and leaned back against the doorframe. He was tall, above six foot, to my five foot four, but our faces were the same, strong jaw, sculpted cheekbones, and the Akillie scowl. The only difference was in our eyes. His were light blue where mine were dark blue. But our coloring we got from our mother. We both had a light dusting of freckles across our noses, as well as our shoulders.

I scowled at him now, and he grinned ruefully.

"Doesn't scare me, Jocelynn." Jacob walked over in his usual "give no fucks" getup. He wasn't even dressed to be here, in his uniform, or even the waistcoat and slacks our mother had pressed him to wear for the state dinner. Instead he wore leather pants hanging off his slender hips and a thick leather belt slung not through his belt loops, but hanging to one side, weighed down with a holster. But there wasn't a gun in the holster. There was a bottle of premium aged whiskey.

"Get me out of this dress before I slash your carotid and drink your whiskey."

He scoffed at me and didn't make a move.

I flipped my blade out of the sheath I wore at all times and twirled it around my hand. He stomped closer, hand shooting out to take hold of the handle mid turn before drawing it down my spine. His expertise with the knife flicked the tip hard enough to shred the thin fabric but spared my skin. I felt the point and knew I would have a scratch from the nape of my neck to the base of my spine. I glared over my shoulder, and he smiled ruefully.

"Ask and you shall receive." He offered the knife back to me handle first.

I was better at close combat than he was, and he didn't flinch as I reached for the knife. As the dress pooled around my feet, he took his own smaller knife to the lace corset underneath. But I held up my hand, signaling for him to leave it. Madden might like it.

I suspected this ruin of the dress was a private *fuck off* to its designer, who had once been a suitor of Jacob's and caused quite a scandal when he tried to out their relationship.

I slipped behind the screen to change.

"How they got you into it in the first place is beyond me." He shoved his knife back into his belt.

I pulled on a light shoulderless shirt that cut down around and showed off the lace of the undergarment in the front, adding to it a pair of my own leathers. Next, I strapped on a belt, but not one like his. Mine was more useful and contained fewer illicit substances. When I was dressed, I pulled up my hair into a twist on the back of my head, scowling over at him.

"Why do women always take so long to get ready?"

"If I could shave off most of my hair like you do I would be faster." I strolled past him, lifting the whiskey as I went. I was almost a better pickpocket than he was. His hands were less shaky and could slip past even the most aware individuals, but my skills were enough to get past his defenses. It wasn't until we stepped into the lift and I had the bottle to my lips that he even noticed.

"Wench." He grabbed the bottle from me and took a swig of his own.

"Where are we going?"

"To a rave. I am meeting some friends."

"Did you tell Mad?"

"Of course I did. I'm sure you can find some place to sneak off to in the dark for your alone time." He gave me a stern look. "But you need to watch yourself. It won't be long before the Baroness catches on to you being absent as much as I am. We've already cut it too close getting caught tonight."

"How come you get away with sneaking around and fucking whatever arse you see fit? Whereas I chase one and am doomed?" I scowled. I thought it was much better for me to be only chasing one instead of the many Jacob seemed to.

"You see, that right there is the problem. If she thinks you're serious about someone and they don't approve, they'll make it impossible to be with them. I don't get attached. I keep my distance, and because I do so, they ignore me with men. If I fell for one, they'd ship me off to manage one of the planets at the edge of the known universe and find me a damn bride to boot." He touched my cheek. "Guard your heart, J. Love is for scabs who don't have an empire to inherit."

"I've already screwed that up."

He looked at me with sympathy in his eyes. "I know."

Madden stood shadowed in the mouth of an alley when we ducked out the servants' gate. He'd also changed from the formal dress attire of the school attendees to well-worn jeans and a thermal. He hadn't taken to the cold nights of our planet yet. The sweltering heat of his Harden was unrelenting even during the night. As soon as the sun dropped below the horizon here, the breeze picked up, and the chill cut to the bone. My arms were bare, welcoming the relief of the fall warmth, but I could see the goosebumps down his neck where the green fabric didn't cover. As soon as we were out of the view of the streetlamps he collected me into his arms.

"Why are you always so warm?" He rubbed his hands down my back, leaching the heat from my skin.

"I'm always warm... Do you think you can forgive me?" I was hesitant to give into his touch until I knew. I hated opening myself up. But worse, with him I knew once I let go there would be no coming back.

"I already have. Now, share your warmth."

I leaned into him, not at all minding sharing the warmth between us as I nuzzled into his neck. With each moment that passed I fell into a more comfortable position with him, learning the familiarity of his body and the way it reacted to mine.

"Get off each other. Can't you wait until you're in the dark with people other than your flesh and blood watching?" Jacob slid a stick between his lips and lit the tip. The scent of tobacco, mint, and cloves permeated the air as he inhaled.

"Come with me," Mad whispered.

"Where?"

"Trust me."

I looked between my brother and Mad, chewing my lip.

"Go, but don't be calling me to save your arse when you get into a stitch." He waved me off and turned his back on us.

"I trust you." I took Mad's offered hand, and followed him blindly.

Chapter Nineteen

Madden

She took my hand when I offered it, and I led her away from her brother. I felt him watching as we faded into the shadows.

"Where are we going?"

"That would be telling." When we passed the turn off for the building I stayed in, she looked around.

"Madden." She stopped.

"I thought you trusted me?" I tried to drag her forward by the hand, but she was surprisingly strong.

"I do trust you, but…"

"There can't be a but in that sentence if you trust me." I slid my arms around her waist.

"It's ingrained in me not to go anywhere with a man alone, more so if I don't know where I'm going." She looked up at me, and I could tell she hated admitting it. "You know what I am, and I'm sure you can use your imagination to decipher what could be done to me to be used against my father."

My brows knit together. "We don't have to go."

"You know I don't think of you like that." She blew out a breath. "I'm not good at trust, but I'm trying. I'm used to Trenton politics and everyone having an agenda."

I gripped a hand in her noticeably new black cloak. "Then have a little faith I'm different."

"You're right. I'm sorry."

It was going to take a lot to get past her walls, but I knew it would be worth it. "I'm taking you someplace I guarantee you've never been before."

She scoffed. "You think you know Trenton better than I do? There isn't a place within one hundred kilometers I haven't been."

When I'd been shown this place I was assured it was the best kept secret of the low life. Otherwise it would have been developed into another hotel or garden or palace bullshit. "Bet me then." I let the smugness show on my face. I wanted to bait her.

"Bet you what?" I could see her mind spinning.

"If you've never been to this place then you will give me one item off your person, when I ask, no questions, no hesitation." It was a low blow, but I couldn't help the images in my mind.

She got an intense look about her and nodded. "And if I've been there what do I get?"

"What do you want?"

She looked up at the sky. "You will take one class of my choosing with me next term."

I stepped back and stuck out my hand. "It's a deal."

She took it and shook, watching me.

"Now can we go?" I pulled her forward, my palm still in hers.

"Lead the way."

I linked our arms back together and took the turn leading to the outskirts of the city. The bike I'd arranged was sitting right where they said it would be, and I couldn't help but grin. Sometimes it's nice to have friends with connections. She looked up at me as I swung a leg over the bike and gestured for her to get on behind me.

Taking the helmet I offered, she climbed on behind me. "Do you know how to drive one of these?" she said into my ear.

My skin prickled as her hot breath blew over the back of my neck. "It's basically a requirement on Harden." I needed this.

Everything here was so different. The familiar would keep my head in check. I gripped the throttle and pushed the starter. She enveloped me with her arms.

"I had no idea," she said over the roar of the engine.

Her grip tightened around me, and I took off, not replying. She laid her head between my shoulder blades, and it felt like heaven. Now I understood why some of the men brought their women on trips through the mine roads on their speeders. The cool wind whipped at her cloak causing it to billow out behind us. But we drew warmth from each other, and I could feel her cheeks pulled up in a smile against my back. The ride wasn't far, and I had to slow when we reached the caverns. The map was imprinted in my mind as I took the tight turns as fast as I could, whipping the back tire out.

I had to give it to her, she never screamed once. She seemed to have as little fear as I did. We started to climb, and the engine of the small bike strained at the degree in which I pushed it. I didn't let up, forcing the bike to her max until we hit the peak of the climb. I let off the throttle, and we rocked down faster than top speed on a straight. The only reaction from J was for her to press her face between my shoulders.

A grin spread across my wind-burned lips. The bike jumped when we hit the flat, and I kicked out to the right. Using my toes to skim the ground, I kept us balanced. The next portion was up again, and we slowed, engine chugging.

"How have I lived my whole life without this?" she screamed against the wind.

"It's freedom in its simplest form." I called back, not sure if she would be able to hear me.

"How did you learn to ride like this?" she asked as we neared the peak.

"Maybe I'll tell you sometime." Chances were she'd disapprove if she knew.

We dipped down only for a few moments before circling back uphill. It wouldn't be clear where we were going until we came out from between the peaks. I could see the moons already, and the stars above us started to brighten the further we got away from the city lights. We took another sharp turn and came out on the cliff ledge. I cut the engine and rolled to a stop on the expansive flat of the large rock.

The view was breathtaking. I'd been told nothing rivaled it, but I hadn't believed anything could be this beautiful. I waited for her response as I drank it in. The city glowed warm with the hint of smoke rising from fireplaces. The twinkling lights created the illusion of a romantic backdrop. I felt her climb off, so I kicked out the stand on the bike and followed.

She walked right up to the edge. I stayed back a few feet, my stomach growing tight. Height was a whole different thing when I wasn't on my bike. She turned back toward me and gestured for me to join her. Hesitantly, I stepped forward, taking her hand. I tried not to think about the ground crumbling beneath my feet or losing my balance. She squeezed my hand in hers, and I noticed mine was sweaty.

I glanced over, seeing the wonder and disbelief in her eyes.

"I was right, wasn't I?" I whispered.

"You were." She turned into me, resting her hands on my hips.

I turned, trying not to look over the edge as I brushed my lips over her forehead. "Do you like it?"

She nodded, gazing up at the sky. Then her eyes went past me up to the heavens. "The sky is even lovelier."

I traced my fingers down her slender arms, then grabbed her under her arse, lifting her off her feet. She looked down at me, giggling, before resting our foreheads together.

"Thank you," she said over my lips in a whisper.

"You should trust me more often." I licked over her lips.

"I do, I really do." She rubbed our lips together, still smiling.

"Come on, there is more." I set her down on her feet and backed toward the bike, glad to get away from the cliff.

"More?" There was a skip in her step as she followed me, her eyes still scanning the stars.

I dug around in the packs and pulled out the blanket then the pre packed meal. "Much more." I spread the blanket out over the ground and took a seat, beckoning her forward.

She lay back, placing her head in my lap. "What did you bring?"

I pushed my fingers into her hair. "A late dinner, if you're hungry."

"You're so damn romantic."

I lifted her head and moved it gently to the ground so I could lie out next to her. She shifted to lay her head on my chest. I covered us with the spare blanket, and we stayed quiet, looking up at the stars for a long time.

"Why me?"

"What do you mean?" she asked, her voice laced with sleep.

"I'm not so ignorant I don't know you could have invited any guy to your bed, and they would have come."

She glanced up at me. "Because you don't treat me like they do."

"Because I didn't know who you were." I laughed it off.

"No, even after. You're intelligent but not superior. Kind but not soft and witty but not mean. The attitude of those born here is entitlement. You're refreshing." She paused. "Plus you don't pander to me to stay on my good side. You say what you're thinking."

I winced a little. "You mean when I yelled at you?"

She chuckled.

"Why do you seem to love all the parts of me I hate?" I brushed my lips over her temple.

"Because you see them as weaknesses, and I see them as strengths." She rolled half on top of me to set her chin on my chest.

I grew semihard, trying not to squirm too much under her when we were having a serious discussion. "Because I want to be seen as strong, not weak. I want to be respected. The qualities you like about me don't bring that about."

She shook her head. "You're wrong. You can be kind and well respected."

"It's seen as feminine. I don't want to project that."

"You don't have to be macho to be manly. I hate when men are like that." Her stare was harsh.

"Well you must be the only one." I slid my hand down her spine, painfully aware of how close we were and what we could be doing up here so far from both our realities.

"Do you care what anyone else thinks?" She raised both brows.

I wasn't sure how to answer her. "I do care how people see me. But I don't care if anyone else feels the way you do."

"Good, but you should stop caring what everyone else thinks." She pushed her knees between mine and slipped between them.

I parted my thighs, welcoming her there. My arousal grew hard against her stomach.

"You're so easy." She rocked over me softly.

"I'm not easy, you're good." I lifted my head to chase her mouth, demanding a kiss. She gave in, slipping her tongue into my mouth.

When she broke the kiss she looked down at me with heavily lidded eyes. "Let's go back."

My heart sank. "I'll take you back, if you want." She always pulled back when we got heated. I was starting to think she had no interest in more.

"You ask me to trust you. Have a little faith in return."

I nodded and waited.

She blew out a breath. "I trust you, and I need to get back. Come to my chambers with me." She looked right into my eyes as she said it, and it may have been the most alluring thing I'd ever heard.

Chapter Twenty

Jocelynn

I could hardly breathe. My heart raced as I pushed open one of the side entrances to the palace. The door was the closest one to my suite of rooms, but it was still a long walk down a vacant hallway. I looked into his eyes. He was instantly calm. Jacob did this all the time. What did I have to worry about?

I slid my hand into his, and he squeezed my fingers. "Let's go," I said under my breath.

I took a step out into the hall, and he followed close at my back. I could feel the heat radiating off his body as we made our way through the dark. I had to fight the urge to sprint the length of the hall, knowing my boots would clatter against the stone. A creak sounded at the other side, and I froze. A shadow moved at the other end, but I couldn't make out whether it was human or animal. I backed up, hitting Madden, who stood still. I pushed back into him wishing he would get the hint and back up with me. But he stayed where he was.

"Jacob?" he called out, entirely too loud.

"Yep." My brother slipped out of the alcove he stood in, much closer than where I had seen the movement.

My heart was beating out of my chest, and I didn't know how to caution them as Jacob stalked forward.

"Little late getting back." My brother stopped before us and leaned against the wall.

Mad tightened his grip on my hand and wrapped his other around my chest. "We went a long way. What's it to you?" The words sounded like a challenge.

I looked between them and to where I'd seen the movement. I wanted to say something, but I also didn't want to give away I'd seen them. I cursed under my breath.

"It's nothing to me, but you do know people pay attention to where she is. I am expected to fuck off, but when you have her missing meetings and events, notice is taken." He shook his head. "That's not normal for her. If you two were smart you would make sure to keep her as normal as possible."

I felt the tension bleed out of Madden. "I'm sure you're right."

"He's staying?" The question was directed at me. I nodded.

"Don't be stupid." His eyes were hard, and I knew what he meant.

"I'm not ignorant."

"Never said you were, but we don't need more issues than we already have, do we?" he asked.

"What are you doing here slinking around in dark hallways anyway?" Madden added before Jacob could leave.

"I was making sure you brought her home." Without another word he left in the same direction I'd heard the noise from. I wondered if he'd run into some eavesdropper.

"Let's go," Mad urged, pressing his groin into my back playfully.

"I see my brother hasn't deterred you at all." I didn't need a second prodding. I was as anxious as he was.

"I compartmentalize, and I think it would take a lot to deter me from my need for you." He kissed the back of my neck as I waved my communicator over the lock. The door clicked open as I felt his warm tongue.

It was barely closed before he had me pinned to the wall just inside. The weight of his much larger body was intoxicating, and I could feel his hard length against my stomach as he shamelessly rubbed it into me. He grabbed me by the throat, not harshly, forcing my chin up so he could claim my mouth. I gave into him. Need dripped from his every gesture. I pushed my hands under the edge of his cloak, forcing it off his shoulders, and he released me only to let the fabric fall to the floor. The room was warm because I'd left a fire burning, and it intensified my need to get out of the layers of clothes.

I teased my fingers under the hem of his shirt, tracing over the sculpted muscles there. I dragged my nails back down his skin as I elicited a deep moan from his mouth. Inch by inch, I eased up his shirt, and he happily lifted his arms to let me peel it from him before doing the same to mine. He didn't resume the kiss. Instead he rested his forehead against mine while his fingers traced the lace pattern covering my chest.

"I almost want to leave this on you." His voice came with heavy breaths.

I tilted my chin up, taking another demanding kiss. "You can." My chest heaved under his touch.

"Another time." He brushed his fingers down my throat. "I want to taste every inch of you."

The thought sent a shiver down my spine, and I trembled against him. "Only if I get to do the same."

He stepped back into the glow of the moonlight filtering through the hangings. The light aged him, and I could see lines of worry etched into his hard face. I followed, pulled by some unseen force. I didn't want to be out of reach of him.

"Where do you want me?"

It was a large sitting room where I hosted guests. There were chairs and loveseats around the fire place, as well as a small table in an alcove and a writing desk in the far corner. It was in the same style of the rest of the house, reds and silvers.

I wasn't sure what I wanted, but I didn't want him to think I'd led him to a place that would restrict us. "Not here."

I tucked my hair behind my ear and left his side to open the door which led to my bedchamber. He followed me inside. With a trembling hand I reached to turn on one of the lamps. He stopped me and shook his head before pulling open the hangings on the windows. It was something I seldom did as the window looked out into a large courtyard where anyone could peer in. At this hour it was deserted. My bed was positioned so the moonlight glistened over the sheets giving them a ghostly purple glow.

He stood there, bare-chested, waiting for me. My breath caught in my throat. I'd never needed to be possessed like I did with Madden. He unhooked his belt as I crossed the room to him, and the click made me flush. He watched me as he pulled it from the loops. The fabric of his jeans caused the leather to whistle slightly, building my anticipation. I caressed the skin beneath his open fly, tracing the soft patch of hair that led into his boxers.

"Take them off."

He looked down at me, but I was focused on his hand gripping himself as I said the words.

"Going to order me around?" he asked as he hooked his thumbs in the waistline of his pants.

"I am, and you're going to like it." I was sure of myself. I didn't have to second guess how he'd feel about it. We both knew which one of us would be in charge.

"I already like it, ma'am." He shoved his jeans down and stepped out of them to stand before me in shorts barely covering his arousal.

I didn't make another move to touch him as I stood there. "Those off, too."

His eyes bored into me as he slowly lowered them, revealing himself to me. His length hung heavy between his thighs. As I reached out to touch him, he dropped to his knees at my feet, nuzzling into my stomach.

"I want to take yours off you." His fingers crawled up the back of my corset until they found the ties. He undid them one by one, loosening the fabric around me. He cast it aside and looked up at me. The height difference between us was so great his face was level with my breasts as he knelt. He stared at them for a moment, and my cheeks started to pink. But then, slowly, he lifted a hand to cup the underside of one breast and touched his lips to my nipple. My skin prickled, and pleasure washed through me at the simple touch. He parted his lips to flick his tongue over the taut peak. I thrust my hands into his hair, wanting to keep him right where he was for the rest of the night.

His fingers skimmed down the center line of my stomach to trace around the hemline of my pants as he parted his lips around my pebbled nipple, sucking it into his mouth. I let loose a whimper as his teeth met my flesh. The room was void of air, and I couldn't draw a deep breath. Before I knew it, he had undone the clasp to my leathers and drawn down the zipper. He gripped the waist and tugged, leaving me standing there in lace boy shorts. He dropped his head to my stomach, and I could feel his labored breath over my skin as he skimmed his nose over the thin fabric.

"I want you," he said through a gasp as his fingers traced the curve of my arse.

"You have me." I tugged on his hair, tilting his face up to look at me.

His eyes searched mine. "No, I want to be inside you."

"What's stopping you?"

He ran his fingers down the back of my thighs eliciting another soft moan from me. "I'm conflicted."

Before I could ask, he went on. "I also want to stay down here and worship your body." He flicked his tongue out to trace the delicate line of lace at the crease of my leg.

"We have time. Take me to bed."

He didn't hesitate, grabbing me under the ass as he got up, carrying me toward the bed. I kicked off my pants as he laid me out, before he crawled up to hover between my thighs. He was hard and leaking when he lowered his body to mine, leaving a warm trail of sticky fluid on my stomach. His lips parted for mine again as he rocked into me, pushing his thick head up my slit. I pushed at his chest and forced my hands between us so I could get rid of the last barrier we had.

He pulled back, frowning. "What's wrong?"

"Nothing. I just want these off." I lifted up my ass to slide the lace down, but he grabbed my wrists and stopped me.

"I want to take them off you."

I lay back and dropped my hands. He slid down so his face hovered over me as he gently removed them. I lifted up, giving him easier access. Once they were gone he brushed his fingers up the inside of my thighs causing heat to pool between my legs. I wanted him. He skimmed his nose over my lips, moaning softly.

"You are so beautiful." He teased his tongue just past my folds.

I arched my back, pressing myself into his face, needing more. "Madden..."

But he didn't give in right away, tracing a hot path over my lips with his flattened tongue. I gasped, needing so much more. He pushed his tongue deeper, finding my clit, and I shuddered with pleasure. It wouldn't take him long to push me over the edge if he stayed there. But he didn't. After the single taste he resumed his position over me. I could feel the heat coming off him in waves, and he was so close. I grabbed at his shoulders trying desperately to pull him down to me.

He tilted his head and rubbed the scruff on his jaw under my ear as he spoke. "Do we need protection?" He words stuttered, like it took every ounce of effort he had to hold off with me naked beneath him.

I shook my head, wrapping a leg around his ass so I could lift up into him, trying to feel every last inch of skin against me. "I want to feel you."

He drew in a shaky breath and reached between us to grip himself. His tip brushed over my entrance, and I melted. Every touch was like a jolt of electric pleasure infused into my veins, and like an addict, it wasn't enough. It would never be enough. He nudged his hips forward trailing his tip over me. I clawed at him, needing more.

"You're killing me, Madden," I said as he teased another pass between my lips. This time he pressed hard, massaging his head over my clit. I tilted my hips, begging for more of him with my body.

He laid his forehead over mine. "Killing you? I don't think so, but close to death will suit my purposes." I could see the playful glint in his eyes.

"Do I have to order you around again?" I gasped and grabbed his ass as he circled himself over the tight knot of flesh.

He looked me in the eyes. "Your wish is my command, Mistress."

I wasn't sure if he was teasing, but the idea of telling him what to do to me struck a chord deep inside, and I was willing to try anything at this point to get what I needed.

"I want you to fuck me. Now."

He groaned over my lips and lined himself up, pausing only for a second before he eased himself inside. He didn't stop until he was fully sheathed, and he stilled for a long moment. His girth stretched me wide open, and I squeezed down around him, reveling in the feel of him filling me so fully.

"I want to live inside you and never leave." He pulled back and drove forward seamlessly, finding a slow, punishing pace that tightened the knot in my stomach until it was intolerable.

"I might be okay with that." I rocked up into him, meeting each of his thrusts as I pulled at his muscular arms.

He grabbed my thigh roughly, pulling my leg around him, changing the angle so he could force his length deeper. The new position caused his tip to hit all the right places making me writhe against him. He brought me to the brink but didn't let me come, changing his strokes to short jabbing ones. He swelled inside me, and I dug my fingertips into his flesh, knowing they'd leave bruises. The action seemed to heighten his desire as he let out a low groan.

Madden pushed one hand between us, tracing his fingers around his base to coat his fingers before he spread my own silky lubricant over the outside of my lips. The light touch was torturous, leaving me whimpering. Working his way toward my center he found my clit, kneading his fingers around it in slow circles. He dragged his lips down my throat and found my breast. His teeth pinched and tugged my nipple before he soothed it with his warm tongue. Between his fingers and his mouth, I was hovering on the edge, completely under his control.

"I want to feel you come around me." The tone in his voice almost did me in. Pleasure mounted deep in my stomach, and he pushed me over the edge with his fingers against my swelling clit. I exploded in ecstasy, and my muscles gripped him, pulsing with every wave of my orgasm. I threw my legs open, welcoming him deeper as I rode out the seemingly endless release. He gasped against my neck, and his strokes faltered telling me he was close.

I knew it wouldn't take much to throw him over the edge, so I turned and nibbled at his ear as I whispered, "Come for me."

He shuddered in silence, giving a final thrust before his own orgasm seemed to wreck his whole body. He collapsed on top of me, our hearts pounding together in sync.

"Jocelynn." He exhaled slowly and kissed up my neck until he found my lips.

I cupped his face with my hands, keeping him there. We kissed with him still inside me, throbbing with the last of his release.

"I don't want to move," he said into my lips.

I tightened my legs around him, holding him there. "Then don't."

He maneuvered us around a little until I was half draped over him, and his tip was still nestled half hard inside me. I reached for the blanket and pulled it over us, giving in to sleep.

The next voice I heard was not the one I wanted to wake up to.

"It's like I have to give you pointers on how to sneak about."

When I peeled my eyes open Madden was bare-arsed and face down sprawled between me and where my brother sat eating a bowl of fruit. I threw a blanket over Madden, smiling to myself as he snored lightly, then pulled a sheet up over myself before I climbed out of bed.

"I wasn't expecting my nosy brother to pick my lock." I took a seat across from him and dug into the extra bowl waiting for me.

"You left it unlocked."

"Shit. But why are you here?" A third bowl sat in front of the empty seat. As simple a gesture as it was, it told me Jacob had accepted Madden.

"I had to make sure you made lecture this morning. I don't want to have to deal with you sobbing for days over that one. Better to head it off at the pass and keep you in line."

"I don't sob." I stood, leaning over the table to kiss his cheek. "I love you, brother mine."

"Yeah, yeah, yeah. Eat, then wake him up so I can sneak him out of here then meet you." He shoved another spoonful into his mouth.

"Can I wake him up with my lips?" I batted my eyelashes like all the women Jacob hated.

"Only if you're putting on a show for me, and even I can't handle the idea of us getting *that* close." He made a face.

I burst out laughing. "God, no. You already know too much about me."

"If you want to have morning fun, which is the best way to start the day—I should know." He winked, and I gagged on my food. "Then you need to train him to get up an hour early."

"I am not taking notes on this from my brother." I shuddered.

"Taking notes on what?" Mad had one eye open and was staring at us both.

"Notes on how best to go about getting laid in the morning. Believe me you don't want to know." I grinned, loving the way he looked all sleepy.

He pulled the blanket over his head and muttered into the pillow. "Did your brother come in here and..."

"I can see why she likes you. You have a great arse," Jacob said before I could reply.

Mad groaned. "They always tell you families are the worst part of being in a relationship, and I am getting screwed from every angle."

"You've not been screwed yet, but if you want to see how good it feels up the arse I could help you out." Jacob gave a toothy grin, and I reached over and smacked him.

"You say that like I haven't."

I looked between them for a moment, then hit my brother. "You have enough conquests. Stay away from the one I like."

He rolled his eyes and huffed. "If you insist, dear sister." He turned to Mad seamlessly. "Come eat, and then I am getting your arse out of here before we all get in trouble, and if you sleep here you need to be out of here before first bell. It's so much easier to sneak out before the servants are about."

It was my turn to groan. "I have to walk him out of here so early?"

Jacob dug in the pocket of his tunic and pulled out a ring of keys. "No, but if he wants to spend the night in your bed he will drag his arse home that early." He tossed the keys at Madden. "These should open all the necessary doors."

"You trust me that much?" He looked from the keys to Jacob.

"No, but she does, and it's good enough for me."

Mad pulled the sheet around himself and sat up. "Bathroom?"

I nodded toward the other door in the room, and he collected his clothes and disappeared inside.

"You're turning into a softy. Keys?"

"I called in a favor to get an extra set. You owe me." He tipped his bowl to his lips, drinking the remaining nectar.

Mad reappeared a moment later and inhaled the contents of his bowl. Jacob wiped his mouth and watched with one eyebrow raised. I glared at him, knowing what he was thinking.

"Let's go. I'm going to have to take you a rather roundabout way, but it has to be done." Jacob led the way out to my sitting room, and when Madden headed for the door he grabbed him by the arm. "Not that way." Jacob instead pushed one of the bricks on the fireplace. For a long moment nothing happened, but then the stones started to rumble, and the back side parted opening, revealing a dark passage.

"Really?" Madden glanced back at me. "And you didn't show me last night?"

"Over what we did?" I raised a brow.

He looked a little sheepish. "You act like the two are mutually exclusive."

"It leads to his room. It's rather boring."

Jacob sighed. "You had to give away the intrigue."

The fire had burned low enough so it could be easily stepped over. When they were in the passage I called out hastily. "Let me know when you get out, okay?"

"I'll be fine, don't worry," he called back.

Chapter Twenty-One

Madden

I was playing with fire. I knew I was, and yet I had to know more. The meeting place was different. Another long hike through the city to a seemingly abandoned part and then we went underground. You'd never know by looking at it, but the city was built over the shell of a much older city. Underneath, there were passages, abandoned buildings, and the lessers. Those not even fit in the eyes of the Akillies to be servants, and the people who wanted to live outside the law. Or perhaps those who rejected the government like the Red Stars did.

I suspected this was a lot closer to home than the first building I'd gone to. Every step I took in the two inches of water echoed off the curved walls and made me tenser. The note I'd received told me two rights then to walk past thirteen turn-offs before taking a left. I checked my comm. I was going to be late for the ball tonight. I'd promised Jocelynn I'd be there, even if she couldn't spend the night with me.

Sweat started to bead on my forehead. It was a lot hotter down here than on the surface. At this rate I was going to have to shower before I went out again. I took the turn once I found the right passage and walked right into two men standing there. Both had red badges on their jackets. I straightened up and tried to look them in the eyes, but they both also wore silver polarized glasses.

I waited for them to speak, but they seemed content with silence.

"I was told to come here?" I was also sure I sounded like an idiot.

"Wait," one of them said and pressed his fingers to his ear. "Are you ready for him?"

I slid my hands into my pockets and did as I was told. No sense in stressing since I would already be late.

"All right," the guy spoke into something. His wrist maybe. Then he looked down at me. "You're going to press this into the back of your neck. It's a way for you to get in touch with some of our leaders, without risking them coming onto planet."

My mind started to whirl as he spoke. Speaking to people off planet? Couldn't I have used a comm for this?

"There is no risk for you, but it will take you into an altered sense of reality. It's normal to feel slightly nauseated the first time."

No risk for me? Who was there a risk for? I really didn't like this. I swallowed past the lump in my throat and tried to listen to the rest of what he had to say.

"Don't ask. It's tech we don't share. If we find you trying to steal, duplicate, or even suspect you've spoken about it to another living soul we'll eliminate the risk."

"Eliminate the risk?" I asked.

"By any means necessary." He held out the device, and I took it.

"Just press it to the back of my neck?"

He nodded.

"Where am I doing this?"

They stepped aside to reveal a tiny lounge area. "We'll protect your body while you're in."

"Protect my body?" Panic rose up in my throat like bile. This wasn't a good idea. I could feel it in my gut. I never let anyone have control over me. Not again, not since what I withstood as a child. I had a hard time even sleeping without one eye open. "And if I refuse?"

"I'm sure now that you've come this far refusing to talk will be seen as hostile and a threat to our safety."

"I thought so." I stepped through the space they'd made, and dropped to a seat on the sofa. I pressed the tiny device to the back of my neck before I could decide how bad of an idea this really was.

When I opened my eyes I was in a lounge. It looked like one of those expensive smoking lounges the elite on Harden liked to frequent. A place where someone like me would be turned out just for looking like I did. I wanted to explore the room. The floor under my feet felt as real as everything looked, but it wasn't possible. Tech like this didn't exist. They couldn't have transported me all this way, could they?

The guards had said something about watching my body so I couldn't have been transported. I did a slow turn spotting the only three occupants of the room. They sat, relaxing on the posh sofas. While two looked perfectly at home, the third looked—winded—strained maybe. Something wasn't quite right.

I knelt to brush my fingers over the ornate floor. Stone under my fingertips, even the texture was perfect. "How is this possible?"

"Whereas it may feel real, none of it actually is. We are currently residing in a program built inside the mind."

I looked at the men again. "His?" I nodded at the sickly looking one. "It's a strain?"

"I told you he was quick," the sickly looking man said.

"So, your mind is supporting this world?" I took a step forward, still barely believing this was a program.

"Yes, but you have used up your questions. Take a seat. We've been watching you for some time, and we have an offer."

****

I tugged on my knee high boots before I straightened up to tuck in my shirt. My mind was still reeling from the meeting, and she had sent me one message today. One. I opened my comm and looked at the message again.

J: **I'll be at the ball until late, but I want to see you after. Please don't make a scene, whatever you see. I'm still going home with you.**

It hadn't sat right. What would she be doing tonight that would upset me? Between the stress of the Reds and J's sudden coldness I wanted to crawl into a hole. I scrubbed a hand down my face. I wouldn't get answers unless I finished getting dressed and went to the ball. It looked like it was going to be an uncomfortable night all around, since I wasn't happy about the attire. Not that I hated dressing up, but I knew I didn't pull it off as well as others did.

Next I put on the vest, then the waistcoat, and all were topped with a cravat pinned into place with a tiny black star. Under the right kind of light, it would shine red, or so I was told. I hadn't tested it, and I wore it for the perks more than anything. It was also an easy way to spot friends. A top hat was the final touch, and it was the most fun. A hand-me-down from my grandfather who had been given it when he worked as a manservant to one the lords on Harden.

It was a short walk to where the Akillie ball was hosted, welcoming everyone to the start of the fair. I was starting to wonder if the Worlds' Fair was more a show in strength and power than what it masqueraded as. I was greeted at the door and handed a plain black mask, which I strapped on. More cloak and dagger shit to let the nobles have their fun. The Red Stars told me this procedure allowed the Baron to invite prestigious guests like the Emperor's son, who was rumored to be here tonight, without forcing the Emperor to show favoritism over Jok.

My eyes scanned the room for her before I even knew what I was doing. She was easy to find, her golden hair wrapped up in a twist on top of her head and a floor length black dress. The dress was stunning even from afar. It was two layers, the top being hand-woven lace which sat over a thin shimmery sheer fabric of the same color. Every time the light caught her dress it gave a tease of her porcelain skin hiding beneath. A long slit ran from mid-thigh to the floor, giving a tease of her every time she moved. She glowed with radiance, and I looked down at myself, knowing I didn't deserve her.

She didn't wear one of the masks handed out at the door. Instead, hers was molded to her face and accented with jewels, silver, and her house red. Jacob stood next to her in the only red mask in the room. I wondered if he'd done it on purpose to stand out. Between his roguish smile and the way he stood I figured he had.

A man taller than me approached her and offered one of the two drinks he held. A grin curled over her lips as she gave a slight bow and accepted it. He seemed to wave off her bow, leaning in to whisper in her ear. As he pulled back, his lips touched the place under her jaw.

I saw red. Everything else in the room vanished as she placed a hand on his shoulder. They laughed, hers ringing out across the room. I needed a drink. I stalked toward the bar and ordered a Dragon blood. The alcohol would either make my mood volatile or it would calm me. I shot a look back over my shoulder. He had his hand on her hip, and their bodies were even closer than before. My chest tightened, and my hand shook as I picked up my drink, throwing it back. A hand touched my shoulder, and I spun around to confront who ever dared touched me.

I softened a little when the red mask was staring back at me.

"You need to calm down."

"I'm calm," I snapped.

"That is Phillip, and I'm sure you're not so daft as you don't know the name. She has to do this." His voice was low, barely more than a snarl.

I knew she did. I knew the name. It was the Emperor's eldest son. A marriage like that would immortalize the Akillie House. But there was a catch. The younger sons of the Emperor could be married for treaty, and usually were, but by law the heir could not be. The law made it so the Emperor had no way to show bias toward one of the houses. It kept the peace. The Empress usually ended up some lesser noble from the imperial city. That was the worst part. He was here of his own accord, and Jocelynn was beautiful. If she'd caught his eye it was for good reason, and I knew she had to act like this. I knew she had to put on a good face, but yet here I was letting it get to me. I blew out a breath through my nostrils.

"I know who it is." I looked at J again.

She was giggling. Giggling! He had his arm around her waist now.

"You know this is never going to work out between you two, right?"

I looked back at him with my jaw set. "I know."

And I did. I hated the fact, but I knew we couldn't have the happily ever after I wanted so badly.

"She's going to end up with him or some other Baron's son, and I'm going to end up with Aubrey, or even worse her seven-year-old sister." He paused setting his glass down on the bar. "It may be the most horrible injustice we have to suffer to live a life of leisure, but we feel it. We made a pact to never fall in love, years ago, she and I, and she's never broken it for a handsome face. Then you came along. She wouldn't be doing this, knowing how it has to end, if she didn't really have feelings for you."

I knew everything he said was the truth. "Why are you telling me all this?"

"Because he," he gestured to her and Phillip, "is work. If she stays in the Baron and Emperor's good graces she can have the time with you she does. If she's lucky it will be years before she has to marry anyone. That is all time for you two."

The bartender refilled his drink, and Jacob brought it to his lips before going on. "We all do what we have to, to survive. Don't doubt her feelings."

"I don't." He was right. I'd needed the wakeup call. It didn't make it any easier to watch, but at least I'd calmed enough to not make a scene.

Something apparently caught Jacob's eye because he was up and moving across the crowded room chasing a young man serving drinks. As there were plenty of these servers I figured he liked the way that one looked. He did have a nice ass.

I shook it off, returning my attention to Phillip. He certainly acted the part of the interested party. He stayed at her side, always with his hand on her arm, kept her drinks refilled, and he was enthralled by everything that came out of her mouth. It didn't surprise me. I knew she was amazing. It was stupid of me to think no one else would see it. She'd have a good life if she married him. I started to wonder if Jacob would get control of Akillie. Could she maintain her duties as Empress and still keep the Akillie House? I was sure the Baron would find a way to make it best suited to him.

Hours passed, and I'd had too much to drink. I sat at the bar, glass in hand, staring at her out there. She danced, and laughed, and chatted with the other dignitaries like she hadn't a care in the world, or a thought of me for that matter. It was my own demons talking, and I should have ignored them. I knew who she was going back to her room with tonight, and I hated playing the part of the jealous bastard, but it ate at me. How long could we keep this up? I wasn't a part of her world.

She took her leave of Phillip, and he watched her walk over to the bar. She took a seat next to me and without looking said, "I'm famished."

My heart rate picked up. "Decided to take a break from your fun?"

"You mean a break from my job?" She snuck a glance at me.

"It didn't look like work from here." I snapped, and then kicked myself. She didn't deserve the way I was acting.

"I'm at fault for being a good actress? I've been doing it for years, Madden." Fire burned in her eyes.

"You're right, I'm sorry. I don't want to fight with you." I brushed my fingers over her arm. "How long do you think you have?"

She looked back at him. He'd chosen another dance partner. "I told him I was feeling faint and that I was going to sit for a while."

"So I have you for at least a few minutes."

She nodded. I got to my feet.

"Let's go sit in the shadows."

She followed me to the far end of the bar where a few stools sat completely in the shadows. There were better spots for what I had in mind, alcoves that were shaded and balconies, but I knew she wouldn't want to disappear. She took her seat against the wall, and I scooted the other stool closer to her so our knees touched when I sat.

"Tell me why you didn't find your own partner to flirt with." She laid her hand on my thigh.

"Because I only have eyes for you, Mistress."

"You call me that a lot. Why?" She leaned on the bar, bringing her face closer to mine.

"Because it's how I see you. I want to be a good boy for you, Mistress." I could see the change in her when I said it. It was like flipping a switch.

Her gaze pierced mine. "You must know what it does to me when you say it."

I ran my tongue over my teeth. "Yes, it's one of the best parts."

"Evil. You're so evil. You push all my buttons." She dug her nails into my leg.

"I have to be able to combat your flirting somehow," I retorted adding, "Mistress," with a sly grin.

"Do you know what you do to me?"

I shook my head.

"You know I saw your eyes on me all night. You look at me like you own me, like you want to possess me, and it makes me flush." She bit down on her lip. "So, I'm wet talking to a man I want nothing to do with." She drew in a steadying breath. "That's what you do to me."

I instantly went hard. Knowing I made her feel those things was so arousing. "I know what I want," I growled right into her ear.

"What?" She leaned forward to whisper, looking around to make sure the Emperor's son wasn't in earshot. I knew she couldn't tell what I was talking about.

"The bet, I know what I want." My chest expanded, and I wanted to mark her in the most primal way.

"Well, tell me." She scooted closer to me looking right into my eyes.

The world around us vanished as we shared the moment. I pressed my lips right to her ear so only she would hear. "I want your panties."

Chapter Twenty-Two

Jocelynn

I thought I'd heard him wrong, and I turned into him trying to read his face. "What?" My heart was pounding out of my chest. If not for the intense beat of the music, I knew someone would hear.

He flicked his tongue over my ear. "Take your panties off."

I looked around, my heart pounding in my chest. "Here?"

He nodded, silver eyes boring into mine. "Right here." His fingers skimmed up the inside of my thigh.

I knew we shouldn't. I knew I was going to get us both in trouble, but I couldn't stop my fingers from inching up my leg and pushing under the slit of my dress. I uncrossed my knees as I turned the stool I sat on toward the bar. The shadows allowed me to lay my other hand over my lap, disguising my movements. I looked over, and he was staring at where my fingers crawled up the gap in my legs.

I dropped my gaze to the bulge in his slacks. I shivered, instantly wet knowing what I was doing to him. I loved that I could do this to him. It was a power I had never experienced. I'd always been treated like I was beautiful. But he treated me like the elixir of life, and he'd die without a taste.

I hooked my finger in the black lace scrap that hardly covered anything. I wore them not because the dress required them, which it did, but because I knew there was a chance Madden would see them. I started to drag them down my ass, pressing my heels into the rung of the stool to lift ever so slightly. The fabric pulled as it skimmed over my skin. I sat back when they reached my thighs, slipping easily off. Now was the tricky part. They sat hidden by my dress, but would easily be seen as soon as I dared to push them the rest of the way down. I glanced over my shoulder, scanning the crowd for anyone paying too close of attention to us.

He stood to stand near my shoulder to brush his fingers down my spine. "Chicken out?"

I smoothed my hand over my dress before pulling over the slit enough to show him where they sat. "Not a chance. When I lose, I follow through."

His eyes flashed with amusement as he leaned forward, placing his forearm on the bar top like he was going to order a drink, but it was clear it was an act when his fingers of his other hand drifted up to skim over the lace.

I turned into him, using his large frame to shield what I was about to do. Carefully I inched the material down over my knees. Leaning on the bar like he did, I rested my head in one hand, looking bored as I worked between us to pull my panties off one foot then the other. I tucked them in his pocket then brushed my knuckles over his bulge as I pulled back.

A low growl emanated from him, and his fingers took a walk up the inside of my thigh. My breath caught in my throat as he ventured closer to my soaked lips. Gently he brushed over my slit and his eyes pressed closed.

He turned his face into mine, lips on my ear, as he spoke. "You're so wet." He tried to move his hand under the cover of my dress, but the fabric was too restrictive. "Does being in public do this to you?"

"No, knowing I do this to you does." I risked parting my knees a hair more to give him more access, and he flipped his hand around to brush his thumb over my clit. I dropped my face to his chest, trying to bite back a moan.

I felt the sting of his teeth on my ear. "I'm going to lose it. Can we go?"

I looked up at him. I couldn't go. I had a speech to give. Phillip waited for me. My father would be looking for me any moment … but I didn't want to be here. I wanted to be with Madden.

"Let's go," I said.

His fingers lingered there, stroking over the tight knot of flesh, and pleasure ran up my spine. I grabbed his wrist, whimpering softly. If he didn't stop, I was going to come right there. He met my eyes, and I could tell he knew. He slid his fingers out from my dress and brought them to his mouth, licking my taste from them. I clenched and rubbed my thighs together.

Chapter Twenty-Three

Madden

Once back in the room, she dropped her face, brushing her lips over my collarbone, lighting on fire the places she touched. I pressed into her, grazing my hips over hers. She groaned over my skin, and I pressed harder into her, showing her what her mouth was doing to me. There was hunger behind her eyes when she looked up.

Not wasting another second I grabbed her by the back of her thighs and picked her up, carrying her toward the single bed. Our mouths met again in a clash, and she grabbed onto my ears. I laid her back, settling between her hips, pushing her thighs wide open with my knees. It was clear what she wanted as she tilted her hips and rubbed herself over my length. All the air left my lungs, sucked out by her, but it didn't stop me. Her back came off the mattress as I slowly slid the material down exposing her ribcage. I traced my fingers over the lines of her tiny bones, skimming the bare, milky white skin.

I broke our kiss, glancing down at her. She chased my lips, but I turned my head so her lips stroked over my stubbled jaw. I nipped at her neck before moving lower to inhale her scent. She smelled of paper and fresh strawberries. I dragged my tongue over the hollow in her throat.

I didn't want to focus on anything but feeling her. I wanted her skin pressed into mine, and all thoughts of leaving for one more night vanished. I inched her shirt up, slipping down further between her legs to lick over the underside of her breast. Her shoulders lifted off the bed pressing her chest into me as she threaded her fingers into my hair. She squirmed when I rubbed my chin over the sensitive skin, making me grin.

"Damn that stubble of yours."

I glanced up smugly. "I'm sure you'll be singing a different tune when it's between your thighs."

She picked up her head, arching a brow. "So confident?"

"I'm an expert," I said, then winced at how it sounded.

"Drag lots of Baronesses in waiting to your chambers to ravage, do you?" She half sat, yanking at my hair as I tried to slide lower to distract her with my tongue.

I licked over her hip bone, but she stopped me from going any further. "I…" I groaned inwardly. Did she really expect at twenty-two I hadn't touched another woman?

She shook with laughter. "If you expect us both to be virgins like bad teen literature where we saved ourselves for each other, you're a few years too late."

My mouth fell open as my stomach tightened, filling me with a jealous feeling. "You've been with others?"

A half smile curled over her lips, and she yanked me back up over her by the hair. I crushed myself over her, growling.

"Did you really call yourself an expert whore, then try to get possessive in the same breath?" I could tell by her smile she wasn't mad.

I dropped my head to her neck, grumbling as my cheeks heated up. "Yeah, maybe a little."

Hooking a leg over my hips she rolled us over, coming up to sit on top of me. "Even if you are a professional pleaser, I shouldn't stay." She set her hands on my chest, rubbing lightly over my clothed skin.

I cupped her face with both hands, sticking out my lower lip. "You need to get back before they figure out you've gone?"

"You are so hard to say no to."

"Then don't say no," I wasn't above begging. Whatever it took. I had to get inside her again.

She took my lip between hers and groaned. "They will notice my absence eventually."

I hitched her skirt up as she spoke. I already had her panties in my pocket. It would be so easy to take her right here. "Then let them notice."

"And what will I tell them?" She grabbed a handful of my hair and rocked into me.

"Tell them you're sick?" I found her bare thigh, under the layers of fabric and dug my fingers into it.

She whimpered, "Yes…"

"Yes what?" I released my hold on her thigh and worked open the catch on my pants.

"I need you."

I stroked over myself. It took all my control to hold back. "I thought you had to go?" I had to feel her need. I wanted more than words. No, I *needed* more than words. My self-doubt ran to my core, and being who she was didn't help.

"I don't care. I need to be here with you."

"How badly?" I brushed my tip over her opening as I pressed down into her, bringing my face next to hers.

She looked into my eyes. "Make me come. That's an order."

I did as I was told. Like a good boy.

We basked in the afterglow of our shared orgasm, and the doubt crept back in. The thought of losing her to the Emperor-to-be would slowly kill me. I didn't know how to begin to deal with knowing we had an expiration date.

"It's going to be him, isn't it?"

"Who?" she asked.

"The Emperor's son."

"Yes, no, who can tell?"

I pressed my face into her shoulder, fighting off the tidal wave of emotion. "Okay."

"Don't, please. We've had a good night."

I forced my head back up. "It would be easier to let me go now. You know that, right?"

She cut me off. "I don't want easy. I want you. This can't be it. I'll figure out a way."

"Jocelynn." My brows fell.

Before I could finish there was a pounding at the door.

Chapter Twenty-Four

Jocelynn

"Shit." I pulled my shirt down and slid my hands in my hair, trying to smooth the lumps out as to not look like we had been rolling around in bed for the last hour.

Mad practically shoved me off of him getting to his feet as he thrust a hand into his pants, smoothing out the wrinkles. I tried not to laugh at his predicament.

"I'm sure it's just my brother. No one else knows where to come looking for me."

He growled as he stalked over to the door. "He could have given us a few more minutes." He wrenched it open, and I gasped backing away when I saw who it was.

The Baroness stood there flanked by my brother, who looked apologetic, and two guards. Her cold blue eyes landed on me, and I swallowed. They swept down my body, and I knew I had been found unsatisfactory. Her blood red lips parted, but no words came. Jacob's gaze flashed to me. I pleaded with my eyes for him to give me some hint as to what she wanted to hear from me. But I knew it wouldn't come. He couldn't say anything.

We stood in a silent standoff before I broke it. "I forgot the time." I tried to smooth out the wrinkles in the front of my dress where Madden's hands played a moment before. It was useless. The dress would have to be steamed for any hope of removing them.

"You mean you disregarded the time and blew off your father in the months leading up to your coronation?" The Baroness had never been motherly, but now she was icy. I was a disappointment.

"No, ma'am." I lifted my chin, jutting it out, holding my ground. Even if it was true, such an admission would be equivalent to disrespecting my house and stomping on the title I was soon to receive.

Her eyes flickered from mine to Madden. "And why are you here with this tainted man?"

The room stiffened, and Madden's lip curled at the insult. I lifted my arm like I could stop him from doing anything to worsen her opinion of him. He took a step forward to stand at my side, and I silently begged him not to say anything.

"He's a friend in the advancement program."

She looked him over again. I knew she would pick out the flaws in him, from the ink decorating his arms, to the facial scruff and unkempt hair, down to the silver-tinged ring around the outside of his iris. It could have been worse. Had he worked in the mines, his eyes would have turned pure silver from overexposure.

Something seemed to click in her mind, and she touched her tongue to the edge of her teeth. "How long has this been going on?"

I crossed my arms over my dress. "There is nothing going on. We should return to the party."

She turned to Jacob. "How long?"

He shrugged one shoulder.

"The Baron will hear about this." She turned on her stiletto heel. "Make sure she comes, and that the tainted blood doesn't follow."

I pried my teeth apart, taking a deep breath. "Wait, I won't see him again. Don't tell the Baron." I looked at Madden, trying to convey with my eyes what I felt. If he got kicked out of advancement it would be my fault, and he deserved better. I couldn't ruin his life because I was selfish. "It was nothing more than fulfilling a need, which I'm sure you can understand."

Jacob cracked a smile because he knew.

She whipped back around, narrowing her dark shadowed brows. "I see…" She paused, pursing her lips. "I don't want to hear a word of you within ten feet of him again." She looked disdainfully at Madden again. "I have no illusion of you remaining pure in this day and age, but to risk tainting our bloodline with rumors of such things." She let out a high pitched scoff. "Fix it."

As she walked out, the guards stepped into the room. I turned to Madden knowing I didn't have much time. How could I explain without them hearing? I searched his face, but there was only sadness there.

"Madden…" I took a step closer to him.

"Don't." He held up a hand. "Go."

I couldn't read him. His expression was blank. He had to know I was trying to save him.

I took another step toward him, and a heavy hand landed on my shoulder closing around it painfully.

"Please understand."

He turned his back on me. "You should go."

I sank to my knees. The guard hauled me to my feet. I tried to fight, but Jacob grabbed my other side and helped drag me from the room.

Chapter Twenty-Five

Madden

Part of me knew she had to say what she did. But the tiny insecure part at the back of my mind told me I was never anything more than an itch she had to scratch. My mind tore at itself. She couldn't make a scene, and my answers were cold, but it was all I had left. I turned my back so I didn't have to see her being dragged out of my life. When the door clicked closed I picked up the nearest thing I could grab and threw it. Despair blackened my thoughts as I tore apart the room.

I came to myself on my knees in the middle of the room. The faint morning light peeked through the window coverings. My knuckles hurt, and I had blood caked around my fingernails. I sank back to a seat. I'd had my grief, and now I had to make sure it didn't affect the rest of my life. I was here for a reason. I came here because I hated my life on Harden, and I thought making something of myself would replace the seed of unhappiness I carried in the back of my mind. But only she had made me forget it existed on the darkest nights.

I cleaned myself off, wiping away the worst of the blood. I had to be at class in under an hour, and the walk there itself would take me thirty. I dressed in worn clothes and shoved papers in my bag. I hadn't done the homework, expecting to have started it after J passed out on me. She always fell asleep after the midnight hour, and it was easy for me to work long into the night and then sleep late. But I would never have her sleeping in my lap again. I grabbed a hat and shoved it down on my head and walked out the door. I missed Colton. I needed someone to vent to. Fishing around in my bag, I dug out my communicator. Since coming here I had been horrible about keeping in touch. I would be lucky if he replied. I couldn't remember the time conversion between the two planets, and for all I knew he would be sleeping or in the mines where he wouldn't have any signal.

M: **Hey.**

I sent the message without a second thought as I ducked into class.

I slid into my usual seat, and my eyes instantly scanned the room for her. In a room of four hundred people it took me less than ten seconds to find her. She had chosen a different seat with her brother. I expected to see the mask she wore so easily, the one I had to work to get behind, but it wasn't there. Her eyes were ringed with red, and her normally perfect makeup was smudged. I pressed a hand into my chest. The sight should have made me feel better, but I hated seeing her in pain. I slammed my head back against the rest, determined to get through this lecture without focusing on her.

It didn't work. By the time the professor called time, my notebook was blank, and my head was full. My thoughts were dark and only grew worse. I had just enough time to duck back to my room before the afternoon lecture. My stomach had turned, and I wouldn't eat, but I walked to stretch my legs.

My comm buzzed, and I pulled it out of my pocket, hoping to see a message from her, but I knew it wouldn't happen. She would be stupid to contact me so easily.

The message was from Colton.

Colton: **Hey, man, long time. You doing okay?**

M: **Not really, call me later?**

I replied quickly, waving through the swarm of students as I typed.

Colton: **Yeah, might be the middle of the night your time. I'm just heading into the mines for the day.**

His responses were almost instant. It was a weird feeling getting a message back like we lived two clicks away when in reality we were across the universe, and the message was nothing more than a blip of information.

M: **Wake me up.**

Colton: **Will do.**

I closed my communicator, but it pinged again.

Colton: **Chin up, bro. You're making something of yourself.**

I didn't reply and carried on getting my keys out. When I looked up, she was standing there. Her face was splotchy, and her eyes were bloodshot. Jacob wasn't in sight, but I knew he wouldn't be far off. At times I felt like he was her guard dog.

She didn't come to me as I approached, and I didn't move to touch her.

"Hey." Her red lips were cracked.

"Jocelynn…" There weren't words for how this felt. If I'd doubted last night how much pain she was in, I couldn't now.

"I had to see you again." She tucked her hair behind her ears.

"How did you even get here?"

"Jacob is covering for me." She stepped closer to me so I could feel the heat radiating off of her. "This is all my fault." She dropped her face to my chest, and I wrapped my arms around her shoulders.

"No, I didn't have to do it. I was trying to be better for you." I blew out a breath, and kissed her forehead.

She looked up at me, and I melted. All the anger I'd felt at getting my place revoked morphed into utter despair at the thought of leaving her. Everything I had believed about soul mates crumbled as I lowered my mouth to hers. Her silky lips parted as they touched mine, and our warm tongues teased together. I crushed my arms around her as I deepened the kiss, suddenly needing more from her. Her back arched as she pressed into me. A universe so cruel it separates you from your other half the moment you find her, forced all hope of happily ever after from my mind.

She pulled back, rubbing her nose over mine. "I'm sorry."

"It's me, not you." I pushed back the hair that had fallen in her face. "I have these issues, and you were trying to help. It's not your fault."

The sorrow behind her eyes told me she wouldn't believe me.

I dropped my bag and grabbed her by the arm, forcing her body to mine so I could wrap her up in a hug. I lifted her tiny frame off her feet. She pressed her face into my neck and slid her arms around me. We held each other, forgetting the universe existed or anything else mattered. I tightened my grip when she pulled back, feeling like the moment I let go she would vanish.

"I'm going to be late for class." She pulled back to look me in the eyes.

I melted into her gaze, but I didn't let her down. I shoved the key, still in my hand, into the door and stalked to my bed, tossing her down. Climbing in after her, I covered her body with mine. She pushed her hands into my hair, forcing my head up.

"You're incorrigible."

I nodded, sticking out my lower lip. "Fake sick with me?"

The corner of her mouth turned up at she smiled a little. "I have half an hour, but then I have to go. If I miss any more meetings of state…" she trailed off.

"I know. I never expected to see you again." I couldn't look at her. I pressed my face into her chest.

She yanked my hair hard. "This isn't an itch for me."

"Are you sure?"

Her gaze was hard. "I'm sure."

I swallowed past the lump in my throat. "It's more for me, too."

"I know because of the way you look at me." She released my hair and playfully smacked my cheek. "Please believe it when I say this is real for me, too."

"It's hard for me to believe anyone can feel that way about me." I'd felt it as long as I could remember, and it wasn't easy to look her in the eyes and say it.

"Then I'll prove it to you every day." She rubbed her thumb over my cheekbone.

I turned my face to kiss her palm. "You can't."

"I will. Trust me." She brushed her lips over mine looking right at me.

I parted mine, teasing my tongue over the seam of her lips. "You taste good," I murmured.

"I don't know why." She laughed, letting her lids fall shut as she tilted her head to deepen the kiss.

My hands roamed her body, needing to touch every inch of her in a primal possessive way. She clawed her nails down my shoulder, and the pain soothed my mind, forcing me to focus on the contact and none of the anguish. I rolled us, coming up half on top of her. I rubbed my scruff over her neck, skimming my tongue over her skin to get a taste.

There was a light knock on the door, and she broke the kiss. "That's Jacob. He was keeping eye out. I have to go."

I sat back on my heels and looked down at her. "What are we going to do?"

She got up on her knees and pressed her body to mine. "We will figure it out. This is not the end."

I wound my arms around her again and whispered into her hair, "Thank you."

A crease formed in the center of her brow. "For what?"

"Coming back when I acted like a dick yesterday."

"I couldn't not." She smiled and took another kiss before detangling our bodies. "I'm sorry I had to say what I did in front of the Baroness."

I nodded.

"We'll talk later." She glanced back then slipped out the door.

Knowing I would be late and not caring, I picked up my bag and left behind her. I ducked my head as I walked down the corridor and out the door at the end of the hall. I looked up and almost ran into two men standing there.

Before I could gather what was going on, one of them punched me in the temple. I sank to my knees, my vision blacking for a minute. A bag went over my head. One of them jumped on my back, shoving me to the ground, and my hands were forced behind my back and bound. The other man kicked me repeatedly, and all the air went out of my lungs.

Blackness took over.

Chapter Twenty-Six

Madden

I came round to the sound of thrusters. My head throbbed, and I was thankful for the dim light when I opened my eyes. I blinked a few times trying to get them to focus. A bottle of water was shoved in front of my face, and I looked over at the man holding it out to me. He had a full red beard and deep wrinkles in a young face. His clothes were crumpled and his hair matted like he'd been sleeping against it.

"I was starting to think you'd never wake up," he said in a deep familiar voice I would have placed to a logger from the seven moons of Vega.

But what would he be doing on Trenton? It all came back to me in a rush. I stiffened and looked around, finding I was shoved in the last seat in a transporter with a harness loosely strapped around me.

"Where am I?" I asked the man.

"On your way back to Harden. Now drink up, yer gonna need it."

I ignored the bottle, stomach dropping to mingle around my intestines. I glanced at my wrist. My communicator was there, and I punched it on and saw I had no signal. "How the fuck can we jump across universes in the blink of an eye but can't keep a communicator signal?" I said to myself.

"We are in transition behind the asteroid belt. You won't have shit until we land."

It had been a whole day. She would know I was gone. My chest was tight, and I couldn't breathe. I would never see her again. I would never hold her in my arms again. Tears welled up in the corners of my eyes.

"Take the water and stop being an idiot." He turned toward me, and a tiny silver star pinned to his collar caught my eye. I knew I'd heard the voice before.

"Following me back to Harden?" I scoffed. What could I be to the Red Stars now that I'd been kicked out of the program?

"Friends aid friends." He shoved the water in my face again, and I took it.

I drank down half the contents, and my headache eased. I hadn't realized how thirsty I'd been. Finishing the bottle, I offered it back, and he waved it off.

"What aid could I need now?" I blew out a breath and laid my head back against the seat. I'd blown it all for a woman, and I would do it all again.

My heart ached. There wasn't just a piece missing. The whole damn thing had been ripped from my chest, leaving a black hole in its wake.

"You threw away the chance of three generations to be with a girl." He lowered his voice. "I'm guessing you want my help in seeing her again."

My mouth fell open, and I stared at him.

"I thought it might get your attention." He glanced around then leaned in, still speaking softly. "We are willing to help you, our brother."

I knew I couldn't say no if there was a way, but I bit my tongue, forcing myself to think through it rationally when I wanted to scream yes, I'd do anything. "What's the catch?"

"As with the rest of the brotherhood, when we call on you to do something for us, you will do it." He licked over his cracked lips, not wavering.

"So you people want me indebted to you?" My heart pounded in my chest, and I thought he could hear it over the rumble of the engines.

"Not at all. We want to use you to further our cause of course, but you have a say in the matter. We've found through the last century forcing our agenda will only leave us in ruin. When we have loyal supporters who will do anything for their brothers, that's when we can affect real change, and we already have, Madden." His voice was smooth, urging me into a false sense of security.

"I want the details." I looked around to make sure no one was eavesdropping, but the few people on the transport were snoring.

He reached into the inside of his jacket, and when his hand reappeared he held the spider looking thing I'd used before. The weld marks were showing, which told me this wasn't some factory made device. It was homemade somewhere. "It's as easy as this and some minor set up. You've already seen how it can work."

I held out my hand for it, and he dropped it into my palm. I picked it up to examine it. "Tell me how?"

His hand disappeared again. "Combined with this." He now held up a tiny silver microchip. "Program it right and you can be anywhere, with her, you want."

My mouth went dry. "How do I know this is at all safe?"

"Since our own council uses them, as we couldn't be traveling all over drawing Empirical attention, we needed a way to have private meetings outside the scope of the Emperor on the nets. This is what we use smart guys like you for. They figure out a different way. Did you find it safe yourself?"

"Why would you share tech like this with me? It could mean your head if it falls into the wrong hands?" Jocelynn was in my grasp, but it sounded too good to be true. "That disk has got to be worth more than my life."

"One, because this one can't be linked back to us, and two, because, like I said, we need guys like you on our side. You know the reason you can't be with the woman you love is because of the classes and how they keep your planet as a basic slave world." He dropped the device into my hand. "Use your head. You gave the Baron a key to get around our raids. We can't risk letting his side exploit you. We gain nothing by hurting you."

He was right. They'd wanted me all along, and this just appeared to be an extra incentive to what I would have done anyway after the Baron had me deported. One thing struck home. I was worth more than I'd realized, and I had to use it to my advantage.

"How do I get it to her?" I closed my hand around it.

"We'll take care of it. Just broach the subject, and we'll get it into her suite."

Both my brows rose. "You have that kind of reach?"

"You have no idea." A crooked smile formed on his lips, showing off two silver teeth in his smile.

"Thanks." My heart wouldn't slow down. I wanted to get off this damn spacecraft and talk to her. Apologize and then see her.

"There are a few things you need to know."

My eyes darted back to his. I knew it. "Go on."

"Hosting the program isn't easy. Because of the way we had to work it into the neuro receptors, there are a few things we are still trying to work out." He kept his voice calm.

I growled. "If it's dangerous, I won't let her do it."

"It won't be as bad for her. Since the program uses your subconscious you will have to deal with the brunt of it. You already knew all of this." I couldn't read

145

anything in his eyes. They were just as hard laying out the facts.

"That's why he was in pain?"

"Yes." He exhaled slowly before answering. The first real sign he gave me. "Our subconscious minds work out our fears and worries for us. Because we tap into it to from a matrix into the network, you have to fight through your own mind to make contact to the world we've created."

I stared at him not quite understanding. It was more, or different than I expected. "Fight my own mind, what the hell?"

"To get to the world, one or both of you can write the program for the starter, which will be you. You will have to fight through your worst fears to make the connection. She'll have some mild discomfort of facing a much shorter challenge, but you will carry the brunt of it," he said. "There will also be a point where your mind will reject the program and kick you out. When it's used too much this will happen more frequently, and it's dangerous to use again before a forty-eight hour time period."

I swallowed hard. My worst enemy was already my mind. "Dangerous how?"

"You can reject it for good, or your mind could become damaged if you try to force yourself back in too soon. When all the rules I've given you are followed, there are minimal risks. Like I said, our highest council has used the program regularly for the last five years."

I nodded trying to take it all in. "How real is it?"

"You were there. You tell me."

"I mean with her. I didn't touch anymore while I was there."

"You will think you're really there. Your mind will be completely connected to the network. All input your brain will accept as real."

I forced my face to remain blank.

He went on, "Every touch, every look, the whole program will seem real."

"How can we write the program?" I wrung my hands.

"The information will be placed in your quarters before you return home this evening. With your mind you shouldn't have trouble creating a reality for the two of you to enjoy."

I was shocked at how fast they worked. "So, you assumed I would say yes, despite the pain involved?"

"If she means as much to you as you claim, nothing would keep you away."

The ship dropped, and I knew we have broken through the atmosphere. I looked at him again, and he had turned away, pretending to be asleep.

I leaned forward pressing my forehead to the seat in front of me. If this worked I could at least see her. Touch her in my mind. It would have to be enough for now.

Chapter Twenty-Seven

Jocelynn

Two days had passed. Two days. I felt hollow. I hadn't left my room in over a day, feigning illness. I'd avoided Jacob, clutching my communicator as I stared at the walls. I couldn't eat or sleep, and one question haunted my mind. Was he dead? At first I'd wondered what I'd done. But his room was empty. I'd had Jacob check. He could be dead because of me. I wouldn't put it past the Baron. I had to get my revenge. It was just a matter of biding my time.

A fist struck my door, causing me to jump. I looked up and then said, "Go away. I'm ill."

They tried my knob, and it was still locked, which made me breathe easier. A low growl came from behind the door, telling me it was my brother there. I ignored it. Jacob barged into my room a moment later holding up a pick.

I scowled. "That is a brand new biometric lock. How the hell did you get past it?"

"Anything which can be locked, can be unlocked by hacking."

I wanted to smack the smug expression off his face.

"I needed to make sure you were still alive." He took a seat on the edge of my bed.

"You see I'm alive. I could have the plague. Leave." I pulled my knees into my chest and pressed my face into them, hiding in my blankets.

He grabbed one end of my cover and yanked it away, leaving me exposed. "Well now that I see you're alive and clearly not ill in the slightest, I am to tell you to make haste. You have a visitor."

"There is no one I will see."

"This you have no choice. You're lucky the Baron isn't here holding you down to paint your face."

I looked up at him. "It can't be. He was here not four days ago."

"He has returned and has asked for you."

I closed my eyes. My chest ached. To anyone else, the handsome son of the Emperor might be a good replacement for a man the Baron banished, but for me it made things worse. I knew he was a consolation prize. "I guess I have no choice." I had to put on a face. If they suspected my motives it would ruin my chance of finding him again.

"None, but if it makes you feel any better I wish he would bend me over." He winked and climbed off my bed to grip himself.

I had to put on the mask I'd worn my whole life and fake it. I could do this. I would search for Madden to the ends of the known worlds and bring him back. Jacob had his secrets, and I would have mine. I just had to figure out how.

I wrinkled my nose as I stuck my tongue out. "You can have him." I followed him out of the bedroom and went to my large wardrobe. "Tell me what to wear. I can't be arsed with it."

He pushed me aside and scavenged through, picking a shocking combination. They were my usual leather pants which the Baron hated and a light purple t-shirt, boasting an all lace back.

"Really?" I took them behind the screen before he could answer.

"You don't want him to be attracted to you, so why do you care?" I could see his shadow through the divide, and he leaned against the wall looking entirely too smug.

I chose my words carefully. The Emperor's son's favor would afford me many more ways to find Madden than even my own rank. "Because maybe I should just get on with it. Better match than I'll find anywhere else, and at least he's funny." I blew out my cheeks as I stepped out. "Do my hair?"

"What would you do without me?" Before I could respond he went on. "Be a ragged mess, that's what."

"At least I show up to my meetings and pay attention to state affairs," I shot back. It was easy to fake things with my brother. To return to our banter, like my entire world hadn't changed.

"But no one would pay you any attention if you went like you want to half the time."

I growled at him, and he smirked.

Thirty minutes later, I stood at the private landing strip we reserved for dignitaries coming in secret. My brother flanked me on my left as we disembarked. The Baron and his full guard would have drawn too much attention to the arrival, not to mention he would be missed from his usual meetings, so it was just us. Phillip stalked down the gangplank, and his lips turned up into a foxy grin when his gaze landed on the pair of us. He was striking with blond hair that fell to his chin and violet eyes, a trait only still existing in the royal blood. Most of the rulers over the last two centuries had them, and Phillip was no different. It made me wonder if at birth the firstborn was rejected if it looked different.

He was tall, even taller than my brother, and thin. He had some muscle tone, but not the rugged look Madden had from hard labor. Phillip was soft from his lifestyle. When he approached he inclined his head at me, bending his knees to sink lower.

"You are all kindness." I offered my hand as was customary and curtsied. "Why ever would you bow to me?"

"I will always bend a knee or be on them for you, my lady." He met my eyes, and his smile had turned flirty.

I smiled in spite of myself, and he brought my hand to his lips to kiss it. "I must say, I do prefer men on their knees."

His lips spread open to show off his gleaming white smile. "Men?" He placed a hand over his heart. "You crush me with words, lady. But I will not give up. I will have to revamp my advances and plan a trip to your winter castle."

My mouth almost fell open. There would be no way to hide from his advances if he came to Gavin 9 with my family. "Determined are you?"

"Very." He turned to my brother and extended a hand, which Jacob took. Phillip pulled him close and clapped him on the back. They lingered there a moment longer than necessary, and Phillip turned to speak into Jacob's ear.

They broke apart, and Jacob laughed. "Who said I'm willing to help you?"

Phillip scoffed, "Is everyone against me?"

"Our father's not," Jacob shot back.

Phillip shuddered. "Thank you, no."

I broke out laughing as he linked his arm through mine. We walked back inside and through the tunnels to the suite of rooms he would occupy while he was here.

"Now, what boring thing shall we do so I am seen all over Trenton with the two of you?" Phillip flashed a smile, and my mouth dropped open.

Jacob pushed his tongue into his cheek, reappraising him. "You weren't kidding last trip, were you?"

Phillip shook his head slowly. "Not at all."

I looked between them. "What did I miss?"

Jacob looked at me harshly. "While you were absent at the ball Phillip and I had a discussion about how tedious duty can be."

"We share similar views on fucking off, as you call it," Phillip cut in.

"I am all astonishment." I looked at my brother. "I see you two had a lengthy talk."

Phillip went on. "We had hours, and we agreed you took the brunt of it from your brother, but mine cannot do that. How lucky birth order and a matter of minutes can make you."

"Indeed." I didn't know what else to say.

"Across all the great houses, and half the galaxy you two are the only pair I've found who don't buy into the crap. Sure you put on faces, don't we all, but more women who meet me are interested in my title than what comes out of my mouth." His gaze bored into mine, and I thought I saw a hint of weariness behind them. "In fact, you're the first lady who snuck off on me."

I blushed a little. "My apology."

He waved me off. "Don't be. I've been thinking of it for days. I enjoy your company, but I've had too much bad company forced on me to understand the desire. So, I have a proposal. Give me another chance, my lady, and if I disappoint or you have no interest, I will take no offense to you fucking off as you will."

For the second time in so many minutes he made me really smile. "Is this an offer of sorts?" I paused to choose my words. "I do not wish to soil our position in the eyes of the royal house." I thought my words were candid enough, but I waited to see if my meaning came through.

He didn't reply right away, turning to look out the window as he folded his hands behind his back. "I think I can speak for your brother when I say we will be a strong alliance."

I looked to Jacob, and he nodded.

"You two did have a productive night." He hadn't answered my question, and since he seemed to be on good terms I decided to push it. "And the offer?"

He turned back around and took a step closer to me. There was a something in his expression I couldn't read. "I think it's up to you. If you'll have me." He took my hands in his. "Now, tell me what you wish of me, and we will get the visual part of today done, then we can find some fuckery with your brother."

I kept my hands in his, even though it felt like a betrayal. He was charming, regal in all the right ways, and he had a personality not wholly off-putting thus far. It was the best I could expect, and maybe I should take the offer standing right in front of me.

"What do you think, Jacob? What will please the Baron?"

"Shall we take a stroll through the ornate gardens? They will be packed with lovers at this hour since the weather is reasonable." Jacob grinned. "Then I do think we need to play a drinking game."

Phillip laced his fingers through mine and looked over at my brother. "Why does this sound like an utter disaster?"

"Because it usually is," I laughed.

"Oh it will be. I am thinking blasters and swords. Losers drink."

We were fully intoxicated by the time we returned to Phillip's suite. I collapsed on the sofa, kicking my feet up. All of us were laughing and had been since my brother had downed more liquor and still outshot us both. Phillip discarded his suit coat and cufflinks on a table, then undid a few buttons on his shirt before rolling his sleeves.

"Much better." He turned on me, cheeks rosy from the spirits, and he had a foxy look in his eyes. "I feel like a monkey done up as such." He stalked forward and took a seat, then lay back resting his head in my lap. "Now, this is the view I've been waiting for all night." He grinned ruefully.

I gasped and smacked his shoulder, uneasy with his position. "You are cut off."

He rubbed the back of his head over my thighs. "Has anyone ever asked the two of you for a threesome?"

Jacob and I burst out laughing, and he said, "Is that why you're after my sister?" He licked his lips. "Trying to get at me, eh?"

I laughed. "You two."

My communicator vibrated on my wrist, and I jumped. I placed my other hand over it to silence it. I begged the universe for it to be him.

"Don't deny my nasty charm is endearing me to you."

I didn't move to check the message. "It is one of the reasons I agreed to your proposal."

"Shy to check your messages in front of me?"

Jacob leaned forward placing his elbows on his knees. I could tell he knew who I hoped the message was from.

"Not at all." I brought up my wrist and clicked the screen.

M: **Jocelynn, I am so sorry.**

Phillip sat up, but Jacob shoved him out of the way, a gesture I would have found exceedingly funny had I not been gasping for air.

I pushed them both away and dropped my head to my knees to take a few deep breaths. I could feel them hovering so I looked up. "I am fine."

"Can I get a healer?" Phillip looked truly concerned.

"No, it was the news. I found out a friend who had been injured is pulling through." I plastered on a fake smile, which came easily from years of practice.

I found my brother's gaze like we always did in times like these. I was sure he could tell by the glance what it meant.

He took his seat next to me again but didn't lie back down. "Well that is pleasant news."

I struggled through the rest of the night, and the ease with which the evening had been going was lost. As I walked back to my room, arm in arm with Jacob, I hoped I hadn't ruined things with Phillip. Even if my heart wasn't in it, he was the best possible match I could find, and I did like his company.

"Was it him?" Jacob asked when we slipped into my room and the door was closed between us and any spies.

I nodded, placing my hand over my communicator, wanting desperately for him to go so I could talk to Madden.

"I'll go so you can return it. For the record, I'm glad he's okay, but I'm guessing he's light years away." He turned to go but added, "Give Phillip a chance."

"I already decided to."

"Good." He turned back and crossed the room before taking a seat on the sofa. "I'm too curious to go find a bed to sleep in. Get on with it."

My fingers flew over the controls, and I sent back, **Are you okay?**

I took a seat next to him as we waited. I tried to calculate the time difference between our planets, but I'd never been any good at those problems.

M: **I am fine, back on Harden but unharmed.**

I showed Jacob the message, and he nodded.

J: **Were you taken? What happened?**

Sometime later he sent me a long explanation, and my heart sank. I knew who was behind it all.

J: **I have no words… I'm sorry.**

M: **Don't be, it was as much my fault as yours.**

I started to type out another message but got another from him. **What if I have a way for us to see each other again? Would you?**

My mouth dropped open, and I gasped.

"What?" Jacob asked.

I showed him then sent back.

J: **How?**

Another long pause then,

M: **It's not easy to explain but I have a way through a world of our creating. It's made in the back door of the nets.**

I received message after message of explanation. My mind was reeling. I couldn't believe what he had just told me. This could be my escape from the life I was trapped in.

M: **I was told you would receive information from a trusted source as well. Have you not?**

"Shit," Jacob said when I showed him the message. He pulled out a micro disk from his pocket. "I was going to give it to you this morning, but with Phillip showing up I forgot."

"You trust the person who gave you this?"

"With my life, and I think it's as he says." He paused. "Don't make me give this to you."

I put my comm down and stared at him.

"How long have you known Madden was okay?" I could barely get the words out.

"I had no clue about him. I can't believe you'd doubt me. What I know about is that this tech is not only dangerous but completely unknown except to…" he trailed off. "I wasn't sure why they wanted you to have it. If you take this you owe them." His words hung between us.

"What the hell is it?"

"It's a way for you to see him."

I held out my hand for it. If there was a way to see him nothing would keep up apart.

"Are you sure?" he asked.

"Jacob, what can they do to me?"

"Nothing once you inherit, but think about Madden."

"When I inherit he'll be here with me."

"And Phillip?"

"I'll figure it out," I snapped.

He placed the disk in my hand. "You need to be careful."

I looked at the micro disk and grabbed my tablet.

"Are you fucking daft?" He knocked my hand away and grabbed his bag. "You think you can do an off network program on a network tablet." He pulled out a piece of transparent strong glass from a case in his bag and set it in my hands.

"What do you want me to do with this?"

He tapped the upper left hand corner, and the screen came to life. "You don't even know what exists outside this little world you live in." He took back the micro disk and set it in the other corner. The space under it glowed, and a screen game up that read: Master Builder Program 6.8.

He'd been holding out on me. If I wasn't so happy to have a way to see Madden I would have been livid.

"Now, tell me how it works."

He took the disk back out of my hand and set it over the reader on the screen. "You have to build a world. Don't use one of their prebuilt ones." He gave me a pointed look.

"Okay, and then what?"

"Then you load it into this." He took a tiny spider-like device out of his pocket. "You load the world then press the spinal transmitter to the back of your neck. His is A, and yours is B. He has to go in first. This is imperative."

"What? Why?" I demanded.

Jacob took a deep breath. He never lied to me, but I knew he was about to. "He's the host. I won't let you do it, and the way the devices are set up you can't, so it doesn't matter."

I chewed on my lip. I'd get the answers out of Madden. "Fine. Tell me the rest."

"Then you'll be together. It will feel as real as I'm sitting here before you."

I searched his face. "How long will it take to design a world?"

Jacob shrugged a shoulder. "I didn't take a real good look at it, but you could get a rough one done in a day with my help."

J: **What are you doing tomorrow morning?**

A nervous ball of excitement built in my chest. The thought of tasting him, of seeing him, of the warmth of his arms around me soothed all the fear I'd felt in the last two days.

M: **I have to work, it's midday here... Maybe we can see if it will work tomorrow night?**

I sensed hesitation.

J: **What's wrong?**

M: **Nothing. I know you have places to be and I have to get up as I have to report first thing in the morning.**

J: **Madden.**

M: **I have to go. I'll message tomorrow night.**

I had a full day and night to wonder what his problem was, and it made me sick to think about.

I pressed my eyes closed and held out my hand to my brother. "Show me how. I want to work on the world building."

I opened one eye when he didn't answer.

"Not going to sleep? You know you have a full day with Phillip tomorrow."

I lifted my lip as I snarled. "I can handle it. It's not like you ever get much sleep."

"But it doesn't wear on me like it does you. You were missing meetings."

"Only because I wanted to stay with him. I don't need more than five hours, you know that."

He took the glass from me and started working.

My mouth fell open. "Who has this?"

He lifted his shoulders. "No idea, but it's not us, and somehow the fringe groups got a hold of it. Or maybe they invented it. We may never know."

I stared at him a moment longer. "How did you get it, and how come this is the first I'm hearing about it?"

"I know the right people, and I keep my mouth shut."

I narrowed my eyes at him. "Jacob, what are you involved in?"

"Nothing. I don't ignore the rebels as the Baron does, but they don't know who I really am."

I took his word and returned my attention to the program as he started to pressing buttons.

Chapter Twenty-Eight

Madden

I held the communicator in my hand and cursed myself. I was an idiot for being scared of this. It was only fear. How bad could it really be? But I knew how bad it could be. My mind had haunted me for a long time. If I let it loose, I didn't know what it would do.

I tried to forget about it as I ducked out the door. I had to meet Colton. He promised me a space on his diving crew. It would be a big change from the control room I was used to, but maybe the dark tunnels and the dangerous work would keep my mind off what I gave up and what I'd lost over the last week.

When I closed the door to my single room, my bike stood outside shining. It hadn't been there when I'd gotten in, and I'd expected months of dust coating it. Colton must have cleaned her up after I called him and told him I was back. He hadn't asked, but I knew he would, more so now that I'd asked him for a job. I swung my leg over her and brought her to life. She purred, and I suspected he'd been riding her. The first sun was above the buildings, and its mate would be peeking over the horizon before I reached the mines.

Barely past dawn, I had to squint past the harsh light. Billions of years ago the binary stars had collided, and the planetary system around them had formed in the aftermath. It had crippled the smaller star leaving it a white dwarf, while the other had become a green giant. Because of the pair of them it was light here fifteen to twenty hours of our twenty-six hour days. As most other planetary systems in the known worlds had light twelve or fewer hours a day, it was hard to handle for outsiders. Toward the poles I was told the suns never set, rather dipping lower in the sky before moving up again. The unique circumstances under which the planetary system was created had been the birth of the element Ore and the mines of hell.

Panic ran like blood through my veins as I approached the pits. The weeks away returned to full force, the panic I'd spent most of my life working to dull. The large pits dipped hundreds of miles toward the core of the planet. Only thin roads existed between them creating a special kind of hell between my fear of bridges and heights. All the breath went out of my lungs as my tire passed over the edge. I had ten kilometers to travel weaving through the over road then down into the blackness. I got there before most of the day's workers having made good time. I left my bike in the dusty lot and took the elevator down. The high speed elevator traveled one hundred kilometers in the span of a few minutes.

I closed my eyes waiting for the drop. It didn't disappoint. My stomach jumped to my throat, and air rushed passed me though the grates in the floor. This never bothered me. I was surrounded by steel, and I welcomed the dark which hid the view. I stepped into the tunnel, taking in a lungful of the stagnant air. Track lighting lit the path with barely visible colors for navigation, while protecting night vision, which most relied on here. I needed to regain my cave sight and recall the meaning of the colors. They'd lain dormant for so long it took me a few moments to remember blue was toward the office.

Colton waited there, hands clasped around a large mug of what I guessed was spice coffee.

"Got one of those for me?"

Colton gestured to the mug next to him, and I picked it up. Bringing it to my lips I groaned at the pungent aroma. Another part of our world few outsiders understood. But the spice in it would heighten my senses for hours, helping me with the dangerous work ahead. Arguably the more dangerous jobs in the mine would be impossible without the stimulant. I took a sip, and the liquid dried my tongue and tickled my throat on the way down. I held my breath resisting the urge to cough. I was a lightweight.

Colton shot me an amused look and kept chugging his. The more it was used the less it worked, and the more was needed to get the desired effect. My months off would do me good in the long run of addiction to the stuff. I didn't meet his gaze, finishing my mug before he did. I set it aside and went left of his office to hit up the supply closet. When I returned I wore magnet bands around each of my limbs and a pair of Nightsight goggles resting on my forehead. I skipped the gloves and other protective padding half the men wore. It helped with bruising but fucked the reaction time.

"Look at you not scared of a few jagged shards or unseen outcroppings." He left his cup next to mine and grabbed his key.

"You mock me for things you refuse to wear?" I followed him out of the low lit room back into the relative darkness. It took my eyes a few moments to adjust to the nearly invisible track lights, but I followed the clumping of Colton's boots.

"Well for starters I'm not a pussy." He flashed me a grin, and I rolled my eyes. "I've been at this a lot longer, and as captain I'm not expected to do the hard jumps anymore."

I scoffed. "Bullshit. I bet you do all of them, and if your training is any good I'll be fine."

He turned on me with a jackal-like smile I could barely make out with his closeness. "Think I'd still be here if that wasn't overlooked by my higher ups?"

"Not a chance." I adjusted the magnet bands on my wrists. "Where are we going to today?"

"I figured I'd scare the shit out of you inspecting a fissure sixteen hundred or so kilometers down on the east side."

I swallowed. The number corresponded to a drop that would shatter every organ and bone in a human body. I reveled in the safety of the darkness. There wasn't any drop if I couldn't see it.

"I saw that." He turned back, and I had to jog to catch up to him.

"What?"

"You don't have it under control anymore." He didn't stop until we were at the next set of lift banks.

"It will be."

"This isn't the control room. You asked for this. Someone could fucking die if you don't control it." He studied me as we waited for the next express down. "From the floor we are going to have to go down two hundred meters to find the fissure."

"Put me on the team."

He laughed as he stepped into the metal box that would take us down fourteen hundred kilometers in the next twenty minutes. "Your first day you want to watch my back?"

I held my ground staring at him, ignoring the drop. My feet lifted off the ground, and I reached for one of the handles on the ceiling. Colton leaned back against the wall, having hooked his toes in a curve in the floor.

"Let's do it," he said but paused and pointed a finger at my chest. "But you get nothing deeper until you've gone through all the bullshit safety training."

Chapter Twenty-Nine

Madden

I was dirty, sore, and covered in bruises when I walked in my door. My small cot had nothing on the bed I'd slept on while on Trenton, but it looked like heaven from where I stood. I'd promised Colton I'd go race, but maybe I'd just go to sleep. I kicked off my boots, not bothering to change out of my clothes before collapsing onto the thin mattress.

My comm beeped, and a smile crossed my lips. God, I hoped she was up, finally. I never thought a pin across thousands of light years, a stupid bit of data that was a random scrabble of letters until it showed up on my screen, would mean so much to me. I had never been so attached to my communicator. I typed in my passcode, bringing up the screen to see it was a message from her.

J: **Hey**

The simple word made my stomach flip, sending sparks flying through me.

M: **I miss you.**

I could instantly see she read the message. I sat up, too on edge now to lie down. I watched the dots scroll across the screen, telling me she was typing. I was so wrapped up in watching the screen, picturing her sitting curled up in a chair thinking about me that I didn't notice Colton standing over me.

"Dude."

I looked up, shaken.

"Watching porn?" He licked his dry lips. They were tinged blue and cracked from the mines. "Because I can't think of anything else that would have you that distracted." He leaned over trying to see the screen.

I clicked the power button at the top feeling it buzz in my hand a moment later. I was anxious to read what she had said. "Something like that."

"Ready to go the race?"

I noticed for the first time he had his bike helmet tucked under his arm. I gripped my phone tighter, pushing the fingers of my other into my hair.

"Oh, shit. Was that tonight?" I scrunched up my face as I glanced up at him, trying to act like I forgot. "I can't tonight, man. Got an early shift." I wanted to stay here with J.

"You can't use that with me anymore, bro. You're on my team, and we are off rotation tomorrow." He licked over his lips again. "You've been like this since you got back."

Fuck. I half shrugged not wanting even my best friend to figure me out. "Getting back into things. I've been off. It's only been a few days. Get off my back."

He turned but looked back over me. "You can't keep this up."

As he walked out I knew he was right, but how could I turn off these feelings? I opened my communicator seeing the message.

J: **I miss you. Going to be around tonight?**

I typed out a quick reply.

M: **I have nothing more important going on than spending the night with you.**

J: **Good, I need some time to talk and decompress.**

Something happen? I replied.

J: **It's too much to type, bad day yesterday.**

I wished I could get tone from her messages, but it didn't translate. I could feel her hurting through the words.

M: **I wish I was there to hold you.**

J: **Me too…**

Her short response had my mind whirling. Did I make it worse?

She typed a messaged but didn't send it. I frowned. There was a way I could hold her. I was holding back. I hadn't yet told her. I didn't know if I should. I trusted the contacts I'd made, including Hornsbee, but I knew those groups always had an agenda. Then there was the fear.

Her message sat there for a long time blinking on my screen. There was something she wasn't saying.

J: **You know there is a way. So why not use it?**

M: **It's backdoor into a virtual network the Reds use for secret meetings.**

J: **Why are you so hesitant?**

M: **Because I've been told there are side effects, and it's not always easy to get in.**

I would have given anything to have a real conversation with her at that point. I didn't know what was right or wrong.

J: **Give it to me straight please. You're not telling me why you're hesitant. Let's go live there.**

I laughed at her reaction. I loved when she was annoyed with me.

M: **Because the host has to fight through our subconscious to get there. I looked and looked, but no one has found a way around that part. Then it's fickle, you can reject it at any point and because of the setup, your brain rejecting it and bandwidth you can't go back right away once rejected. It couldn't be an everyday thing.**

J: **Okay… That doesn't sound horrid. Is this why you were so hesitant last night?**

M: **I don't know if it's a good idea to owe these people, J.**

J: **Are you scared of your mind? I'm not. It would be worth it for you.**

M: **Most of that will be on me as I'll be the host and the world will run in my mind. You might get a little residual. It's different for everyone. They couldn't really tell me.**

J: **I get it now.**

She could read me so well. I wasn't surprised. She started typing again so I waited.

J: **Jacob gave me the program and helped on my end. I'm not surprised, he loves those hacker types. I figured if you do it on your days off and lock yourself in your room... Or on my days off and your nights.**

M: **It would be nice to hold you.**

J: **We are losing precious days. I don't want to miss time with you.**

J: **I don't think you understand how much I need you.**

The last thing I wanted was to disappoint her. I was torn between being scared of my mind and wanting to please her. I needed to race to get my head straight. Tasting death might give me enough reprieve to face this.

M: **I guess we can try it.**

I was like a desperate drug addict without her, but I regretted it as soon as I sent the message. She was right. My head was a mess, and I didn't want to deal with it.

J: **I can tonight. You'll be off right?**

My chest got tight.

M: **Maybe we should talk about it more.**

J: **How many of our limited days do you want to waste?**

She was right. I knew she was, but it didn't help the wrenching in my gut.

J: **You know every day you put off things with me is another day we are never going to get back. I know you're trying to get your head straight, but think of all these days as subtracted from our total. We are here for such a limited time, and you want to keep wasting them because you're nervous?**

I said nothing. I could tell how mad she was. She only ranted when she'd been pushed to her limit.

J: **I have to go soon.**

J: **I'm not trying to be mean, but I've realized I already lost you once and I don't want to waste anymore time.**

M: **I'm sorry I'm scared.**

J: **I'm trying to hold on to anything we have left, and you're pushing me away.**

M: **I'm not trying to.**

J: **Don't tell me you want me. If you want me prove it, if not let me go.**

She exited out of the message. I picked up my comm to throw it against the wall, but I paused and reined myself in.

M: **Please don't do this.**

She didn't reply, but I could see she read the message.

M: **Jocelynn I'm begging you.**

I scrubbed a hand over my face. "Fuck." I swallowed hard. It was fear that was holding me back from her. She was right about everything. I was wasting what we had. I was an idiot.

M: **Let's do it now.**

M: **You're right.**

M: **I'm sorry.**

My hands shook as I sent the three messages in quick succession. I put my comm down when she didn't reply right away. I felt like I was coming out of my skin.

I paced the small room. What if it was too little, too late? She might have gone to her morning classes or meetings, or maybe Jacob dragged her off. He had never wanted us together. I rubbed my hands together then scrubbed them down my face. I looked at the clock. It felt like an hour had passed, but it had only been minutes.

My comm buzzed, and I dove for it, glad to see it was her replying and not Colt. I opened the message to read.

J: **I can't now.**

The message hit me like a weight, and I staggered back, falling to a seat. If I waited I wouldn't do it. I reached into my pocket and pulled out the tiny device that would link me to the nets. Holding it in my palm, I typed out a message to her.

M: **Get Jacob to help you with one of the pre-gen worlds. I'll meet you there first thing in my morning. Load up the program.**

Everything had already been linked by the Reds. All we had to do was load up a world and go. The words of the old man lingered in my mind. I would have to face my worst fears to get through this. I didn't even wait for her reply. I had to do this. Not even racing helped me sleep. As soon as I closed my eyes, sleep evaded me. I tossed and turned all night. I couldn't sleep. My mind kept coming back to one thing. What were my worst fears?

When dawn awoke me, I'd guessed I'd only gotten an hour or two of sleep, but it was now or never. I pressed the piece to the back of my neck and closed my eyes.

Chapter Thirty

Madden

Bugs, I was scared of bugs. I hated bugs. I'd opened my eyes to find myself standing in a metal hallway and my personal hell. There was a door on the far side, but it was a long way through a sea of tiny crawling things. My skin was clammy, and my hands shook at my sides. As if separated by an invisible barrier, a foot in front of me started the insects. They covered every inch of the room before me except the square foot in the back I woke in. I had a feeling the moment I stepped out it was open season, and they would swarm me.

This is the worst part, I told myself, over and over.

Jocelynn would be on the other side of those bugs. I would walk through them again and again to get to her.

This is all in your mind. It's not real.

But it felt real. The buzzing beat of their wings filled the air. I could feel it against my face, and I twitched. It was time to get it over with. I took a breath and held it as I stepped around the barrier. I closed my eyes and mouth, covering my nose with my hand. My hood stayed up, protecting my ears as best I could. Exoskeletons crunched under feet, the sound radiating through my body worse than nails on a chalk board.

They started to land on me, crawling over my bare skin as well as clothes. The ground-bound ones clung to my feet trying to get a grip as I sprinted across the room. I stretched out one arm, searching out the wall ahead. I would run headlong into the wall on the far side, and I didn't want to knock myself out in this room. The noise intensified around me, as if my mind made it worse the closer I got to the exit. I tried to imagine being with her as tiny legs moved over my hands. The bugs hadn't bitten me yet, and I kept that in the back of my mind, but it didn't diminish my fear.

My fingers smashed against the opposite wall. I tried to stop myself, skidding over the slick ground. Things crunched underfoot and against my body as I slammed into the wall. I stumbled backward, trying not to fall. I caught my balance and opened my eyes, squinting through the swarm. I leaped toward the door, grasping the handle and wrenching it open. The insects disintegrated as I stepped through the opening. Brushing myself off, I squirmed, still feeling them on me. I took a few slow, deep breaths convincing myself they were gone.

Why did I make it so impossible for myself? I fought my own happiness at every turn. My heart hammered against my ribcage as I turned to look at what punishment my mind offered me next. I looked down to a sheer drop lined with water and jagged stones at the bottom. Over the water was the longest rope bridge I think I'd ever seen. The boards were slick, by the look of them, with moss or some other wet substance. I scrubbed a hand over my face.

I'd almost forgotten my fear of bridges. If this had been after months in the mines it wouldn't have bothered me so much. I dropped to my knees, knowing I couldn't do it. I'd failed her on the second task. My own mind was preventing me from getting to her.

My head hit the cool stone floor, and I ground my teeth. We hadn't seen each other in a week. It had been a week since I tasted her lips. She deserved more than me. This would always be a struggle. It would be hard for her to stay awake all night to be with me. It was easy enough for me on my days off work to sneak away, but she had every minute of every day planned for her.

I was wasting time. Every minute I was weak and stayed here was another one I wouldn't get to spend with her. Forcing myself to my feet, I surveyed the bridge. The ropes were frayed from rot, and the boards were splintered and thin in places, some broken altogether.

Could I die in my own mind?

This wasn't who I was. I had to be strong for her even if I couldn't be for myself. I growled, forcing one foot forward to step out onto the bridge.

The wood swayed under me. It creaked and groaned but held. A light breeze picked up rocking the bridge as I took another step. I kept going, not allowing myself to look down or stop. The ropes creaked under my hands as my palms slid over them. Each step onto the moss covered boards disrupted my footing. I felt like I had to jump from board to board to avoid losing my balance. About three-fourths of the way across I started to breathe easier.

I didn't really believe I could die in my own mind. This was all an illusion.

My body lurched forward as the board under my foot gave out. I saw the drop below for the first time. I tightened my fists on the rope and fell halfway through the open space, grasping at anything I could with my hand as the rope burned through the fingers of my other. Air rushed by me, and I screamed, begging myself to wake up. I would gladly go through the bug room again to not fall. Bile rose in my throat as I jerked to a stop, both feet dangling in the opening of the board once stood. I hung by my one arm, fingers barely grasping the rope. Bracing my hand on the board in front of my face, I found a grip for my free hand. I worked my way up slowly with both hands, until I was sitting on it.

My breathing came in ragged gasps. I had to crawl the rest of the way across the bridge. My legs were too shaky to do more than that. When I got safely to the other side, I collapsed and hugged the ground, so thankful I didn't have to return back the way I came. I looked up and knew what was coming next, a jog through the dark. This was mild on my fear list.

I held my head high as I walked into the darkness like it was another day in the mine. Nothing could hurt me—unless the darkness was concealing another one of my fears. My skin crawled, and I felt watched by unseen eyes. Anything could be out in the darkness, but I didn't allow myself to dwell on it. Thoughts kept popping into my head.

What if I get lost in here?
Could I be stuck here forever?
Can I die in here?

But I forced them aside. This task was as much a war with my imagination as anything. There could be a madman hiding ahead with a knife or any other weapon I would never see coming. In the end, I had to trust my brain not to kill me, which was easier said than done. It seems we never get over those childhood fears we all have. I could remember racing to my bed in the dark and jumping the last few feet as to not step near the hidden under-space. This was no different.

My outstretched hands hit rock. I blinked, trying to look around, but nothing was visible. I placed my hand on the wall. The fear I had taken a wrong turn was now eating at my insides as if I had swallowed the bugs from the first room. I followed the wall and came to a corner. Dragging my fingertips over the rough surface, I continued. In three paces I came to another corner. I took in a sharp breath. Something wasn't right. I reached out my other arm feeling a wall. I turned frantically and to my horror found I was enclosed in a box. As I braced my hands against the walls, my fears were realized. They closed in around me. I curled into myself in the dark waiting for the end. I pressed my palm into my chest, rubbing over my heart. The fear ached, but worse than that, Jocelynn would never know what happened to me. She would never know I had died fighting my way to her. I sank to the floor and pressed my face into my knees, shaking, feeling like the air was being sucked out of the space.

"No!" I screamed.

I couldn't die like this. I scrambled to my feet. Digging my fingers into the rock, I clawed my way up the wall.

Kicking off the ground I dragged my body higher. I didn't stop or let my fear of heights sink in. My nails broke against the jagged stone, but I kept going ignoring the pain. Higher and higher I found handholds, and footholds in the dark. I battled against my mind until my fingers found an edge. Excitement surged through me. But I didn't let the hope hold. I had been here longer than I'd expected. It felt like days at war with my mind, and I knew I had more to go. I hauled myself over the side, lying stretched out with my eyes closed.

When I'd calmed I pushed the heels of my hands into my eye sockets wondering what other horrors my mind would throw at me next.

"Madden?" Her voice was like the calm after a storm, and the moon in my darkness lighting the way.

Panic hit me. What if it wasn't real? Could I handle Jocelynn as a nightmare?

Chapter Thirty-One

Jocelynn

"Madden!"

He pried his eyes open as I approached. He looked broken, bleeding from his fingertips, coated in sweat and hollow. His normally tanned skin was ashen, and I dropped to my knees in the sand at his side as he looked at me strangely.

I couldn't make him do this for time with me. I couldn't torture him like this. I pushed my fingers into his hair urging him closer to me.

"Convince me you're real." His voice cracked, and he buried his face in my lap, inhaling sharply.

I wrapped my arms around his neck curling over him. "Of course I'm real, Madden."

He clutched at my shirt, nearly tearing the fabric. "Don't let me go."

"Never." I tightened my grip, and we sat there holding each other until the tide started lapping at his feet.

He pulled his face up at the first feel of the icy water, looking me in the eyes. "Next time you need to put this place in an area with warm water."

"I was short on time!" I laughed grabbing him by the ears to pull his lips to mine. I whispered over them. "That's the first thing you have to say to me when you haven't touched me in how long?"

He pushed up on his knees to dive on top of me, knocking me backward into the sand. Attacking me with kisses, he wrapped up around me. My knees fell open allowing his hips to meet mine.

"It's been too long." He gasped between kisses.

I parted my lips to speak, but his tongue delved into my mouth cutting me off. I nipped and sucked at it, tasting him. It was so close to what I remembered. The hint of those cloves he smoked mixed with Axel whiskey. I slid my hand from his ear into his dark locks. He didn't lift up, pushing a hand under my ass to hold me to him as he rocked his groin over mine.

By the time we broke apart I was gasping, and heat flooded between my thighs.

"I need you," he groaned, working his soft lips down my neck. The light dusting of facial hair on his face burned.

"I'm here." I clung to him as emotion washed over me. "I'm not going anywhere."

"Promise?"

"As long as we can stay." I didn't know how to put into words the suffering I'd been through thinking he was really gone from my life. The thought of losing him crushed my soul. It took all the joy from my life. I was left without purpose, and nothing I'd cared about before seemed to matter.

He looked into my eyes, searching. "Are you okay?"

"No, I'm not okay. I lost you, by my own stupidity. I have to hold onto this because it's all we have."

He grabbed me by the hair and captured my mouth. We lay there in the sand reacquainting ourselves with each other.

"I have to have you."

"Like this? Here?" I arched my back meeting his rough thrusts, feeling him harden against me.

"I don't care how…" He flicked his tongue over the hollow of my throat. "You taste like the sea." He skimmed his nose back up my neck, peering down at me.

I hooked a leg over his hips, not allowing any space between our bodies. "And you taste like cloves."

He licked over his lips and narrowed his eyes. "Sorry."

I picked my head off the sand crushing my mouth to his. "Don't be sorry. I like it." Sucking his lower lip into his mouth I rocked my ass, teasing my stomach over his arousal, feeling him pulse between us.

He groaned under his breath, eyes fiery as they met mine. "Are you trying to kill me?" He lifted off me a little, and I pressed my heels into the ground chasing the contact, but he hovered over me to work his fingers under the hem of my shirt. I shivered under his light touch. The sun started to dip below the horizon, casting colors across the water and sky. A light breeze picked up, drastically cooling the warm day. But I wasn't cold. His body and touch warmed my bare skin as he inched the fabric high up. His fingertips trailed over my ribs, and I shivered.

A grin spread over his face. "Like that?"

I bit down on my lip and nodded as he slid lower replacing his hand with his mouth. My lips parted in a silent gasp as he hooked his thumbs in my shorts inching them lower.

"Yes…" My toes curled as I pulled my knees up, opening up for him further. "Too much."

He explored my stomach with his mouth, blowing his hot breath over my skin. My eyes slid half closed as I toyed with his hair.

"If you keep saying too much, I'm going to start thinking you want me against your will." He glanced up as me as he pushed my shorts even lower still with his chin.

"It's not that…" My words trailed off turning into a soft moan when he bit at my hip.

"Then what is it?" His voice was low and husky, laced with need.

I had visions of us hot and sweaty, all wrapped up in each other. I flushed all over at the thought of how he would feel against me.

"It's…" I pressed my eyes closed, tilting my head back. "I'm afraid no one else will ever feel this good, that this is my only chance, and you're five hundred light years away."

He lifted up, brow knit. I clutched at him, trying to get him to return to what he was doing, not wanting to turn things heavy when they were so lighthearted and fun.

"Forget it." I pulled at his shoulders. "Come back here."

He crawled up over me, pushing his knees into the inside of my hips, spreading me wider open for him. "I can't forget it, and I know you're right. But there has to be a way. I can't believe that we feel this way for nothing. It's too depressing."

I nodded picking my head up off the ground to brush my lips over his. "I want to believe that." And I did. But I was a realist. I knew marriage for my kind wasn't for love. The world was that cruel. But that didn't mean I wouldn't keep trying to get to him.

"It's all we have, so believe it and enjoy this. For me?" A shadow crossed his face, and I knew his mind had gone some place dark.

"What's wrong? And what took you so long to get here?" I stroked my fingers down his cheek.

He turned his head, kissing my palm. "Nothing, and it just took me longer than I expected to get through the nightmares."

"Was it bad?"

"It was what it was." He shrugged.

I knew he was hiding something. He'd looked like death when he appeared on the sand. "Let's talk about it."

"Not worth dwelling on, baby." He sat back on his heels, grabbing my hands to pull me toward him as he rose to his feet. He started to drag me backward toward the water. "Let's go rinse off before we warm up by the fire."

The wind picked up again blowing my hair up around my face. "But I'll freeze."

He didn't relent, using his superior size to keep us moving. "I'll keep you warm." He wore a playful grin.

I dug my feet into the sand, trying to stop my progress. In an instant, he reversed his position and grabbed me around the middle, hoisting me off the ground. He threw me over his shoulder like I weighed nothing and turned to sprint toward the water.

I playfully fought against him, knowing I had already lost. When he was knee deep he threw me into the waves. The cold water sent a shock through my body, and I cringed against it before I started to get used to the temperature. When I resurfaced I glared at him and instantly sank my shoulders back under the waves, feeling the air hit my bare skin.

"You're right, we need a location with warmer water." I splashed him.

As the water hit his chest he growled, diving forward to take me under again. We played and wrestled in the water, which quickly turned into another heated kiss. We lingered in the cool water, too caught up in each other to notice the sun had fully set. He used both hands to pull up my soaking shirt only breaking our kiss to remove it. I found the hem of his doing the same. He brushed his fingers over the patch of lace between my breasts, resting his forehead against mine.

"We should go warm up." He skimmed his fingers along the underside of my breasts.

"Yeah…" I watched him looking at me.

His free hand gripped my hip holding me in place as he lightly brushed his thumb over my lace covered nipple. "You're so beautiful," he whispered, barely audibly.

I leaned into him as my nipple pebbled, and pleasure enveloped me. I had been with others, but no one's touch had ever felt like this. It was an ember glowing inside me which only got hotter with every simple gesture.

"You feel so good."

He met my eyes for a second before ducking his head to suck over where his thumb had just been. I pressed my chest into his mouth, his arm around my lower back supporting my weight. He paused moving his forehead to the base of my throat, his whole body stiff.

My brow fell. "What's wrong?"

Chapter Thirty-Two

Madden

I shuddered in her grasp, and I knew I was scaring her with how I was acting, but it was hard to get out of my mind that anything could be real after all that I'd gone through.

I laid my forehead against hers. "Nothing."

She cupped my face with her hands, shivering in the cold water. "I don't believe you, Madden, and I hate saying that."

I closed my eyes. "I need you," I said again.

"You have me."

"That's not what … never mind." My breathing came in heavy gasps, uncontrolled. "Let's go inside."

"Madden…" She tilted my head up. "Tell me what's in your head."

"Let's get you inside and warm first. You're shivering." I could feel her shaking in my arms. But there was more to it than that. I didn't know if I could handle her turning me down. It wasn't even about a release at this point. I would have given anything to be as close to her as possible. I wanted to be under her skin, filling every inch of her mind, and buried inside her. It had been so long since I'd been able to touch her I didn't care if this was all inside our minds. I wanted to touch every inch of her again.

"Okay…" I could read the disappointment on her face.

"J…"

She turned away from me. I grabbed her wrist, pulling her back to me.

"Tell me what's wrong?"

She looked at me, and her eyes had turned hard. "When *you* won't tell me what's wrong?"

My lips parted, and I swallowed a few times, not sure what to think of her turning it back on me. She lifted her arm, which I still grasped and roughly twisted it out of my grip with surprising force. She must have had combat training, which made sense when I thought about it further. The stubborn streak I had seen before showed itself, and I knew there was more to that path. I didn't think I would ever be able to make her do something she didn't want to do. It was handy knowledge I filed away.

I carried her inside and laid her across the fainting couch. She leaned closer to the fire in the hearth, still shivering. I guessed her work. I stripped off my wet clothes as I walked deeper into the house. They weren't real, so I could cast them off with no fear of actually losing them. When I was yanked back to reality I would have them again. I searched the closet in vain. There were blankets, but not a towel to be found.

I wrapped one of the blankets around my waist and gathered the rest, wondering if this was her oversight in the program or a basic flaw. The places our minds wander when we don't want to deal with what's in front of us. Coming up behind her, I draped one over her shoulders before I took a seat on the hearth in front of her.

"Thank you," she said in a whisper. Her elbows rested on her knees as she stared into the flames.

I took another blanket and draped it over the both of us. "It's cold."

"I guess when I chose the atmosphere I wasn't thinking straight. I thought this would be..." she trailed off, rubbing her hands up her arms.

"You wanted it to be cool so we'd have more of a reason to be close."

She looked up at me through her lashes. Right there she looked so small and innocent. Not the powerful woman I knew. I pulled her into my arms and wrapped up around her.

"Yes," she said into my chest.

I adjusted the blankets, and even though she was light years away I felt her, really felt her, for the first time. She was here with me as much as I was with her, and everything I'd been through to get here was worth it and I'd do it a hundred times over.

I slid a finger under her chin, tilting her mouth up to mind. She welcomed the kiss, parting her soft lips as soon as they touched mine. This wasn't a clash or a battle, it was a joining. Her fingers slid into the hair at the back of my neck, and she held us together, not just physically. I needed it as badly as she needed to hold me at that moment.

When we parted, both breathing hard, she rested her forehead to mine, still clinging on to me.

"What are we going to do?" she asked.

"We have this, and we have it as long as we want it."

"Is this enough for you?" Her lower lip quivered as she spoke, and my heart broke all over again.

"Hours with you will never be a waste." I wouldn't say it, but there had to be another way. There had to be something I could do to get back to her.

"Let's not waste anymore time." The look in her eyes told me everything.

"Yes, ma'am."

"On your knees."

I dropped down in front of her, letting the blanket slip off of me as I did.

She stood and started to peel off her wet clothes. When I tried to help she shook her head, and I dropped my arms back to my sides.

"I want you to watch." First she freed her breasts, and if I hadn't already been hard the sight of her still nipples peaked from the cold would have done me in. I wanted to touch so bad, but I made myself wait.

"It's hard to be patient, isn't it?"

I nodded.

"But you're a good boy, you can wait." Her power was back, and it did things to me.

"I am."

She played, taking her time to strip off her bottoms, but leaving her panties in place. There were a tease in themselves. Black and all lace, giving me a preview of the skin hiding underneath. I couldn't help myself. I grabbed her by the back of her thighs and pressed my face into her. She squirmed but didn't fight me too much. Instead, she tugged at my hair until I looked up at her.

"Now, you don't get the rest of your show."

I curled the tips of my fingers into the top of her panties. "I'll make my own show."

She didn't stop me so I slid the lace down her thighs, and when I put a hand on her stomach to push her, she took the hint and sat back on the chaise. I brushed my lips along the inside of her thigh as I parted her legs.

"I should make you wait for this." Her head fell back as she spread herself wide open for me. I looked up at her as I skimmed my tongue along her slit. Her body tensed, and I knew she was putty in my hands.

"Make me wait. You letting me be here is enough of a reward." I dipped my tongue between her lips to emphasize my point.

She shook. "You can spend all day down there if you like it so much."

It didn't take all day. I had her shaking and screaming my name in a matter of minutes. As soon as she finished she tugged me over her, a sated look in her eyes.

"I thought you said you were making me wait."

"If you don't fuck me right now you will be waiting a long time."

I slid a hand between us to position myself. "Shouldn't I be begging?"

She bit my lip. "Are you trying to make me come again?"

"Always."

"Good, because I expect you to ask for your orgasm." She dug her nails into my ass, mixing my pain with my pleasure.

I shook with need. "Please."

"The way you say that word." She lifted her hips forcing my tip inside.

"Please," I said again as I entered her.

She arched into me, and I tried to go slow, I really did, but something in me snapped. I fucked her into the chaise. My hips slapped into her skin, and I stretched her wide to accommodate my girth. There was no holding back now. Her nails dug into my shoulders, but she wasn't fighting me, rather she was urging me on, lifting her hips to meet my strokes, and telling me she needed more. She brushed her lips along the base of my neck, before turning her head to bite my shoulder. Her breathing started to hitch, and I knew she was close to losing it again. Between her nails, teeth, and impending release I lost myself.

She fell asleep with me still inside her. We were both emotionally drained. She needed it. But I wouldn't let myself sleep. Every fucking minute that passed felt like one less I would get with her. I wanted to take in as many of them as I could.

I was screwed. I knew I'd never feel this way about anyone again. This was a once in a lifetime kind of love, and I was going to let it destroy me. Because some things were worth losing your soul over.

Chapter Thirty-Three

Jocelynn

I gasped, bolting up. My head was spinning as I reached out for Madden. Had I fallen asleep? I tore my bed apart searching for him, but he wasn't there.

"He's not here." The cold voice of reality spoke.

I whipped around to find Jacob staring back at me. I dropped my face to the bed, balling my hands into fists. "How long was I there?"

"Three hours maybe. It's good for a first time. I've seen people reject it much faster. A lot of people's brains don't like the simulated reality. Did he not tell you the first time wouldn't last? "

I looked up at him, knitting my brow. "How do you know?"

He ignored my question and went on. "You must have written the program well."

"I followed your parameters." I searched around for my comm, finding it on the floor. "What did I miss?"

He came over to take a seat on the edge of the bed. "All your morning meetings. I was told to bring you this."

He set a gold tied folder on the bed next to me. I didn't pick it up, instead sending a message to Mad.

J: **Are you okay?**

I stared at the comm waiting for it to be read.

M: **I'm fine. We rejected the program?**

J: **Yeah. I guess we did.**

M: **Probably better you don't miss a full day.**

J: **Yeah, I do need to get going. You should sleep.**

M: **I need it. I can barely keep my eyes open.**

I clutched the phone to my hand trying to ignore the packet Jacob held under my nose.

J: **Sleep well.**
M: **I'll message you when I get up.**

I ripped the packet from Jacob's hand and tossed it across the room. It hit the far wall harder than I expected and exploded gold paper all over the surrounding floor. Jacob burst out laughing and lay back.

"You know how it will turn out if you don't plan part of it." He yawned and closed his eyes.

"I know." I rubbed my wrists absentmindedly. "How annoying do you think the bands are?"

He shrugged one shoulder. "I'm sure if they were that bad they would have switched to something else two centuries ago."

I got up and glanced in the mirror as I crossed to pick up the papers. I looked like I had lain abed all morning, which I had. The only trace of where I had been was the slight bruising on my neck. I brought my hand to the mark, tracing the pads of my fingers over where his lips had been. I hadn't known any of this could transition through the nets, but I loved seeing it there. I wondered how many of my marks would be on him.

I didn't linger in front of the mirror, bending to collect the sheets. They were plans for the hall and menus, and it was planned down to the sketches for the dress I would wear and how my makeup would look. I collected them, looking at every page as I put them back in order.

"You suggested it wasn't already all planned." I set the stack back on the bed next to him.

"That was this morning's session. You still have a full afternoon which the Baron has invited Phillip to."

I flopped back. "Do you think I can encourage him to kidnap me?"

Jacob raised a brow.

"Holy universe. Not for that reason."

Jacob got up, glancing down at his comm. "I have a lunch ... meeting. Sure we'll go with that."

"Enjoy your mid-afternoon drilling."

"Do you have to be so crude? I haven't drilled anyone since we were on Slade." He flashed me a grin as he ducked out of the room.

Phillip made the afternoon manageable, making me laugh as he made faces behind the Baron's back.

Madden worked the next four days, and it was painful to only be able to sneak in messages between our reversed schedules. But I couldn't take the risk of missing any more meetings as the coronation approached. I didn't want the Baron to look into what I was doing any closer than he was already watching me after things with Madden. At least I had Phillip to pass the time with, even if he would never be a passable substitute for Mad.

His first night into a day off came in sync with our state day of rest. I woke before either of the suns had peeked above the horizon. The city outside my window was still with predawn dew lingering. It would freeze soon, and everything would turn to ice. I had spent my nights talking to Madden, working on tweaking the program so we could spend the day in warmth. I was hoping he would be up for staying up late even though he'd worked the last five days in a row. The twelve hour days were hard on him, and he usually passed out soon after he walked in the door.

My comm blinked to life, and I ran across the room to grab it.

M: **Ready?**

J: **You're late.**

M: **Little bit.**

M: **Bad fucking day.**

J: **Want to tell me about it?**

M: **I don't want to here. I want to hold you. Can we go?**

J: **Yeah, let me get the program loaded up and we can go.**

M: **Wait!**

I got up as his messaged clicked through. I was about to put the micro disk into the spinal transmitter, but I paused.

J: **Okay?**

M: **I've been working on a little something. It's not as good as yours, but it's a place my parents used to take me to and I wanted you to see it.**

J: **I don't understand.**

M: **I wrote a program. Meet me there. I'm going in.**

I was about to put my comm away and grab the transmitter when another message clicked through.

M: **Wear a coat.**

I grabbed my coat, sliding my arms into it before I pulled it tight around myself fastening the magnet connectors before I picked up the transmitter.

I set the disk aside and waited for the connector to turn green. Once he entered it would open to me. I'd been told more than once he had to go in first, and I figured out why. My brother had a hand in setting this thing up, and he didn't want a record of my fears anywhere that could be traced. So Madden had to open the way, building the matrix in his mind before I could go in.

The tiny light clicked green. I swallowed and pressed it to the back of my neck.

Chapter Thirty-Four

Jocelynn

Before the transmitter could rip me out of my world and into the secret one my mind preferred, someone barged into my suite.

"Good, you're up." The Baroness looked disheveled like she hadn't slept. "Get dressed in your uniform. You're needed in the council room."

I snatched my comm as she pushed me toward my dressing chamber. I sent a message to him in the matrix using the code Jacob had given me in case something like this ever happened.

J: **I got grabbed by the Baroness. I won't be there for a while.**

I pulled on my clothes quickly and tied my hair up in a knot at the back of my head. He was going to go through all that and leave. He had to be exhausted after working all day. I strapped my comm to my wrist and sent another quick message.

J: **Stay, please stay. You can sleep there. We won't be able to go back until your next set of off days and I don't want to miss you. Just please wait for me.**

I pressed my eyes closed and stepped out to face her.

"What are you waiting for? Hurry up." She turned and left. I pushed my hands over my face and stepped out, closing my door behind me.

I hurried toward the opposite end of the palace, and Jacob caught me before I could duck into the council room.

"Stop." He hissed, pulling me into a dark alcove. "What is this about?"

His hair was mussed, and he smelled like sex. "It's not good whatever it is. There have been whispers."

"Of what?" I pulled my arm back from him, staring into his bloodshot eyes. But I couldn't get a good read on him.

"If you'd been paying attention for the last month maybe you would be able to tell me. You sit in on more of these than I'm allowed. But we both have been woken before dawn on the one day the Baron takes for rest. What do you think that means?"

"Jok?"

He shook his head. "It means something is going on. I saw Phillip walk in before you."

I brushed my hands down the red of my formal uniform shirt, smoothing out unseen wrinkles. "Which means the Emperor knows."

"I think your idea for the new trade routes is causing problems."

"What? How?"

"Keep your ears open. It's going to be a long day." He peeked out from behind the flickering half drape making sure no one else was in the hall. "Wait five minutes before you come in after."

I grabbed the back of his shirt. "I don't want to be here all day. This is the first day."

He spun around grabbing my arm harshly, hard enough I knew there would be bruises under his fingertips. "This isn't all about you. There is more at stake here than your heart."

He shoved me back half a pace and slipped into the hall. My heart pounded in my chest, and my knees shook. It wasn't just about my heart. He'd gotten to fuck off for the last four years while I went to every damn meeting and earned my position on the war council. He had no room to talk. I took a slow breath. Nothing I said to myself in the hall would make a difference. I had to see what was going on and assess if I could get away. He was only right about one thing. I needed to change my attitude and behavior, if only so the Baron didn't catch on to where I was spending my free time.

I straightened my back and held my chin out as I stalked into the council room. All eyes turned to me as I did.

"Good of you to finally join us." The Baron scoffed. "It seems I have two children who choose to slack off now."

His comment was uncalled for in front of the entire full council, and he knew it.

I crossed my arms over my chest. "Thank you for waking me before dawn without a pervious engagement and expecting me to show up in full dress uniform in five minutes flat." I met his eyes. He would have never made a comment on me showing up ten minutes later than everyone else in months past. I knew I had a long way to go to get back into his good graces before I was granted my full freedom again.

I took my seat at his right hand side and swiped the glass table to access the brief pages. I scanned it and lifted my gaze to my brother. He had just finished reading the same thing.

"We had an unknown attack just after five local time at one of our outposts, as you can see." The Baron adjusted his seat. "It was the outpost close to Harden, which is why I called you all here out of your warm beds on the holiday." He looked over at me, but I didn't flinch. Years of his stern gaze had made me immune to it.

"What happened?" I asked flipping to the next page of the rushed report.

"Briggs," the Baron said, referring to his Admiral of Defense.

"Reports are still coming in from our ships that survived the attack."

Both my brows rose when he said *survived,* and a few members of the council gasped.

"We were attacked by an unknown vessel. One my men have never had experience with, which appeared out of the unexplored side of far reaches of the outer planets." Briggs commanded the attention of the entire room as he spoke. "It traveled at a speed also unknown to us, but of course we know the Emperor has new tech from Jok and the Time4." He nodded at Phillip.

"That is correct. Do you have the readouts so I can compare them?" Phillip held out a hand as Briggs handed over a paper thin tablet.

"You'll see on the readings, which I suspect you'll come to find yourself, I believe the speeds we clocked the ship at were quite a bit faster than what I understand even Jok uses for trade."

"I have my compatibles on me." He reached into his bag and pulled out a condensable square. He expanded it so the screen projected on the table and started to pull things up. "I'm sending the reports over."

"One ship came out of folded time and attacked the base?" Phillip pressed, keeping his eyes on his screen.

"That is correct," Briggs answered.

"What was taken?" I flipped to the next page of the report, skimming as I waited for the answer to my questions.

"Nothing."

I glanced up at Briggs. "How can that be so?" Raids were always for supplies.

"The first responders are saying they took nothing and that they didn't respond to open channel calls," Briggs replied.

Briggs clicked his own light tablet, and the scene rose out of the center of the table. It was broken in places from where sensors were destroyed before they could give their readings. But a general three-dimensional image of the space around the base came into view. I stood to get a better vantage point and inspected the scene.

"They took scans?"

"Yes, ma'am, which was why we sent out crews from the base."

"And the crews were attacked?" I asked.

"That is correct." Briggs swiped his hand over the tablet, and the scene changed to a partial piece of the battle.

I kept my expressions blank as I watched. It was a grim scene. Nothing our ships did seemed to touch them.

"Replay it."

He did, and it occurred to me that this wasn't an attack. I was about to open my mouth to say as such when Jacob caught my eye. He shook his head, and I remembered his warning to listen and not comment. What did he know? But I didn't think this was an attack at all. I think whoever we were dealing with wanted to test the ship against our defenses and put us on high alerts.

The room was silent, and when I looked up I found all the eyes in the room locked on me.

"Do you have a hypothesis?" the Baron demanded.

"I suspect this won't be the end of these intruders, and we need to do everything in our power to prepare for next time." I watched Jacob out of the corner of my gaze as I spoke. He knew more than he was letting on, and I wanted to know what it was. He was rarely rough with me, and there were too many red flags going off in my head about the entire situation. If I didn't get answers as soon as we were alone I was going to be livid.

I tore my attention away from Jacob to watch Phillip closely. There were reasons he was in this meeting, one of which was being an attack it was mandatory we report the incident to the Emperor as his kingdom was at risk. But this wasn't the normal protocol. After a council meeting he should have received a report, and then the Emperor could appoint a representative to sit in on further meetings. But of course the Baron would never let any spy for the Emperor sit in on the real meetings unless he thought he had something to gain by doing it.

Again, Jacob had been right. I had missed much with my head in space over the last month, and now I had a lot of catching up to do. I was only putting myself at risk by not knowing the politics of my own house.

The meeting came to a close, and we were told we would all receive updates during the day. We would meet again in the morning unless there were any developments. Only two hours had passed, but I was emotionally drained. When the rest of the council dispersed I grabbed Jacob by the sleeve.

"Care to explain to me what you hinted at before the meeting?"

"I can't." He pulled out of my grasp. He'd never been like this. I felt like my one ally had abandoned me.

"You know I covered in there for you. I saw what you did. Someone is testing that thing."

He growled, leaning in closer. "Not here and not now. Go play house, and I will explain when I have time."

I narrowed my eyes at him. "I swear to you, brother mine, I will go to the Baron with what I know this instant."

"Will you trust me?"

We stared each other down until I broke it.

"Fine, but if you don't explain when I get back…"
I didn't know what I'd do, but I wanted answers.

"I don't know as much as you think I know, but I
know the same thing you do. Someone is testing
something. Now go play, and we'll talk later. I am going
to go see if I can find more answers." He was lying. I
knew he was lying, but there were more important things
than the truth.

My head was full when I closed myself in my
room. I picked up the spinal transmitter and pressed it to
the back of my neck. I opened my eyes to find a white
wilderness.

It was bitter cold. I'd left with a coat like Madden
had instructed me to, but I'd imagined the cold of my
world. This was bitter. A shiver ran down my spine, and I
wrapped my arms around myself. I turned a slow circle to
find I was in a thick forest. I'd only seen pictures of such
a thing before, and I reached out to touch one of the
massive trees. The largest were as big around as one of
the castle towers while the smallest would take many
men linked at the arms to span the base. I looked up to
find out an overcast sky through the bare trees. Tiny
snowflakes were falling from the clouds adding to the
meter of snow under foot. I looked harder through the sea
of trees, trying to figure out where Madden could be.

My gaze finally landed on a small cabin
camouflaged in the distance. I tucked my hands into my
sleeves and started in that direction. It wasn't as far as I
first thought. The trees created an illusion, but walking
through the snow was tiresome. The lights were on when
I got there, and my heart picked up.

I tried the handle to find the door open. He was
standing there with his back to me, looking out the
window. I stepped inside, and closed the door quietly
behind me, watching him. A smile took over my mouth

as he sighed and checked the contents of the old-fashioned oven again. I couldn't see past him, but the aroma wafting from it made my mouth water. I shrugged out of my coat. My cheeks already rosy from the difference in temperature, I was starting to become over heated.

I tiptoed across the room and slid my arms around his middle. He leaned back into me as I stood on my toes and brushed my lips over the base of his neck.

"Jocelynn." I could hear the smile on his lips. "You got away."

"It took a while. I'm sorry."

He turned in my arms and picked me up. I moved my arms from his waist to his neck. Our lips met needfully, and he pulled my legs around him. I crossed them behind his back, and we stayed that way for a long time. The kiss was desperate and rushed, but then it slowed as we explored each other's mouths like it was the first time. By the time we broke apart my cheeks were stained with tears I hadn't known I'd shed. He rubbed his face against mine.

"It wasn't normal stuff keeping you away, was it?" He didn't look at me when he asked.

My lips trembled. "No."

"Tell me?"

I closed my own eyes and forced my voice even. "Life is never going to be with us. So we have to make the best of it."

"Do you always have to be stronger than I am?" His voice gave him away.

"I'm your rock, remember." I laughed, trying to get him to calm down.

"I remember."

A soft beep ruined the moment, and he set me down to grab a pair of oven mitts.

"You designed this place with an oven?"

"I wanted to make something." He pulled a tray from it and set it on the counter above.

"You could have written whatever it was you wanted into the program or made a materializer."

He pulled off the mitts on his hands and picked one up of the items off the tray. He winced a little but held it close to me. The smell of the spices wafted up to my nose. I leaned closer trying to get a better breath of them.

"What is that?"

He broke it open so I could see flaky pastry and what looked like cooked fruit. I grabbed at it, and he lifted the thing over his head.

"Share." I tugged at the sleeve of his flannel shirt. He really had played up the part.

He lowered it slowly and held it out. "Because some things are better done by hand."

I tried to take it from his hand, but he shook his head, holding it to my lip. I looked him in the eyes as I took it with my mouth, brushing my lips over his fingers. We moaned in unison. The richly flavored spices assaulted my tongue, and he pulled me in for a kiss. He teased his tongue over my lips, mixing his flavor with that of the fruit.

I thanked the universe for his distraction, not wanting to talk about the things to come, and what it would mean for us. He wrapped his arms around my waist, pushing me back toward the sofa. Even the pastry was forgotten as he tugged me into his lap.

I gladly straddled him, sliding my knees down around his hips, settling into his lap. Our mouths never broke apart, nipping and sucking at one another. I forgot for a moment this wasn't real. Mad pushed his hands under my shirt, breaking apart the kiss as he skimmed his fingers up my ribcage. I lifted my arms, locking our gaze.

"I want you," I said.

I could see the hunger in his eye, but he hesitated.

Chapter Thirty-Five

Madden

I'd known she was off from the moment she walked in the door. I could feel it in her body. She was holding back. There was stress woven into her muscles. The delay this morning had been more than she let on.

I slid my hands from her shirt, letting them settle on her hips. "Tell me what's on your mind."

"Nothing." She shook her head, but I could feel her distance in every movement.

"You can't hide your feelings from me. I can read you like a book, J." I pulled her body closer to mine. She was tense. "What the hell happened this morning? Why were you late on your off day?"

"There was an attack on your outer base this morning." She let out a long breath, going into a brief explanation, and I stared at her.

"I know nothing about this."

She shook her head. "I doubt you will. They don't like to tell the masses these kinds of things."

I still couldn't read her. It was like she'd closed off all emotion. It scared me.

"What's changed? If you're worried about me, I'll be fine." I felt even more helpless than I had before. I could feel something lingering under the surface, like her emotions were pent up behind a dam.

She put on what I knew was a fake smile and touched her lips to mine. "Those smell really good."

It was a clear dismissal, in a way only a member of the great house could. There was no getting anything out of her until she wanted to tell. I decided to ignore it and try to enjoy her.

"You need to eat more, and I need to build the fire."

"I thought we were doing warm this time." She got off my lap and smiled again, but it was vacant. Most of her mind was elsewhere, and it hurt.

"Next time. I had to show you this place." I put all my focus on the fire.

She walked over to the stove and picked up one of the mini fritters I'd made and took a tentative bite. She moaned softly. The sound went right through me, stirring my need for her. But I remembered how she'd acted about contact last time and swallowed back my desire. It was better to have any part of her than none at all.

I added another log to the fire and took a seat in front of it. I hadn't been cold since I left Trenton. It was novel after the unrelenting heat of Harden. I almost wanted to let the cold seep into the cabin. J slid her fingers down my back as she took a seat next to me. She passed me one of the pastries and then laid her head on my lap.

"I was thinking hot chocolate and hot dogs for dinner." I pushed my fingers into her hair.

She looked up at me. "What are hot dogs?"

"Peasant food." I wiggled my brows at her. "Willing to try?"

"All right."

I brushed her hair out of her face. "We can't keep doing this. You're stressed when you're here. Talk to me."

"It worries me to think I'll never love someone as much as I love you, and I can't have you." Her words didn't break my heart. They shattered it into so many pieces I doubted it could be repaired.

"Don't say that," I whispered. "Saying it makes it too real. We have to find a way."

She buried her face in my chest, and I dropped mine to press my nose into her hair.

"How can you believe that?" she asked at length.

"It's the only thing I have to hold on to." I nodded leaning into her touch like I craved it. I did crave it. "I love you. Across a million miles, and thousands of worlds, I will never feel like this again."

"And I love you, like I have never loved anyone before. I can't lose you." Hearing her say those words filled me with hope. It was nourishment for my soul. It gave me hope, and hope was all we had.

She took a shaky breath, and I tightened my arms around her. We held each other in silence for a long time as the weight of what we'd just said crushed my soul. I had to find a way. It had been an impossible situation before I knew she returned my feelings, and now that I knew, I would sell my sanity and my life to get back to her.

"What did you have to go through to get here tonight?" she whispered into my chest.

I knew she was desperate to change the subject, and I thought I knew why. I chewed the inside of my cheek, and my eyes went vacant. In truth I had clawed my way through the darkest parts of my mind to get here, worse than the first time, but I wouldn't tell her. I feared she wouldn't come back if she knew how much it hurt to get to her. How much I really had to face myself and open up to give her a piece of me.

"Are you going to tell me what you've been hiding all morning?"

She growled. "Don't answer a question with a question."

I knew she was tense, but it was hard not to return the attitude. "I didn't think so."

"Tell me, you wouldn't last time."

I lay back, taking her down to the rug with me. "It was bees tonight. Bees and then, God, you'll love this! I

stepped into the matrix, and right onto a crack in the
sidewalk, snapping my ankle. There was no treatment, no
painkillers. I had to crawl through these fields of bee
infested flowers…"

Her eyes fell closed, and she curled into me as I
spoke. I told her almost everything, except the very end.
Being buried alive and having to try to claw out of a too-
small wood box was not something I wanted to share
with anyone. Most would have turned and fled at the idea
of a battle with their minds to get to her.

When I trailed off she looked up. "Don't stop, I
like listening to your voice."

I rolled my eyes. "You accent whore. You can
play the recordings of my voice any time you want."

"Doesn't mean I get sick of it." She purred, not
denying it.

I turned to face her. "You're scaring me."

"I'm trying to enjoy this. Don't make me talk."

I clenched my hands into fists and growled.

"Sometimes I feel like you're a figment of my
imagination." She dropped her face refusing to look me
in the eyes. "A cruel trick played by the universe."

My face fell. I couldn't help it. I tried to be strong
for both of us, but sometimes it was near impossible. Her
doubt was another burden I bore whether she saw it or
not. "Feel me. I am real." I moved her hands to my face
and kissed one palm.

"But this isn't real. You are thousands of light
years away." She dropped her forehead to my chin and
exhaled a shuddering breath. She was good at masking
her feelings, but it hadn't taken me long to work out her
cues.

"I am real. What more can I do to prove it to
you?" I stroked my finger through her hair, doing
anything I could to let her know I was real.

"Nothing. I don't know how to stop feeling this way."

Her words cut my chest open like a knife, but she was right. All of this was based on faith in another person, which was close to impossible.

"I'm here. I'm not going anywhere." I brushed my fingers down her spine.

She gripped on to my shirt. Why did something so amazing have to cause so much pain? The universe wasn't fair. Life wasn't fair. How cruel to meet your other half and it be impossible to be with them. She wasn't even half of me, she was all of me. I was an empty vessel without her.

"If two people are meant to be together they will find a way. They'll find a way to cross the universe and be with each other."

"How can you really believe that?" she whispered pressing her eyes closed.

"It's the only thing I have to hold onto," I said using my thumb to brush a tear from her lashes. I turned back to her. "Listen to me. I love you, and I'm going to try and make this work as long as it's possible, but you need to have a little faith in me. I can't give you a happily ever after. But I'm going to give you everything I have."

She took in a shaky breath. "Okay. I'm bad at opening myself up, but I'm trying." She dropped her face to my neck. "I told you how I feel."

I pushed my fingers into the hair at the back of her head. "You scare me when you're like this. Please tell me what's going on."

She fisted her hands in my shirt.

"Please…"

"They've moved up my coronation because of what's happened. I'm of age next week, which means he can announce me as the heir to his Barony and band me, so he can marry me off to get rid of me." Her voice was barely audible, but the words echoed in my mind like she'd screamed them.

"To him?" I kept the emotion out of my voice. She wouldn't have an ounce of power until her father died, and if she was married off she would have to play by her husband's rules.

"I don't know, but they've moved it up to next week. We leave for the winter palace soon…" Her voice was cold, void of emotion. There was more she wasn't telling me.

I knew what she wasn't saying. It hung between us. "Say it."

"He's escorting me as the Emperor's representative."

I fought the moisture that pulled in my eyes. "So, a coronation and engagement celebration all rolled into one, and you'll only be light years from me to boot."

She picked up her head, and I could see the pain in her eyes. "How do you know where the winter palace is?"

"You don't think everyone on Harden knows where our overlords watch us from?" I laughed without humor.

She pressed her face back into my neck. We sat holding each other as snow started to fall outside my window. The fire burned low, and the chill through the walls started to encroach on us. I knew I would have to get up to build it back soon, but I felt like if I let her go she would vanish. Her words echoed in my mind, "Every day you put it off is another day wasted." I regretted every wasted minute. They rested like a weight on my shoulders. I'd squandered half of what we had with fear. I would never get that time with her back. I swallowed past the lump in my throat. It was a lesson I would take to my grave.

The words my father had said before his death came to mind and finally made sense, "At the end, when you're laying where I am, you'll only regret the chances you didn't take and the wasted opportunities. Don't forget that." I'd taken some chances, but most I'd wasted out of fear. The most important one I'd fucking blown. There was going to be nothing left when she was gone. Nothing. Darkness seeped into my mind, filling every crevasse. I couldn't let it win while she was still here.

I took a slow breath. "It's going to get harder to see each other, isn't it?"

She nodded into my neck. "We should talk about this."

"What?" I asked feeling like I was losing her, no matter what she said.

"You're here now, but our schedules are opposite. Would it be easier just to end it now before…" She trailed off.

I cupped both sides of her face, forcing her to look at me. "You think it's going to be any less painful now?" I scoffed, rubbing my thumbs over her cheekbones. "I don't know about you, but there is no going back for me."

I knew she felt the same. Damn it, I could feel it.

"I know." She pressed her eyes closed. "I'm trying to make it easier for you."

"Make what easier?" I tightened my grip on her face when she tried to pull away. "You think pretending you don't have feelings will make things easier?"

"I just want to turn them all off." Her words were laced with sorrow.

She looked down, not answering. I felt it coming. My gut told me she was going to end things. It was too hard for her. I knew me and my fucked up head were too much work for her. Her life would be so much easier without me.

"If you're done, Jocelynn, just say it." I let the edge show in my voice.

Her eyes flashed back up to mine. "I want this. I wouldn't have just told you I love you if I was done. I was trying to give you an out if you need it. Why do you doubt me?"

I sighed, letting my hands fall from her face. "I doubt me."

"That doesn't make any sense," she whispered laying her forehead against mine.

"I don't deserve you, and I'm waiting for you to realize." I mirrored her tone rubbing my nose over hers. "I'm … I'm nothing. You're strong and have so much coming to you." I shook my head when she tried to turn my face to hers. "I know you see it, Jocelynn, so if you're done tell me. Don't draw it out."

She growled, grabbing me by both ears to turn my face into hers. "You're a real fucking idiot, you know that?"

"What? I pour my heart out, and you can't even wait to tell me I'm an idiot until I'm finished?"

"I don't want this to be over, but I'm trying to spare your feelings. You think I want to be with him?" Her blue eyes blazed.

"I think every female in the universe wants him. I don't compare." My mouth was dry.

"But I am here with you, avoiding him. I'd choose you every time. I'd give up everything I am to be there with you. It's not even a choice."

"You're right. It's so hard to see straight with my emotions." I rested my forehead against hers. "We've gotten pretty good at good-byes. No more. We'll hold on as long as we can."

"Okay."

I tightened my grip on her. "I want to enjoy this. As long as we have here today, and every time from here out … if you can make it back. Promise me no sadness."

"I promise." She wiped her face on my neck.

"We'll always have this." I don't know how I got the words out. But if this was going to be the last time I refused to have it sad.

"I can't stay all day." She pressed her face into my chest.

"Why not?" I pulled back a little so she would look me in the eyes.

She sat back as well rubbing her hands together. "Phillip is escorting me for the departure. I didn't tell you the full truth earlier. I leave tonight for Gavin 9." She chewed on her lip, and I lifted a thumb to tug it free from her teeth. "I couldn't say no to him in front of the Baron. His stateroom will be next to mine."

"I understand."

I detangled myself from her to stoke the fire. The snow outside was unrelenting, and it was just the way I wanted it. Glancing over my shoulder I watched her grab a throw blanket off the back of the sofa and wrap it around her shoulders. She came up behind me and slid an arm around my lower back. I leaned into her.

"He'll take care of you, you know." I knew it would be true. I'd seen it in Phillip's eyes that night. He loved her.

She turned her face into me and pressed her fingers into my hip. "Don't say that. I could never feel about him like I do you."

"But, Jocelynn." I exhaled a sigh. "Maybe you should try?"

Anger more than pain flashed across her face. "How could you say that to me?"

I turned into her once I got the fire roaring again. "I want you to be happy."

"It's like you want me to forget about you and live happily ever after with the prince. Like this is some goddamned fairytale."

"Maybe it is, and I'm the bad guy trying to steal the fair maiden away?" I chuckled, rather liking myself painted in that light.

"I'll tell you a secret."

"Yes?" I quirked a brow, glancing down at her.

"I'd rather end up with the bad guy." She grinned up at me.

I poked her in the sides. "I don't deserve you, but I'll spend the rest of my life trying."

She looked up at me shaking her head. "So, tell me why you wanted to bring me here."

I bent slightly to scoop her up under the knees. I sat down in front of the fire with her on my lap. "This is my rendition of Severus's great forest. The loggers cut these great big trees, and the finest furniture is made from them."

She laughed, and I narrowed my eyes.

"You knew that?" I groaned.

"We have quite a few pieces, but what were you doing there?"

"Some of my earliest memories are of running through the forests here. We'd stay a few days every round trip as my mother was born here. She met my father when he did his first run." I stroked my fingers up her arm, smiling to myself at the memories. I still had family on Severus Six.

"I knew you weren't just from Harden," she said in an "ah-ha" tone.

"I never claimed to be, but that is where I've lived the last ten years or so."

"You were raised on a freighter?" She laid her head on my shoulder.

"First ten years of my life." When I closed my eyes I was on a ship. It was home. The hum of the Time2 bending engines.

"You've been all across the universe?" She slid off my lap, and I grabbed onto her, not wanting the space between us, but when she sprawled out on the rug, I groaned and lay down beside her.

"I have." My eyes half closed. It was the middle of the night for me, and I should have slept while I waited for her, but I'd been too keyed up. Now the drowsiness ate at me.

"You might be better traveled than I am." Her fingertips traced lightly over the curve of my neck and around into my hair line.

"I doubt it, and my travels were not nearly as extravagant as yours have been, I'm sure."

Suddenly I knew the real meaning to intimacy. This was it. I'd never felt closer to someone. I was half asleep, and she had taken over my mind. The small touches, the soft rhythm of her voice, and the millions of unspoken actions that passed simply between us. If I searched the rest of my life I would never find this again.

"But what you've seen is real." Her voice grew softer, and I think she knew I was fading.

"It is different, I'm sure." I drew her in, pressing my face to her neck and inhaled.

"Sleep," she said, wrapping an arm around my head, holding me to her.

Her voice roused me.

"I'll never stop loving you. Remember that." She started to waver, and I gripped her tighter.

"No, not yet," I pleaded. But we both knew there was nothing we could do when we started to reject the simulation.

Chapter Thirty-Six

Jocelynn

I arched and pressed myself flush against him tightening my fingers in his hair. But he blinked. I clutched at where his form was grasping at thin air before he was back, his weight settling over mine as he gripped me as hard as I did him. I squeezed my arms around his shoulders grabbing handfuls of his hoodie until I lost the feeling in my fingers. He shoved his arms under my back and did the same. We lay like that for a few more minutes before he was gone.

I blinked a few times and found myself yanked from paradise and back flat on my back looking up at the painted ceiling of the grand palace. I pressed my eyes closed and balled my hands into fists. It wasn't long enough. It was never fucking long enough, but this was so short. I had counted on hours, not less than one. I forced myself to breathe. How could I go on like this?

Life was too cruel to let something so perfect exist. You could envision this perfect reality and it would be snatched away. Life was pain and suffering. The Baron had told me time and time again to grow up. They said my weakness was how naive I was, and they were right. I was filled with guilt. How could I keep him attached to me when I knew what my fate would be? I had to do my duty and take my place as leader so I needed him here with me. He'd be killed eventually if he was in the way. I couldn't be responsible for his death. There had to be a way to make him invaluable.

"I had to." My gaze flashed to my brother holding the neurotransmitter. I could have screamed.

"Why?" I looked at the clock and knew. The rest of my life wouldn't be enough. He was like no drug I'd ever experienced. A drug that took over my heart, mind, and body. Nothing mattered more than finding a way he could be here with me.

"You look like shit, and you need time to get ready. This is not the time to be out of line. There is so much going on, Jocelynn." He'd taken me from Madden. The last minutes I'd ever get to spend with Madden, and Jacob had snatched them from me. He held out the tiny chip, and I snatched it from him.

I squeezed my eyes shut, biting back the red hot anger threatening to take over. "Then tell me."

"I can't, but J, trust me."

"Get out," I snapped.

He left without another word.

I forced myself to get off the floor, putting one foot in front of the other until I stood in front of my dressing table. Mascara streamed down my cheeks, and my painted face was ruined. All that work and I would have to fix it myself as the servants were long gone, preparing other tasks for the departure. Jacob was right. I had stayed with Madden much too long, but only because it was drawing attention to myself. I needed help, but I wasn't sure Jacob was the person to go to.

J: **I miss you already.**

M: **And I you.**

J: **Comm range will be in and out on the trip, but as soon as I land I want to see you again.**

M: **I'll be counting the minutes.**

In a matter of hours, I was watching my trunks being hauled into the shuttle which we would take to the large luxury cruiser docked above the atmosphere. Jacob and Phillip stood to one side speaking in hushed tones, but I was too depressed to care what they were whispering about. The ship was taking me away from freedom.

I smiled and waved for the pictures, arm in arm with my brother and Phillip. I pretended like I was excited to go to my coronation, but it felt like I was a pig going to slaughter. Phillip kept me close, a constant pressure on my arm. He and Jacob kept exchanging glances. They'd become fast friends, and I had to wonder why. Maybe Jacob thought he was doing my duty for me.

The cameras faded, and Phillip leaned in to whisper. "Shall we make our escape?"

I nodded. "Please." It was painful to keep up the formality when I wanted to scream at the universe for being unfair.

He led me up the gangplank. "Care to have a drink to relax your nerves?"

"Sure." I gave him a fake smile and let him take the lead yet again. There was no point in hiding for the short flight up to the space port.

I took a seat in a single chair in the lounge portion of the empty ship, noticing my brother's absence. Phillip filled two crystal tumblers and instead of taking the loveseat across from me he sat on the edge of the low table causing our knees to touch as he held out my drink. I accepted it but did not bring it to my mouth. Clasping it with two hands I set it in my lap. He downed the drink and set it aside, freeing up his hands. He laid one lightly on my thigh next to my own.

The ship rumbled as the engines powered on. These transports were only used for taking people to and from the station. Their heavy engines were great for breaking through the planetary gravity, but were nothing compared to the Time2 the lighter starships used.

"Are you unwell?" he said at last, brushing his thumb over the bare skin on my wrist.

I looked from his hands back to his dark purple eyes. "I have been feeling under the weather. 'Tis nothing to worry about."

He nodded, but I could see the disbelief in his expression. "I do hope you are well by the time we reach Gavin. I would hope you would enjoy the time with me."

I counted down the minutes feeling the pull as we escaped the atmosphere.

"I'm sure a few days of rest on the ship will put me right."

He searched my face, and I brought my drink to my lips to distract him.

"Don't hide yourself away the entire time and deprive us of your presence." He brushed his fingers further up my arm, sending a shiver through me at the light touch.

The ship shuddered as we came to position at the docking bay. I shot to my feet, knocking him back in the process.

"Excuse me," I said, calmer than I felt.

He stood and stepped back holding out an arm to excuse me. "By all means, I'm sure being ill you're in a hurry to get to your stateroom and change."

"I am." I inclined my head toward him, and he returned the sign of respect. I forced myself to walk slowly from the lounge toward the port.

Deep breaths, Jocelynn. I could do this. I closed my eyes and didn't wait for the escort. As soon as they had the airlock open I slipped through and headed to the cruiser. It was always in reserve at the same port, and the crew knew me well. They allowed me on board with only a few raised brows as to where the rest of the party was.

Once seated in my stateroom I broke down, letting fall the tears I'd been holding back. I'd let myself cry this once. I would get it all out, and then I would put my emotions under lock. I was about to be the Baron in waiting, and love was beneath me. I could throw things, and pound my fists into the walls, but this would be the last time I would cry over Madden. My House did things. They didn't cry over impossibilities. They made things happen. I promised myself.

When I had nothing left I took a seat in front of my vanity, and I picked up a cotton pad to apply the solution to remove the tearstained mask of makeup. I finished giving myself a fresh canvas to start from. I painted from base coat up, and the finished product looked better than the first of the day. I stood shaking out my sore arms, catching a glimpse of a large figure leaning against my doorframe.

"Why don't you come in, Jacob?"

He stepped into the light. "I enjoy watching you."

I lifted my hand to cover my mouth, but didn't dare muss the fresh paint, so I dropped it back to my side, turning my lips into a forced smile.

"Phillip, I didn't realize…" I didn't know what to say to him. My nerves were so raw over Madden it was hard to look at the man I was going to be forced to spend the rest of my life with.

He crossed the room with a swagger, and I could smell the drink on him. He'd been exploring the Baron's wine cellar I guessed.

"I wanted to make sure you were all right after your hasty departure." He towered over me where I sat.

I rose to my feet, but I still didn't come above his shoulder. "I can assure you I'll be fine."

He looked me directly in the eyes, and I didn't back down stepping away from my dressing table.

"Can I be frank?"

I raised both brows. "I would prefer it."

"You're beautiful, and any man would be lucky to have you."

I let out the pent up air in my lungs. I wasn't a trophy. I had a Barony to run. If he was in love with someone else as well then we could live separate lives. But then it struck me. There was no reason for him not to choose anyone he wanted. All the houses would owe allegiance to him when he became Emperor. He had to really like me, and the realization scared me. Being with him was a kink in my plans to find Madden. I kept the shock off my face. It was no matter. I'd decided, and nothing would keep me from my end.

His stare was hard as he took a step into me. He kept coming. My breath caught in my throat, and I stepped back into the wall. He stopped millimeters from me, pressing his hand into the wall above my head. He was twice as broad as I was, and from where I stood I could see the stubble on his face.

I fixed a bored look on my face, one I rarely used but was taught to use on those of lesser rank. "Is there a purpose to this conversation, my Lord?" I questioned his motives, sliding my hand around to the knife I carried in a hidden pocket in my dress.

I worked free just before he pressed his body into mine. He didn't speak. I turned the knife around in my hand pressing the tip into his side. I could easily kill him. I waited for him to make another move. If I was going to gut the heir to the known universe I would have to have good reason, and intuition wasn't it. The cards were all in his hand.

"The purpose is." A smile curled over his lips. "You're exactly who I want at my side." His eyes flickered down to where the knife hovered near his stomach. He dropped one hand from the wall over my head. I thought he was going to grab my wrist, but he closed his hand around the blade. I barely stifled a gasp. He pressed the knife into his side.

"I need someone I know can't be intimidated by those who wish to take me down. Not even by men twice their size." There was lust in his gaze.

He was turned on by this. I felt the tip of my Garian steel slice through his tunic and press into his skin. He was in control of the blade. It cut him like soft butter. He didn't flinch as he dropped his face closer to mine.

"There are not many women who live up to your reputation, but I wanted to make sure it wasn't something the Baron built up." He wrenched the knife from my grasp and brought the knife up between us. Blood dripped down his wrist staining the cuff of his crisp white shirt, yet even still he didn't loosen his grip on it.

He was lucky I hadn't pulled the poisoned one.

"He hasn't." My voice was icy, but there was heat between us. I would never love him like I did Madden, but I would respect him, and I was attracted to him even if I didn't want to be.

He lowered his face, hovering his mouth over mine. "Do you want this?"

Pain engulfed me. My chest constricted, and it took everything I had to stay on my feet. I screamed "*No*" in my head as I said, "Yes."

His smile broadened as he leaned in for a kiss.

Chapter Thirty-Seven

Jocelynn

A female gasped behind us, and Phillip spun flipping the knife around in his hand. I lifted my hands to my face, but remembered the time I'd spent on the paint and balled them in to fists instead. It was too soon. I couldn't. My knees shook, but I forced my expression neutral.

"Sorry," a servant girl muttered to Phillip over and over. "I was sent to find the Lady Jocelynn. I … I … I didn't mean to intrude. The door was open." She stammered her words.

Phillip slid the knife into his belt at the small of his back, keeping it out of her sight. The last thing either of us needed was for rumors of blood play to go through the servants.

"Think nothing of it. I will escort Jocelynn to dinner myself. I do need some assistance. Run to my room and fetch me a fresh shirt as I cut my hand and soiled this one."

She curtsied and hurried away. I moved from the wall taking away that vantage point from him, seating myself on my sofa instead.

"Forgive my behavior. There are not many ways to see how easily a person spooks." His face was a mask as mine was, but there was arousal still hidden in his eyes.

He took the knife from his belt and cleaned it carefully on his shirt before handing it back to me handle first.

I slid it back into the hidden sheath. "You didn't spook me."

I struggled with what to make of the encounter. It hadn't spooked me as such, but after the conversation with Madden my head was full and I was having trouble processing any of it. I needed to speak to my brother if he wasn't already in on this. Maybe he wanted the Barony to himself so he wanted me with Phillip. I was becoming as paranoid as the Baron.

"I thought not." He untied his tie and then worked his fingers down the buttons of his shirt before letting it slide from his large shoulders. He tossed it over the back of the chair then took a seat next to me.

I looked away. He was no stranger to exercise, and his body was proof of that.

"I can feel a connection between us, and I'm not expecting you to act on it now, or soon, but it's there. I need that. I want you to trust me. I plan to spend as much time with you as I can so you do. That is a must for me. I want to unite our families, and if you don't trust me we'll be at odds and working behind each other's backs. My mother and father have never trusted each other. I don't want that for us or for our sons."

I nodded. I was having a hard time coming up with my usual easy replies to all situations for state matters. But this wasn't just for the good of my House. This was so much more.

"I want that, too." The words made me sick as I said them.

The truth was, I would always have a Madden-shaped hole in my heart. Nothing would fill the space, and I would always love him more than any other man alive.

He collected my hand in his and brought it to his lips. "Good." He searched my face, for what, I didn't know, before retuning my hand.

All I could think of was how Madden looked half asleep and how happy just being there with him made me.

****

By the time Jacob and I woke on the fifth day, we were on Gavin, having drunk ourselves to sleep once we got on the starship, and the days that followed were spent in a deep depression. Jacob had tried to snap me out of it for Phillip's sake, but I was too far gone in mourning. Maybe the Baron would disinherit me for the disgrace. I could only hope.

Jacob wore thick glasses as we exited the ship to a cheering crowd. I had been up an hour before him, getting my face painted and hair done for the greeting. We had a ceremonial breakfast to get through, and then I could hide again. Phillip was doting as I was presented at the Baron's side. We greeted all the officials from Harden who'd come to Gavin 9 to meet with us for the month long holiday trip.

All the events were laced with work when it came to my father. The wheels in the back of my mind turned as I picked at my food. I half listened to the meetings going on around me. From this point on not only would I be in all my usual studies with tutors, but I would also sit in on all important meetings and have an opinion in all state matters as the official heir.

Halfway through breakfast I looked over at Phillip. He still wore a smile for me, but it was probably faked after how I'd treated him the second half of the voyage. I glanced around the hall. The politics of the great houses were ruthless. All of these people wanted in my good graces. I faced a lifetime of outsmarting and distrusting all those closest to me. Spies were also a hazard of the title.

I picked up my comm and studied it. I missed him. We'd barely spoken because of both our respective schedules.

"Do you need anything?" Phillip leaned over the back of my chair, his hot breath fanning down my neck.

I glanced back at him and tried to smile, but I didn't have it in me. "Thank you, no."

I closed my hand around my comm and sent Madden a message without giving myself time to think it over.

J: **Hey**

I had no more, and I squeezed it in my hand waiting for him to reply.

Reaching into my bag, I took out my tablet and set it on my lap, because my mind kept flipping from the meeting to a mental checklist of the things I would need as a plan started to form in my mind. I erased all trace of the notes, and turned off the thought tracking function, writing notes by hand instead.

Every time I looked up it was to disapproving stares from the Baron. It was like the guilt was written on my face. I had to do it before he guessed. It was time to decide if I could tell my twin. He would either help me or try to stop me. He'd been so distant and different the last month. I could use his help, but if he tried to stop me it would be impossible.

I was losing my nerve. I had to see Madden again.

Chapter Thirty-Eight

Jocelynn

I clutched my communicator in my hand, willing myself not to send him a second message, as the slaves held a long mirror in front of me. A day had passed, and still there was nothing from Madden. I felt like a caged tiger. At any moment I could snap. The formal attire felt like bonds.

I didn't recognize the woman who stared back at me. She was regal, and I used to see myself as such, but my perspective had changed so much. My long hair was tied up in accordance with the fashion. My lipstick was the same shade as my blood red dress and the color of the House of Akillie. I looked like the blood queen. It made me wonder if the Reds had chosen their color for that reason, taking both the color of my house and the flag of Jok.

"I assure you, you look lovely." Phillip startled me, but I made no outward display. He was getting the best of me too often. It was a sign of my loss of focus. It was dangerous.

I turned and gave a slight curtsey to him, inclining my chin as I did so. "Thank you."

"Your expression would suggest you hate it."

He put me on edge. He always did. "Red is not my preferred color."

"Perhaps Imperial purple would suit your skin tone better." His violet eyes blazed, and I noticed he wasn't in the royal color.

He wore a light gray suit with red accents. We looked like quite the pair. My heart picked up speed as he held out his hand for mine. I offered it, and he brushed his lips over my fingers.

"Perhaps." I glanced over at him as he linked his arm through mine. "I wouldn't know as owning a scrap of the Imperial color is punishable by death."

"Only for those who are not in the direct line of succession to the Emperor himself." He dropped his face and brushed his lips over my bare shoulder.

Goosebumps raised and extended down my arm. "Are you trying to say something, your highness?" I tucked a loose strand of hair behind my ear keeping the eye contact.

"Tonight, but we shan't speak of such things. This morning belongs to you, young heiress." His intentions were clear.

My cheeks took on an involuntary red hue. "Shall we?"

I breathed easier when I found Jacob waiting in the hall for us. He was dressed similar to Phillip, and I knew they'd planned it. He linked his arm through my other, and we continued to the coliseum.

Jacob leaned over to whisper, "Breathe, you look like a balloon someone sucked the air out of."

I scowled. "You try binding yourself into a dress three sizes too small."

"Don't frown, your face will freeze that way, and then you'll have permanent puss for the vids." Jacob grinned.

"You know the best part about corsets?" Phillip added.

We both turned to him, not used to someone interrupting our banter, speaking in unison. "What?"

His lips curled into a roguish grin. "Getting cut out of it later." He flicked his tongue over his gleaming white teeth as his fingers brushed over the ceremonial knife at his belt.

A shiver ran down my spine. By the end of the night we might be bound by blood as well as metal. The blood didn't scare me, but the metal sure did.

Chapter Thirty-Nine

Jocelynn

I had to remind myself to fill my lungs as we neared the coliseum. I could hear the roaring of the crowd from inside the palace. When we stepped outside we were greeted by an even louder volume. A sea of people waving red and purple flags met my gaze.

Phillip smiled over at me. "It seems our secret isn't as much a secret as we thought it was." He shrugged, a wicked glint in his eyes. "Oh well."

I growled. "I think you are responsible for that."

Jacob stepped into the carriage and took a seat without ceremony, but he could get away with it. He was allowed to be the bad boy. "Shocking people hear about official visits and talk about how much time you two spend together. I bet the rumors from the slaves alone are ghastly."

Phillip released my arm and took my hand to help me into the carriage. "Have I been too forward?" He laughed.

My feet were bound into ten inch heels, so I willingly took the support of his hand to balance as I stepped up the tiny stairs. He took my hand and lifted it in the air making the crowd roar.

Phillip liked the attention. It was undeniable as his face glowed. I was perfect arm candy, and he only gained more support from those who were fiercely red. He lowered our joined hands and kissed mine again. There were so many sides to him. It was impossible to know which I was getting, which was real and which was for show.

Jacob kicked his booted feet up on the silk seat next to me and slumped back. The ride was a blur, and soon I was standing behind the veil of the Baron's box in the coliseum listening to him start the winter games. We would see everything from competition of sport competed in by the wealthy merchants from all over the galaxy to slave fights because the Baron had a taste for blood.

The solid metal and stone structure extended out over where the lessers sat, giving our house a front and center view of the action in the arena. The Baron was long winded, but I stood straight backed waiting for him to give the word.

"Ready?" Phillip asked.

I nodded not trusting my voice. My comm sat in my pocket, and I'd checked it three times in since arriving. He wasn't replying. He was probably watching me on some giant screen in one of the squares.

"I give you my children and the prosperity of your great House of Akillie," The Baron's voice was magnified from the din of the crowd.

Jacob and I joined hands and walked out to stand next to the Baron like ceremonial trophies. Phillip would stay in the shadows until the time was right.

"I know there has been much debate on who my heir shall be," the Baron began the beginning of the end.

"Not for anyone who lived on Trenton," I muttered.

Jacob's lips twitched into a grin.

"But after much conference and close inspection of my twins over the years I am proud to announce Jocelynn as the rightful heir to the House of Akillie, both by birth and decree," the Baron said, and his words echoed out over the silent arena. "Supported by the Imperial house." He lifted an arm, and Phillip stepped into view next to him. "Blessed by his highness the High Chancellor to the courts." He used Phillip's official title.

The crowd went wild. If word had not spread from those around the winter palace to the arena, they knew now. There was no delay. He'd announced it, and it would be done. The region would be secure with or without the news of the attacks spreading among the people.

"I bind Jocelynn with bands of Akillie. She will wear them for life, as I have, like shackles binding her in servitude to the people we govern, in accordance with the Emperor."

He took the first of the ceremonial bands and held it over the fire pit. I stepped forward and extended first my left wrist letting him clasp the cool metal there. It quickly heated in fire sealing itself into an unbreakable ring. Next my right wrist was done, and then Phillip stepped forward to stand next to me. A slave stripped him of his jacket and helped him roll up one sleeve.

Phillip pulled the knife from his belt, holding my gaze, and slit his wrist. He held the blade out to me as he said, "By Imperial blood, she is bound into servitude of her people and the royal house."

I slit my own wrist and let my blood fall into the fire to burn with his. The metal around my arms had been forged in a dying sun and exported for only this purpose. It started to glow red. It wouldn't become hot for hundreds of thousands of degrees, but my skin prickled and started to burn from the proximity to the flame. I turned the knife and handed it back to Phillip hilt first.

He took it and wiped the remnants of my blood on his shirt. It would be burned after the night was through. Royal blood was as dangerous as it was precious and could not be risked falling into the wrong hands. But he'd already spilled blood for me. This was a reminder of it.

Instead of resheathing the knife, he brought the tip to his tongue and flicked it over the last drop lingering there. A collective gasp radiated around us as he replaced the blade.

It was over all too quickly, and I was sitting in a seat next to him as the games blurred before my eyes. Madden would see us smiling and holding hands on every vid today. We had to be matching as well. I'm sure it was a well-planned publicity stunt. Either by my father or Phillip himself. All I could think about was Madden watching. How Phillip had shoved the knife through his chest with each small gesture. I wanted to take away all Madden's pain, but he wouldn't answer me. I'd pushed him away, and I'm sure he thought I wanted Phillip now.

Chapter Forty

Madden

"Those can't be the last words we say to each other, Jocelynn, they can't be." I said the words as much to myself as I did to her, knowing she was thousands of light years away, while I was standing back in my shop. I hadn't heard a word from her, and I'd sent more than a few messages. I didn't know if she was ignoring me or couldn't contact me. My chest heaved as I drew in ragged breaths. Tightness gripped my throat, and I sank to my knees realizing I had no way to say the words to her. No word and then this? I had to clear my head. I didn't know what to think about it all. If she followed through with this, I had no means to contact her. She took it all, yanked it away, but yet I wasn't mad at her.

I was a wound, and she was trying to heal herself.

If she didn't forget about me it would never close. But I couldn't. There was no way I could forget about her. I blew my hair out of my face and rested my hands on my work bench. My mind struggled to find a solution for the problem.

"Fuck." I picked up a wrench and threw it as the wall. It hit the stone block, and dust exploded behind it as the metal shattered part of the stone, coating my floor.

My anger was becoming impossible to control. I drew in a shaky breath. What could I do? There was no rescuing her from her castle. I was an engineer on a mining world. What she had seen in me in the first place I would never know. I didn't deserve her, and maybe she'd come to realize it. The thought was like a knife between my ribs. I'd been there with her. I refused to believe she didn't feel as I do.

The door to my room banged open, and I glanced over my shoulder to see Colton standing there with a

bandana over his face. He hadn't knocked, and he didn't
wait for an invitation. I knew what he wanted when I
spotted the helmet under one arm. I dropped my gaze
back to my bench, gripping the edge of the reader harder
than was good for it to disguise the shake in my hand. I
had six open books lying across it, and none of them held
my attention.

"Madden!"

I blinked a few times and looked over at him.
"What?"

After the night of fitful sleep with her arms
around me in the matrix I hadn't slept another night. The
sleep deprivation weighed on me. My eyes flickered up to
the screen.

"You seem distracted. You have something
invested in this?" He gestured at the vids which had been
covering the games.

It was stupid of me to be watching it out in the
open like I was. It was out of character, and I could see it
in Colton's face.

"Just fucked that so much press is spent on this
crap." I laughed it off and tried to focus on one of the
books I was working on. Why did this of all days have to
be a light day?

I could feel his eyes on me, but I didn't look back
at him.

"It is … but it never bothered you before," he
pressed.

I swallowed hard and turned to meet his gaze. "I,
errr." I screwed up my face. I was a terrible liar.

"There is something you're keeping from me. All
your sneaking off and how busy and distant you've
been." He took a step toward me.

I glanced around the junk facility. The others
were packing our gear up for the exploration trip. One I

wasn't going on because I hadn't trained on the type of jump they were doing.

"I shouldn't tell you," I hedged.

"We were like brothers before you went there, and you come back and you're distant and haunted. What the fuck happened to you?" His voice got louder as he spoke.

I owed him everything, the job as I would never get my former one back, my life, more than once, and the distraction I needed after I got back. I would be on the street by now if it wasn't for the job. Hell, he'd even cleaned up my bike and kept her in shape.

I sighed, gesturing for him to get closer.

"It can't be that big a deal…" he said, but he moved closer, humoring me. "Not like you were fuckin' her." He thumbed at the screen.

My face gave it all away.

He staggered back gasping, eyes wide like he'd seen the spirit of his dead wife. "You've got to be kidding me."

I put my face in my hands almost laughing. "I'm not." I had never really thought anyone would believe me.

"She was slumming it?"

I shrugged one shoulder. Jocelynn would never say it, and when I was with her I believed her, but those hours between the darkness crept in and parts of me thought I had been a rebellious streak.

"That's why you got sent home?"

I glanced up at him. "Yeah."

"Shit." He looked back up at her on the screen. I took a breath, hating Colton a little for bringing her up. I shook my head, trying to appear calm. He side-eyed me but didn't say anything.

"It's nothing. It's over. I haven't heard from her."

Colton arched one brow. "There is something you're still not telling me." He crossed his arms over his chest, and his eyes flickered back to the vids going a little wide.

I cairned my neck to find Phillip ushering her into her new title. I groaned inwardly.

"Come on let's go," I said, having the sudden urge to get trained on blind jumps.

"Go?" Colton stared at me. "We haven't trained you for the dark jumps."

I gave Jocelynn once more glance, seeing Phillip cupping her face. He paused for a minute and then kissed her.

I screamed inside. I begged her to push him off. But she did nothing. She set her hands over his on her face like she had done with me so many times and kissed him back.

It was now clear what she'd been doing in the week on the star cruiser with him.

It was like a charge to the heart. I'd lived on ten different worlds, and lived through hell, but I would live through it a hundred times over to never have to see another man kiss her.

"I don't give a shit." I grabbed my gear bag and hoisted it over my shoulder.

"No one is worth this. Come on, Mad." He grabbed my arm, and I spun on him throwing a fist. He blocked it and grabbed me by the shirt. "Madden, I swear to fuck."

"If I stay here I won't be able to take my eyes off that." I pointed at the screen behind his head. "Take me with you. Then take me to see the Reds." When he opened his mouth, I cut him off. "Don't. I've been told you're a part of them."

He knit his brow. "I've been trying to get you to a meeting for years and this does it?"

"Well I went while I was there. They've already helped me some. I know they were there last night. I want off this planet." I swallowed hard after I said the last word. If I left the planet I wouldn't have reliable access to the nets, which meant no more Jocelynn.

"Are you sure? This isn't something you can take lightly, or back for that matter." Colton's usual calm demeanor had turned harsh.

"I'm already in. Now, I just want off world. They won't complain. Make it happen." I shoved out of his grasp and walked toward the crew. I didn't have time to mess with their internal politics. They'd come to collect sooner or later, and I was ready for sooner.

"I don't have as much clout as you think I do."

"Bullshit." I looked over my shoulder. "Do you really think I'm that stupid?"

He stared me down, but I turned my back once again. "Well even if she is the catalyst I won't complain. Let's go."

We loaded the gear into the lift doubt checking that we had everything for a blind jump. We were going to explore a deep vein of Ore that ran off from the bottom of the pit, and was believed to run straight to the core. One side of the vein had been opened up with electron drilling, and the next step was to send a crew in to stabilize the tunnel so the mining crews could get in there.

We loaded in the large temp expanders we would set as we went. All the base structure had to be marked out, and the supports had to be installed and tested. Colton, who usually worked beside us for all the heavy lifting, was missing. He'd ducked off with some excuse of needing to talk to a captain. I wiped the sweat from my brow and stepped out to look up toward the sliver of visible light at the top of the cavern. We were already miles underground, and we were going further. Suddenly the memory of being buried alive in a box had new meaning. I swallowed past the fear and turned to find Colton already rigged up checking over the gear.

"Going to be a long one. I'm thinking three days for the initial at least," he said when he caught my gaze.

"Good." I waited for him to say another word.

"You are a royal pain in my arse, and if you get yourself killed I'm going to celebrate," he said when I looked back up. The job description had the same appeal to most as climbing down an unstable crater in the dark with risk of cave in at any moment. Colton loved it, but he had a hard time keeping people. His losses were less than a team member a year, which was the best of the scouts, but it wasn't a job most sane people volunteered for.

"You and me both." I growled.

He stepped into the lift. "One day I'm going to kill you myself."

I followed him with a swagger in my step. "I look forward to it."

"You better stay by my side—"

He was cut off by a deep rumbling in the ground. Colton's eyes flashed around, and then he started shoving people out of the lift. "Get the fuck out," he screamed.

The floor started to pitch and roll. The lift shook violently, and the inhabitants descended into chaos, clawing over one another to escape. I was near the front and my feet found solid ground, but I fell to my knees as it rolled under me like the sea. I searched the bodies pouring from the lift looking for Colton. He was in the back helping the last of his crew, who was trapped under one of the beams. I staggered through the crowd, trying to get close enough to help.

An eerie groan cut through the yells. The supports to the lift were strained to the breaking point.

"Colton," I yelled, but my voice didn't cut through the noise. I started shoving men out of way as he threw the smallest of his team from the lift. It dropped a meter and tilted to one side as he tried to climb out. I dove forward reaching out for him as it groaned again. I braced one hand on the wall gripping his with the other to pull him out of the lift. We fell back to safety hearing another boom, deep in the center of the planet.

The aftershocks lasted a few minutes, and then the mine went deadly silent. Colton and I stared at each other. In another twenty minutes we would have been down there. I pushed to my feet and helped Colton up.

"Central command?" I asked wiping blood from my mouth. I was too filled with adrenaline to feel it, but I knew later I would be hurting.

He looked around at his crew. "We need to make ourselves scarce." He grabbed me by the sleeve and pushed me toward one of the empty supply closet.

I staggered back, gripping his arms to steady myself. "What the hell?"

"I don't want to be stuck cleaning this mess up for the next two days, and it's better if you disappear. No one will ask questions, they'll assume."

I sucked in a breath. He was right. "You serious?"

"If you want to get off planet, there is a chance."

Chapter Forty-One

Jocelynn

The world moved around me. I sat in the center of my balcony staring at the tiny greenish silver blip in the night sky. He was there. I felt like we were close, but impossibly far. My dress pooled around and I knew it would be ruined as the rain started to fall, but I couldn't move. I was in pieces on the ground.

I beat my fists into the ground until they were bloody. I was so angry, and I couldn't hold it in anymore. I couldn't keep this stupid composure. I had to let out some of what I had bottled up inside.

"He's not real," I screamed. "He's not real." I gritted my teeth hugging my knees. I didn't believe in true love. I didn't believe in soul mates. One person couldn't change that. I'd been resigned my whole life to marry who I was told. Akillie House honor. I was delusional if I thought this could have been more. I had duty and responsibility, and here I was like a stupid little girl upset over a boy not returning my messages. One who now only existed in a world I created in our minds. We could be anyone there. Nothing was real. I clawed my nails over my ruined make up.

He was right. The longer we let this go on the more pain it would cause us in the end. Why was it so easy for him to walk away? Or maybe it wasn't. Maybe he was in the same state I was. I thought I knew him inside and out. I was shattered. I knew he would be, too. This was the worst time to doubt him. I picked up my comm and typed out a third and final message. I wouldn't embarrass myself further.

J: **I'm sorry. Please forgive me.**

When had I become so pathetic? I didn't send it. Vulnerable wasn't me.

A shadow moved over me, and I looked back over my shoulder to find Jacob standing there. I looked up at him, not trying to hide my bloody hands. No shame.

"Madden?" he asked.

I nodded. "You don't have to remind me. I'm an idiot. But even with all the pain it's caused me, I still wouldn't take back the time we've had. I would suffer ten times over for another day with him."

He looked down on the damp dress then shrugged as he walked over the billowing fabric to take a seat next to me. "Come inside."

I reached up to unpin my hair, letting it fall in tendrils down my back.

"I thought you ended things?" Jacob trailed his fingers down my back.

"And to think, I don't do regrets. I was hasty. I can't—" My throat went dry.

"I'm sorry, if I could change our birth order I would, even if it meant giving up all debauchery, but sadly we both know it wouldn't change anything." He laid his head on my shoulder, and I leaned into him. "He would have picked you no matter what. All that looking into birth order was merely him pleasing all those watching." He turned more to look me in the eyes. "But J, it's for the best."

"Believe me I know. He doesn't see your worth." I glanced over at him. "Gavin is the closest I can get to Madden without going to Harden." I pointed at the green planet hovering over the skyline.

"Somehow I don't feel as if I've cheered you any, sister mine."

I looked into his blue eyes seeing so much of myself reflected in his face. He carried the burden better. I knew he would never even be able to be with the gender he preferred, let alone someone he loved. We'd made a pact a long time ago to not let anyone have our hearts, and even when I'd broken it he was still here comforting me.

"I keep wondering how I breathed before. How each day passed and that piece wasn't there. Somehow I functioned, but now that I know that piece is missing I can't go back." I knew I sounded stupid, and I doubted he would understand. I tucked a strand of hair behind my ear and looked up. It would be staring back at me whenever I looked up at the sky.

"When you're Baroness, you can do as you please. The planet is within the stretch of our power. Can waiting be that painful?" He looked at me sternly when I shook my head.

"And I'll be married to him by then." The words tasted bad as they left my mouth. "As if anyone would let me choose who I want if I were Baroness today. It will be a 'suitable' mate that I can wear on my arm like a decoration, even if I wasn't already practically promised to Phillip."

"He's a good match for you. Give it time."

I looked at him hard. "Why are you pushing it?"

"Because he is smart, he doesn't have only air in his head. It's a first love, J, give it the rest of the season and it will fade."

I wasn't an idiot. Something wasn't adding up.

"Too bad it's a little late to disappear and give it all to you." I lifted one wrist to look at the band there.

"As if anyone would let you do that for a fuck up like me." He shook on it then pushed his fingers into my hair, and kicked his feet up on the rail.

I'd never said let. But I didn't press the point. "You know you'll be acting Baron when I am Empress, as Phillip has stated his intentions."

"I guess I'll have to step up then." He rolled his eyes. "But can you do something about the Candor girl?"

I laughed for the first time in days because picturing Jacob with her was beyond amusing. I wanted to see the horrified look on his face when he saw her naked for the first time. At least I could fake this life enough to get by. If my parents knew what he was they would have suffocated him in the cradle.

"I almost think being born a miner on Harden would be preferable to this." I closed my eyes and imagined Madden coming home to me after a long day's work.

"Don't drop your status that far. You're used to quite a few luxuries absent from that world." He gestured around us. The plates of food cast aside, I'd taken from the ceremony this morning. There were two chilled champagne bottles. I guessed he brought in with him still corked and full.

"I'm eighteen, and have thus been crowned. I couldn't get rid of the title if I ran away. Upon the Baron's death I will be found and made to rule." I rolled my eyes, tapping the irremovable bracelets I wore. "I am shackled to it now, anyway."

He traced his finger tip around the thin red bracelets. "I think you're the first person to look at it that way, J."

"I thought about cutting my hands off to remove them. Do you really think that isn't on purpose?"

"At least you can live without hands?" He chuckled.

I glanced down at my dress. The color ran as the light rain soaked it, causing all the pigment to muddle at the bottom creating an ugly brown color. "Do you think anyone would want to be bound to me without hands?"

"You're going to be more than bound to him after tonight." He wiggled his brows.

I wrinkled my nose.

"He's hot. I should be so lucky." Jacob scoffed. "That Candor girl is, too."

It was his turn to wrinkle her nose. "You know what she's missing?"

"Wit?"

He laughed. "Aside from that. A nice thick…"

"Don't say it."

"Like you don't like to be fucked as much as I do." He smiled sweetly.

I held up a hand, wrinkling my nose. "Can we change the subject?"

He was quiet for a moment then say. "You couldn't have said no. You know it as well as I do." He looked me in the eyes. "Don't pretend it was a choice for either of you, and if it was, you made the wrong one. He can't change who he is any more than you can change who you are."

"I made the wrong one." I stared back unwavering. "I am bound 'til death."

"I think there is more to it than that. They started with this procedure so there was a true heir, to end the squabbling. It's not a cage, J. This will give you all the freedom you want. And you know you'll be good at it. You've been preparing for it your whole life." He paused, and I knew he truly thought I was better suited for it than he was, but he was so smart. Smarter even than I was, he was just too lazy to put it to work. "Just the other day you gave the Baron the strategy to reroute the trade ships, and your insight about the attack at Caspian galaxy border."

"You know Madden gave me half the information for that." I hated when he denied what he was for me, and the Baron. I was good at strategy, but he was the science oriented one. He was too eager for me to do my duty. Something had changed. There was something I was missing, and I hated it.

"You still put it together." He pushed to his feet. "Come drink this champagne with me." He stepped off my dress and offered me his hands.

I rose to my feet and followed him into my room. I would drink with him, but he was right. I was a master of strategy, and I wasn't using it. I had been slacking, not paying attention. That needed to change. It hit me suddenly as I watched him get up. As he helped me to my feet I lifted his comm from him.

He turned his back to pour us drinks, and I entered in Madden's scan and sent a message from Jacob's comm. I tucked it into my pocket before Jacob turned around offering me one of the drinks.

"Fuck him on the side once you're settled into your position. Hell, take him as a personal slave."

"You really think the Emperor will let his wife have a dick on the side."

"When you put it that way." He threw back his drink. "When you're the one with the power in the relationship it's different I guess."

I nodded watching him drink. "It would work with a trophy husband, never with Phillip."

He looked annoyed I'd seen through him. He was hiding something.

Jacob's comm vibrated in my pocket. No matter who it was from, I'd learn something from the message. I had a feeling about it.

Chapter Forty-Two

Jocelynn

Phillip pushed open the door.

"You look like hell," Phillip said to me as he took a glass Jacob offered him, his eyes never leaving mine.

"The rain. I stayed outside too long."

"I had to drag her inside," Jacob added.

"Are you a great lover of the rain, my lady?" Phillip was almost too smooth at times.

"That I am."

I went to the bar to freshen my drink, racking my brain for an excuse to get away from the pair of them. Then it struck me. Phillip had given me the out himself.

"We are losing her," Phillip hissed.

I acted like I hadn't heard as I filled my glass.

"What do you want me to do about it?" Jacob shot back. I could hear the grit in his voice.

They were in on it together. Whatever it was. I squeezed my comm in my hand. I couldn't will myself to care what they were speaking about.

"I don't know, but nothing will work out without this." Phillip leaned closer to Jacob, and they studied each other for a moment. "I feel like she she's getting further away from me."

Jacob sighed and said something under his breath. But I couldn't make it out. I moved to get closer, getting curious, but the comm vibrated again. My heart stopped in my chest. It had to be him. No one else would message twice in so little time. I moved my hand away to see the letter M flash on the screen. Forgetting about the hushed conversation, I made my hurried apologies about needing to clean up and ducked into my private chambers.

M: **Jocelynn?**

M: **What is this?**

M: **It has to be you. Only you would message me from your brother's comm. What's wrong?**

J: **You replied!**

M: **Why wouldn't I? I've been messaging you for two days. You're the one who cut me off.**

J: **I messaged you. I swear. I got nothing. Someone must have messed with my comm.**

I almost sank to my knees as emotions washed over me.

M: **Who would have done so?**

J: **I don't know.**

J: **I could barely a day without speaking to you.**

J: **I'm so sorry. You have to know that.**

I was rambling. There was too much whirling around in my mind. God, he was so stubborn some times.

J: **Think about it. Why would I be on Jacob's comm?**

M: **I believe you.**

M: **Are you okay?**

J: **Not really. I'm dreading tonight.**

M: **I know.**

I could feel the space and tension between us. It was like Phillip was the wedge driving us apart.

J: **I need to see you…**

M: **What, why?**

J: **Please just meet me.**

My brother and Phillip were still whispering, so I ducked out hurriedly walking toward my room. I had made up my mind. I needed to talk to him.

M: **I can't.**

J: **I have to feel you. I need you here. I…**

I couldn't tell him why. Not yet. And not in a message this way. I could see him typing. It took forever for a message to appear.

M: **Colton will kill me. We have a dive tomorrow.**

It sounded like excuses.

J: **Madden, we need to talk.**

M: **I'm sorry, but I can't.**

J: **Madden...**

M: **I really can't. I could lose my job, or worse.**

I didn't know what to do.

He didn't reply, and I stood to pry myself out of the horrid red dress. I clawed at the back trying to undo the tied corset back, but I couldn't reach no matter how I bent and twisted.

"Need some help?"

I looked over my shoulder at my brother. "Please."

He'd followed me, and I hadn't even heard the door open.

"I had to get out of this dress." I offered him a fake smile. Everyone was against me.

"Where are all your slaves? I wanted to borrow a few for an afternoon stress release before we have to be back tonight." His nimble fingers worked over the back of my dress, and I felt it start to loosen until I could draw a full breath again. "I don't know how they got you into that dress."

He seemed so normal. An eerie silence settled between us. What had happened?

"They stood on my shoulders and pulled the dress tight." I held the front, turning on him. "How do you think they get their muscles?"

"I don't care how they got the muscles, only how they use them." He flashed me a grin. "Now where did they go?"

"I dismissed the lot of them." I slipped behind the screen to change to sweats. Madden had once said he preferred me in them.

"Well that was stupid before you're out of your dress."

"Clearly I hadn't thought it through." I looked in the mirror as I stepped out from behind the dresser. I would leave my hair and fix it when I returned. There was too much paint on my face to try to fix. I would have to start over for the parties tonight. "You'll have to find some other men for your afternoon orgy dreams."

"Why do you torture me?"

When I turned I'd found he'd made himself comfortable on my bed. "Giving up on sex?"

"Laziness is winning out." He yawned. "Watch a film with me, and tell me how long you're going to make Phillip wait for it."

I kept the shock off my face. "You know my feelings about that."

Jacob laughed. "Poor guy."

Before Madden, I would have fucked Phillip and enjoyed it. But now? I shook my head.

"I don't know. Nap if you want, I have to go," I said.

I slipped out of his room to send a message in the hall. I was going to have to do something now.

Chapter Forty-Three

Madden

There was no point in replying to her. I'd be off world soon enough. If I couldn't be with her I was going to do something to change the universe. It was the only way I could reconcile with fate.

"You know wages haven't been paid, couldn't if I wanted to." I didn't look up. He knew I was as much an addict as the rest of the group. I tried to focus on the words. I had been trying all damn day to no avail. "I only have a few bills left from…" I trailed off, pulling what I had left from my pocket, but he knew what I meant.

He gave a low whistle. What I held in my hand was unbelievable to those who'd never been off planet. We stood in the small room I lived in that held everything I owned in it. I had no second thoughts about leaving it all behind. My comm vibrated again.

"What if someone sees me? I thought I was laying low."

"None of them are on my crew, and if they realize it will be too late. Believe me, more is at stake here than credits." He reached into the hip pocket of his coveralls and pulled out a handful of credits. "I'll spot you. Take the rest of your credits to the exchange and get something you can use." His words were loaded. "There is more than just a race out there."

I rubbed a hand over the back of my head and looked into his eyes. I knew what he was getting at. This was a cover so he could meet with his contacts. "I don't want you to throw away your money."

He scoffed. "You forget you're the best rider out there."

I picked up my comm then tossed it back down. I'd gone over and over our old conversations the last few hours. I couldn't bear to think about where she was and who was by her side. I knew I could never be the guy who got to kiss her in the morning, let alone stand by her side.

"I'm all right, but you know how long it's been? Five months at least. You know what slow means."

"This is important." He looked around and picked up my helmet. It had a long gash across the tip and was missing most of the paint. "I've got a couple o' cans of this color I think. If we go now I can grab 'em on the way." He would ignore me and keep pushing until I did what he wanted.

Shit. I grabbed my keys. "I don't even remember what mods I have on her."

"You've been riding her since you got back."

I shrugged. "I haven't opened her up. You might have stripped her for all I know."

"Test it on the way, quib." He flashed me a grin, and I knew from one look what to expect.

I pushed both hands into my hair. I had to do something. I had to get out of my own head. Racing would do the trick. I couldn't stand to be alone in my mind another night knowing what she was going to be doing. Would he touch her? How long could she really put it off if she was promised to him? Getting as close to death as possible was my only reprieve. It always had been. I yanked my helmet out of his grasp shoving it down on his head. I left my communicator on the desk, knowing she wouldn't have time for me today even if she wanted to make up, which I doubted.

"I don't know why I bother with this anymore." I looked over at my comm before closing the door and touched the key to lock it.

He shot me a glance as we climbed onto the bikes, but didn't ask. I tied the green strip of fabric I wore in the mines over my nose and mouth and brought her to life. It was a short ride to base of the mines. I followed after Colton opening it up behind him trying to get the feel of it back. This wasn't the back and forth to work. This was going to be pushing it to the limit.

The machines used antigravity and hovered a few millimeters over the rough road at full speed. The faster you went the more taxed the servos, pushing the limits of the antigravity. Too fast and the wheels caught on sharp turns. It wasn't bad if handled correctly. But around the mines and the giant holes in the ground one mistake wouldn't mean road rash and a few days at a healer's. It would mean a fall to your death kilometers below.

We slowed as we approached the factories and sheds on the outskirts of the mines. They were boarded on the far side by the space port. Colton wove through the buildings stopping at the one used for spare parts. In other words, junk they hoped to repurpose at some point. He set his helmet on his seat and used the large ring of keys to unlock the door to his shed. I followed him inside, and he went to the ancient color tinter and held a hand out for my helmet. He would infuse the pigment into the metal and restrengthen it. More than I'd expected.

I turned to look around at the large building. If I had free rein of a place like this I could build anything I wanted. As the new engineer for Colton's team I would get to work on the crap after my field training.

"Don't get yer hopes up. You need to make useful shit and not tinker."

I glanced over at him, and his back was still to me. "You don't know what I'm looking at."

"I know you're coveting my shit." He chuckled. "I can see you eying the scrap like a starving man looks at a Baron's daughter."

I winced. "Fuck that was a low blow."

"Too soon, eh?"

I held up my middle finger hissing, "Shut it." I ventured deeper into the warehouse. It looked a little like a dump with mountains piled to the ceiling. I glanced over my shoulder and grabbed a few odds and ends as I walked stuffing them into my knee pockets.

"I see you," Colton yelled from around the stacks.

"Then what am I doing?" I stuck two bolts into my nose and stuck my tongue out.

"Making an idiot of yourself like usual."

I dropped the shit back onto the pile. I made a full circle around the junk and saw Colton was still working on the mod and color refinish. I headed outside to smoke spice. I left the shelter of the buildings, feeling the hot wind blowing across the flat of the planet surface. I looked up to the cuts that went deep into the ground, showing the years of mining.

I took the vaporizer from my pocket and put it to my lips as I neared the closest hole. So much had changed. So much was different. But here I was stagnant staring at another hole, wishing I had courage I knew I would never have. The pieces of my mind were scattered across the universe, and I knew I would never be whole again.

I had to get away. I took another drag from the vaporizer filled with spice. I could feel it starting to tingle down to my fingertips. It forced more oxygen into the blood, binding to the hemoglobin. It sped up the synapses in the brain, quickening reaction time as well. Racing would be near impossible without it, just like the mines. Not that either was exactly safe with it.

I started down the long dark street that stretched out as far as the eye could see. It was the remnants of dirt mixed with sand and Ore with a sheer drop off on either side. At first the mines hadn't been deep, as they extended across most of the planet which was rich with Ore, but as the years progressed they had to dig deeper and deeper into the planet's core to collect the material needed to power starships. The unique feature of Harden, which had not been found on any other plant in the known universe thus far, was the Ore. Before its discovery Light2 ships couldn't travel more than the speed of light. Now, centuries later, with the help of the Ore they could travel many times light speed.

I stood at the edge of the pit, looking down at blackness. The distance was so great it was impossible to see the bottom even in full sun. I had spent years racing the hazardous roads between the pits. I'd seen handfuls of men fall over the edge on a wager of nothing more than a handful of coins. A shiver ran up my spin as Colton approached me from behind.

"Not going to jump are you?" He passed me my helmet now repainted green. He'd asked me the same question not too long ago, and it felt like a lifetime.

Jumping wasn't what I was thinking tonight— riding full speed over the edge was. Now, I had eternity to watch her from afar, on the vids, and I didn't know if I could keep doing it.

I laughed in his face. "Hell no, you know me better than that." With my mask firmly in place, I turned away from the pit and stalked toward the bikes sitting where we'd left them when Colton had gone to repaint my helmet. My hands barely shook. I'd gotten my tolerance back a lot faster than I'd expected.

As I climbed on the bike again and lifted the helmet to shove it down over my head Colton rolled his eyes and shouted. "Look at the back idiot."

Under my usual "Madden" he'd added in tiny block letters, "I was in love, but I conquered it".

J.R. GRAY

I looked up at him. "Asshole."

"I'm hoping it comes true."

I scowled.

"I can read it on your face." He turned and spat on the ground. "Stop watching the vids."

"Yeah, you shouldn't know me that well." I growled.

"Don't mope around like a brokenhearted bastard then."

Most men quit racing when they found someone who cared about them enough to protest. It was his subtle reminder I wasn't in that category. I scoffed and rammed the metal down on my head. It was his "fuck you" for leaving, and how I'd been acting the last few days.

"Very funny." But I hadn't conquered anything. I had barely survived. If I could call this surviving at all. I flipped the kill switch into start and grabbed the clutch. "Ready?"

He nodded, and I brought her to a roaring start. She still purred like a kitten. I'd built her by hand, from scratch, even welding the fame together. I tore off toward the narrow stretch of road. My stomach didn't even drop when I kicked up dust as my wheel caught the first bite of the narrow strip. I'd always been afraid of heights, but after years of racing, and then the dreams, I felt numb to it all. Like it had gotten into my head so much, nothing felt real anymore, unless I was with her.

But that would never happen again. Never was a hard word to swallow.

Chapter Forty-Four

Jocelynn

I felt Madden watching. Even from light years away I could feel his eyes on me. But he wouldn't reply. I'd hurt him too much.

I kept dumping my glass into the bush while Phillip got progressively drunker. After the champagne he had broken out spiced Ore malt. The Ore acted as a catalyst to the alcohol, taking it directly to the blood stream, giving you a high along with intoxication. Two shots and he was staggering. I lead him out of the grand ballroom and toward my own quarters. He went willingly. How much men thought with their cocks.

After five shots all he could do was lie on the floor and stare at the images he saw on the painted ceiling. I pretended along with him waiting until he was snoring before I went about my plans. I assumed Jacob was busy with a slave, and I needed a clear head. I wrote him a note and stuck it to his communicator leaving it on my bed. I wouldn't take mine either as it could be traced too easily.

Chapter Forty-Five

Madden

The path we took wove through the mines. We rode under way stations to the long abandoned sites where no one would notice us. I saw the crowd gathered miles out. Poised under one of the abandoned drains that rusted where it sat was a group of men with bikes and a few brave souls who'd ridden in on the backs of the death traps. There was no other way to get out here. Without a bike, or with one, it required nerves of steel.

I'd been racing for years, and I couldn't imagine the leaders of a fringe group keeping up something so dangerous as a cover, but Colton would know better than I would. As I suspected he'd been a part of one of them for years. I really thought it was the reason he hadn't wanted me to leave. In fact, the more I thought about it the more it made sense as to why I got the offer and the help from the Reds in the first place. It occurred to me I should be mad about being romanced and enticed into this decision, but in reality Jocelynn had brought it on, not anyone else.

As we approached the course, we slowed. These were changed and moved frequently, to keep the illegal activity's cover. A large crane towered over the site, and the dark red warning lights illuminated a group of people standing around the base of it. There were boards laid across the upper levels of the crane, which would be used to watch and judge the races. I could see the course was laid out. Tiny blue flares flickered in the dark for thirty kilometers around the tower. It was a tough course, with some hairpin turns from what I could tell. If we were racing with a big pack people would die.

I didn't hesitate pulling up right under the metal structure. I dug around in my pocket and pulled out the hundred credit bill I had shoved in there.

Colton placed his hand over mine after he removed his helmet. I shoved the note back down and waited for him to lead. We walked up to the group, and there were faces I recognized. Most of them were seasoned racers. Colton had to be mistaken.

"Mad?" Tim stepped forward and held out his hand.

I clasped forearms with him and nodded. "Hey."

"It's been a long time." Tim released my arm and looked me over. A few other familiar faces crowded around me, and we exchanged pleasantries.

"Who's got me first?" I asked anxious to get out of my head.

The men around me fell silent.

"Shit, Mad, way to come back with a bang," Tim said. "But do you have coin?"

I pulled the credit bill back out of my pocket, ignoring the look from Colton.

Tim leaned in to look at the money. "You've got to know we ain't got coin to match that. Even combined we'd barely hit you there."

I laughed to myself, but it wasn't funny. This could have only bought me lunch on Trenton, but here it would feed a family for half a moon cycle. I thought about throwing the bill with her father's face on it down the black pit before me, but put it back into my pocket resisting the urge to toss away a fortune.

"Told you." Colton stepped away from the man he'd been standing with. "Who's first? I see the course is already laid out."

"We're going in five men races. First is filled, you two want second, that is if Mad can supply any coins us normal people use." Tim shot me a look.

Colton pulled out a handful of coins. "I'm spotting him tonight. Get the fuck on it so we can have our go."

"Good enough, you two can have second go with me, C, and Zath." Tim turned back around to call out, "Ready," to the men who had been waiting for his cue. When they were staggered at the starting line spray painted across the road directly under the rig Tim started his way up the rusted ladder.

Colton followed as did the rest of the other men lingering around. There was one off in the corner who waited until everyone was up before joining us. He was shorter than anyone there by a head and wore a teal blue helmet, fully covering his face. A hard color to come by on this planet. Could that be Zath? I'd never heard the name, but a third of the faces were unfamiliar to me after near six months of being away.

Tim sounded the air horn, and the bikes took off. My well trained eyes could make them out as they sped off. But it wasn't easy to see who was in the lead. It was why everyone had a different helmet color. Mine had always been green, and no one else had ever tried to claim the shade. It was easy enough to wait out the color you wanted until its original owner retired or took the plunge. The dust cloud was the best gage of progress billowing up toward the starts. The second lap was the real killer. Venturing back through the dust cut visibility, and if you hadn't memorized the course from the first lap you were screwed. This sport not only took timing and coordination but a sharp memory. I already had it committed to mind as I watched the progress. Three laps in, it would be second nature, then four and five was the time to outshine the rest.

The bikes roared under us, coming around for their second lap, and I walked to the outside edge of the tower. I used to always stay toward the middle, but what was the point now?

Colton nudged me as I passed. "Be ready. They are going to want to talk to you."

"Here?"

"I told you it was important." Once at the edge, I peered down. The sand almost seemed to shimmer with the light of the stars. The silver Ore was in everything here, even our bloodstreams.

"Madden, is it?" Teal helmet was standing next to me on the rail.

"It is." I glanced over at him only seeing his eyes.

"Colton tells me you want a job off planet."

"Not just a job. You guys did me a favor, and I'm ready to repay." I didn't bother with the game. They'd been romancing me since Trenton. If they wanted me they would take me.

"I see you're not one for beating around it." He flipped up his visor and met my gaze. He had hard gray eyes, but I didn't flinch.

"I'm not. You people wanted me. Do you still?" I turned my back on the edge and tried to casually lean back against the rail.

"At first I'm told you were being considered because of your mind, and the potential, but now I'm being told by a little bird that you came up with the alternative shipping strategy."

My mouth fell open, and I couldn't contain my shock. "How did you know that?"

As far as I knew she hadn't told anyone. Or maybe she had. My stomach sank. It could have been the professor even. But it was too close to home. They could have even been following me and seen the whole exchange. With as big as the fringe groups had become nothing would surprise me.

"I have my ways. Now what I really want to know is do you think you can devise a way around it?" He stepped forward, his intensity never wavering.

"I'm sure I can. But that's not what I expected."

"We like intelligent minds, but we use all manner of people." He studied me for another moment. "If you're serious I'll give Colton a time and place for tomorrow night. Be there alone, and we'll take care of the rest."

"Okay ... that's it?"

"Say good-bye to him and leave all forms of identity and means of contact behind. You'll become someone else with us."

I swallowed passed the lump in my throat. Even if she wanted to, she would never have a way of finding me again. "Got it."

The racers roared under the crane. The whole conversation had spanned a few minutes. They started around the track for the third lap, and the guy had gone back to mingle with the crowd. Colton joined me but didn't say anything.

The cloud spread as the pack spread out on the first open stretch of land. I knew the move. The red helmet was trying to cut inside just before the sharp turn. Collectively the bystanders held their breaths as his bike skidded into the turn. The contrast between his wheels and the sand blinked out as he cut too close to the blankness of the drop. The group rushed forward everyone trying to get a better look. I could just make out his bike wobbling, and I bit down on my tongue. Red helmet knew it was coming, and he leaned in. His knees skimmed the ground. The wide tires meant for the packed dirt roads covered in sand spun out a few times as he lost traction at the angle. He made it around the corner, but now he was in danger of sending one or more of the other drivers over the edge. He skidded sideways like a wrecking ball toward the other edge.

I couldn't draw in a breath, but I wasn't nervous. I was excited to taste death myself. I had too much to think about. If I showed up tomorrow night, there would be no going back. I wanted to forget everything tonight. The blood in my veins started to run hot. I could taste the dust in the air. It was the first time I'd been able to take my mind off of her for more than ten minutes. I wouldn't allow her back tonight. I wanted to be selfish. I wanted to be out of pain. This was the only way. I could start a new life and get rid of it all. But she had come back to me. Could I leave my comm in my room and exile myself knowing she still wanted me?

They spun around for the fourth lap, and my palms itched. I ran the course in my mind. I pulled back from the edge pacing the structure, restless. One more lap breezed by, and Red helmet's reckless move paid off as he skidded across the finish line to cheers.

I was the first one down, walking at a fast pace to my bike. They'd told me I'd have to forget Colton, but I could do that easily. It was going to be harder to evict her from my mind. I was ready for a taste of freedom. I itched for it. I couldn't wait any longer. It was the only way to get my mind to shut up. I took the inside position, resting my helmet on my handlebars to wait. Tim came over and collected the purse, before handing it off to be held by the judge. I reached down and touched my left leg, rubbing over the old injury there. I sat back and rolled my shoulders, working out the nervous energy.

Colton took the spot next to me looking over with his brow knit. "You never…" he started, but he didn't have to finish. I knew what he meant.

I never took an outside spot. They held the most advantage, but they were also the most dangerous to ride. Inches mattered instead of feet. If someone on the inside fell, the outside person was the one going over.

I half shrugged. "And?"

He pointed a finger into my chest. "Don't you dare."

I licked over my dry and cracked lips. "Dare I?"

His lips pulled back exposing his teeth. "Madden, I will fucking kill you myself."

"Ready," the judge called.

"Not if I do it first."

Chapter Forty-Six

Jocelynn

I would know if my research had paid off any minute now. I paced up and down the port corridor we'd agreed to meet outside. It was a risk continuing my plan not having spoken to him, but what was the worst that would happen? I forced myself to stop the incessant pacing. I would present myself as calm and confident.

I took a deep breath, just in time to see a commanding man step around the corner. The captain finished and walked over to me with a swagger. He had a blaster hanging off a low slung belt across his hips and a roguish look about him, but I had done my research and while he was an honest shipper by day, he was also known for getting illegal substances for fair fees. He'd never been caught, which played highly into what I needed. That meant his men couldn't be bought and that he kept his word. His business meant more to him than earning a few coins by turning in the people he smuggled.

I had the cowl of my black cloak pulled up over my head. The deep shadow it created hid my makeup and hair. I would have to head right for the ball after the meeting so no one suspected me. The cloak hid all but my boots, and I'd taken my brother's while he slept.

He held out his hand, and I took it, making sure to keep my cloak covering the bracelets on my wrists. He held my hand longer than he should have, trying to stare into my eyes.

"Vex," he said in a heavily Sphinxiced accent, a planet which sat on the outermost rim of the known galaxy.

"Jaq," I said masking my accent as best I could.

"Jaq, tell me why you need my services and don't feed me a line. I've been doing this a long time, and I know crap when I hear it."

I had to listen carefully to understand him.

"I need to get off planet."

He paused. "Take a shuttle."

"I don't want to be traced," I countered.

"What you ask isn't an easy thing."

I knew I had him. It was probably a line he fed to everyone to drive the cost up.

"I can pay."

He scoffed. "Young lass like you? I doubt it."

I grabbed a bag of credits from my pocket and held it out to him. "I'll give you this when I board, and another when I depart."

He looked at me with the hard eyes of a man who dealt with a lot of unsavory people for a living. "How do ya know I won't gut ya for it, lass?"

"Because I've looked into your reputation. You're an honest man." I slid the bag back into my pocket. "Dawn, and this is where I need to go." I held out a piece of paper for him. "Get all the necessary permits and landing rights and make up a good story."

"I haven't said I'll do it." He grunted.

"You will." I turned my back and walked off. The rest of the night had to go smoothly or all would be ruined.

Chapter Forty-Seven

Madden

I shoved my helmet down onto my head, tearing my eyes away from my friend. I could see it in his eyes. He knew what was in my mind. He had somehow read me well enough to see through me. It was something only Jocelynn had been able to do before, so either my mask was fading, or maybe Colton paid more attention than he let on.

I look at him hard as we brought our bikes to life. The horn sounded, and I dragged my eyes away, firing forward like a rocket.

The first turn I took recklessly, using my heels to kick out my back tire, spraying those behind me with dust as my front wheel slipped around the corner. I used a tap with my opposite foot to stop myself from spinning out. Hammering my throttle, my wheel caught and shot me past two of the men who had taken the corner carefully. I was using the freshly settled track to my advantage. Riding forward on my handles I kept my weight evenly spread on the bike. Flipping open the turbo switch, I sat poised waiting for the next long stretch. I flew around the second and third turns passing one more man. Now, only Ted and the Gray helmet stood in my way. I knew Gray. He was a formidable opponent having run more than one man over the edge in his time on the field. Teal was nowhere in sight.

Ted had ten years on everyone, the only person still racing who had a wife and kids at home. I think his wife valued the credits he brought home more than his life, but I could have been wrong. She used to come with him to all the races, so maybe her fear of falling over the side had evaporated with the excitement.

I wove around the large tower coming around for my second lap. This one would be a true test of who was paying attention. I flew into the thick cloud of Ore flavored dust, feeling the burn in my eyes instantly. I fought to see, but it was impossible to catch anything more than the occasional light marking the path, and glimpses of the helmets illuminated by the scant light. I punched the turbo on the first long straight, skidding over the smooth ground. The roar of the engines in front of me got closer, and I passed one of them. It wasn't until I got close enough I saw who was still ahead of me. Gray helmet, and I had a feeling one of us wouldn't survive this race.

What was even stranger was I didn't care. Licking over my cracked lips I clenched my jaw, sucking air between my teeth resisting the urge to cough and lose focus. My palms were wet against the rubber handles of my bike, and my vision blurred with the mixture of dust and Ore now coating my eyeballs. I squinted seeing his back wheel. There was a set of zigzagging turns coming up, and I knew I could pass him there.

I cut him on the inside right, then hit it hard left trying to claim the inside for the second turn. We were neck and neck, and our shoulders touched as he held his balance. I could have sworn he looked over at me large teeth showing in a scowl. I glared back, taking the inside again for the right, pulling ahead as I cut the corner close. I whipped around back to the left, getting half a length ahead of him to take the front path for the corner. He didn't let up fighting as I gained the lead on that turn. But he cut quicker over to the right turn again gaining on me. I took it fast trying to get to the final turn in the zigzag before he did. I was half in front of him as we both took the inside track.

I held my breath knowing what was coming. When our bikes connected we were both thrown, and I tumbled through the air. I landed hard, my momentum causing me to skid across the ground toward the far edge. I dug my fingers into the earth trying to stop my forward progress. But it didn't even slow me. I pressed my toes into the ground, using every part of me as drag. The dust had cleared enough to this point that I could see the blackness approaching. I released my hold on the ground curling into a ball accepting my fate.

Chapter Forty-Eight

Jocelynn

I watched the sun rise over the airfield. The star was an eclipsing binary, two stars circling one another. The bright blue giant created most of the heat for this system, while the smaller yellow dwarf intensified or detracted from the light put off, depending on its place in the orbit. But the effect was this green glow that cut through the atmosphere giving the world an almost eerie feeling at this time of day. This far out from the stars, Harden could barely be seen. Gavin 9 was really a moon that orbited a gas giant planet and was never more than fifteen degrees Celsius on the hottest day. I pulled my black cloak closer around me. I saw the ship I had contracted, powering up. The captain walked around the outside checking it. The trip to Harden was an easy one.

I kept my hood shadowing my face as vids of the coronation would be on replay as well as me shaking hand with every delegate in the system and I dreaded to think what more. I had played my role with Phillip well, but he would wake up and not remember most of the evening. I wasn't sorry.

I would be lucky not to be spotted getting out of Harden's main city. But it was a risk I had to take. I knew the Baron would follow the trail, cold or not, so I had to stay a few steps ahead of him, at all times.

"Everything is set. You have the funds?" He said the last as "foons".

I resisted the urge to laugh and offered him the first of the credits. He took it, opening it to inspect them. When he was satisfied I breathed easier.

"The rest before you step foot off my ship, girly."

"When we have landed safely you can have the rest." I picked up my bag, and he made no offer to carry it from me. It was nice to not be made to feel helpless.

He trudged up the gangway, and people moved at his command as he took the bridge of the massive ship. He had an art to the way he set things in motion, more like conducting an orchestra than the cold command I was used to on a ship. His people worked seamlessly, and the ship lifted off as I took my seat. The scale of the ship was about half what I normally flew on, but it had a massive bridge, as well as all of the same facilities. I wouldn't need to venture into a cabin as the trip would only take most of the day at Light2.

The view screen took on the view of the sky, artificially projected and enhanced on the main screen. We broke through the clouds, and I could see the greenish halo of the atmosphere. Captain Vex called for full power as we approached to break through the hold of it. My fingers tightened around the arms of the chair, and my heart started to race. I was really doing this. I was really getting away.

We edged closer to my escape, and soon we would be out of radio communication, out of even the possibility of being stopped and searched before we left. It was one of the reasons I'd picked dawn as a departure time. The customs agents were lazy, either just ending their shift, or just starting. I never thought for a minute he bought my story of legit business, but it covered both our asses. The closer we got to the green shimmer, the more relaxed I became. We would get through the outer defense shield soon, and then there was nothing between me and Madden.

I exhaled a breath I didn't know I was holding when we passed through. Vex called himself for clearance through the shield, and they granted him immediate departure. I squealed to myself. For all my planning and nerves, this had turned out to be a smooth ride. I laid my head back against the rest and closed my eyes. In a moment I would feel the Light2 drive kicking in.

"Captain, we are getting a call from Gavin central command," one of the men in front of the viewing screen said.

"Are we past the shield?" Vex returned, and I could feel his eyes on me.

Ice ran through my heart, spreading out through my veins. They knew I was gone.

Chapter Forty-Nine

Jocelynn

The heat burned my skin through the wrap I wore. I pulled the cowl further up to hide my face. The sun blazed eighteen hours a day here this time of year, and was just setting. The winter palace was in the same system, but the temperature difference was striking. I kept my head down as I walked, trying to avoid any attention my clothes already brought to me. I was dressed far too nice for this part of town, and the fine cloak was the least of my concerns. When Madden had explained where he came from I never pictured this. On all my tours to Harden I'd stayed in the nicer areas where all the metals were polished and the streets were free of sand. Here, everything had a layer of sandy Ore covering it. It was pushed into all the corners against the buildings, and the metals were dull and worn. The dry wind carried a microscopic film coating me as I walked.

Two men watched me as I walked toward where Madden had told me he lived. Their eyes trailed down my black cloak. I was so stupid. The fabric gave me away. I hadn't even thought when I'd had it commissioned. On Trenton it wasn't anything unusual, but here it was a sore thumb.

"Are you crazy?" I was grabbed roughly and pulled down an alleyway.

I tried to pull away. "Let go of me."

The grip was like iron, so I spun aiming my fist at his throat. But he countered my move twisting my arm behind my back and shoving me into a wall. I gasped in pain as my eyes watered.

His hot breath blew down my ear. "Shut up."

I struggled for a breath still fighting against him. "I'll scream. Let me go."

"So you want those guys to find you?" He released me. "Then you deserve what you have coming."

Out of the corner of my eye I caught a glimpse of the two men passing by the mouth of the alley. They peered down. Instinctively, I leaned closer to the man who had grabbed me. He pressed his hands into the wall behind me shielding me with his body, the air between us stagnant and raising the already sweltering heat.

"You need to do better," he said under his breath, barely loud enough for me to hear him.

I didn't allow myself to look over at the men who I could hear still standing in the mouth of the alley. *What would Jacob do?* I swallowed looking up at the young man. Under the caked on sand and dirt he was handsome. Blond hair which looked like it had been cut with a dull knife. It was slicked up with dirt. His hair extended down his face in a patchy beard, also heavily soiled. I closed my eyes, giggling louder than normal like I had too much drink as I squirmed into him.

His lips turned up at the corners as he used both hands to push down my hood exposing my neck. He lowered his face to my neck, rubbing his facial hair over the sensitive skin there. I thrust a hand into his hair yanking hard as I pressed my body into his.

"Looks like you can act." He nipped at my ear, and his large chest rumbled into mine with a laugh.

I tightened my hand in his hair turning into his to speak in a whisper. "Why are we doing this?"

"Don't scream." He said then grabbed me by the ass, picking me up off the ground to wrap my legs around his waist.

I bit back my scream, letting out a tiny squeal. I was sure I felt his arousal against me, but I ignored it.

Footsteps echoed around the entrance of the alley, and it took everything for me not to look in their direction. He pulled back to meet my gaze. His eyes weren't blue, but the distinct silver that only came from working the mines. He held onto me long after the sounds of the men faded into this distance.

"Why are you here?" he said when he finally dropped me.

"I'm here to see someone." I bit back my fear as I righted my cloak.

He scoffed. "I know who you are. I've seen your face, and more than that I know who you're here to see."

I took a step back and bumped into rough stone behind me. The clouds parted spilling light down on both of us.

"Jocelynn."

"How do you know my name?" I glanced around. Who was he?

He grabbed me by the arm, dragging me deeper into the alley. I started to struggle. If he knew who I was, what would he do to get to my father? Panic clutched at my chest making it impossible to draw breath. His fingers tightened on my arm until I knew they would bruise my flesh. I was going to have a hard time explaining the marks in a dress. If I survived this. What was I thinking?

"Stop struggling. Had I wanted to kill you you'd be dead." He wrenched me forward and I stumbled, but he kept me on my feet, weaving through the back streets.

"Who are you?" I kept fighting him. He knew me, but I had no idea who he was. It left a bad taste in my mouth.

When we ducked around a corner I caught him off guard and pulled out of his grasp, taking off. I was quick on my feet, and in the right shoes I got a lead on him. I glanced over my shoulder seeing him gaining on me. His blond hair almost glittered in the moonlight.

"Shit." My breathing came in ragged gasps as I ducked my head to put on a burst of speed.

He slammed me into the wall of a building, keeping his body between me and my escape.

"If you run again I'll knock you out and carry you. Understand me?" He grabbed me by the arm forcing me forward.

We didn't walk long, and my heart was racing when we stopped in front of a black door. I looked over at him. "Where are we going?"

"He's home. You're lucky you caught him." He scoffed. "Go see for yourself. If he isn't dead from being left alone all day."

My blood ran ice cold in my veins. He couldn't be...

"What happened?" I demanded, setting my hands on my hips as I turned on him.

He scoffed. "You happened. He was happy before you."

I turned on him and ran to the door.

Chapter Fifty

Madden

The door creaked open. I needed to oil it. I needed to get up. I had to finish packing, but I didn't have the energy. The creaking of the floor caused my temples to throb. Blood pounded through my ears. I'd only taken a tumble, but my body was stiff.

"You didn't have to come back," I said. My voice didn't sound like my own, it was hollow and soft.

"Madden…" It wasn't a male voice. It wasn't a voice I ever expected to hear again.

"You can't be real." I fought against my pounding headache to further open my eyes.

"What happened to you?"

"He's a fucking idiot; that's what happened to him," Colton said from behind her.

"Just a fall. I'm only bruised."

"At least you're alive." He closed the door then leaned back against it. "Your royal arse here thought it would be a good idea to stroll down the back alleys of Harden in fabric worth a month of food." He said the last distastefully.

"Jocelynn," I groaned. "Why would you come here? You could have been killed."

"She nearly was. I saved her from a couple of blokes that had been following her." Colton crossed the room taking a cloudy glass off one of the shelves before filling it from the faucet and handing it to me.

I took it gratefully drinking down the silver-tinged water. It tasted of the metal. I'd missed it while on Trenton.

"They weren't following me." Jocelynn glared over at him.

275

"Do you realize what would have happened, had I not happened along?" Colton looked her directly in the eyes.

She shook her head. It was cruel, but she had to know. She couldn't stay here without knowing. J was smart, but she had no idea how to function outside her sheltered life. I wondered if her father would know how to survive in the slums of Trenton. I doubted it. My hand shook as I set the glass aside.

They stared each other down.

She muttered, "No." Glaring at me she skimmed her fingers over my visible scrapes.

I took her wrists in my hands and looked into her beautiful eyes I'd missed so much. "I'm fine. Looks worse than it is." I sighed, not sure how much Colton had told her. "Why are you here?"

She frowned. My words were colder than I meant them. "I couldn't take it anymore. I couldn't be with him." Her voice dropped. "You wouldn't meet me."

"I couldn't." I swallowed past the lump in my throat. "I couldn't watch it anymore." I dropped my face to press into her neck. I'd fucked up.

"It was all an act so I could escape. I did what they wanted of me until I could run." She turned into me kissing my temple. "You don't have to watch anymore."

I picked my head up to look her in the eyes. "Yes, I do, if not him someone else. You can't expect to stay here. You'll be traced here in days at the most." Overwhelming sorrow choked off my voice.

She gripped my shirt, and I had to grit my teeth to not wince as her fingers brushed my bruised chest. "You want me to go back?"

"I'm leaving with the Reds. What other choice do you have?"

Her eyes flashed fiery. "I want to go with you. Life's not worth living without you."

"They are working to undermine your family, the Emperor." She wasn't thinking things through.

"I know. I'm sure I can help."

"Jocelynn, why did you come here? What did you really expect?"

"At some point I realized I wasn't me anymore without you."

I let an ounce of hope seep in. "It wouldn't be the life you're used to. No servants, cooling systems, food dispensers…" I brushed my fingers down her cheek.

"I don't care. I don't need it all."

I believed her. Cupping her face, I brought my mouth down on hers and kissed her for the first time in weeks. She tasted better than she had in the matrix. I couldn't get enough. She grabbed my hair pulling me closer. Nothing existed outside of her lips. I wanted to live and die within this moment. I broke the kiss because if I hadn't we'd end up giving Colton more of a show than he wanted.

"Colton, if they want me I'm taking J with me." He looked like he was going to argue. "Don't say a word. I know she's worth ten of me. Make it happen."

"Are you fucking stupid?" Colton never raised his voice, but his tone carried the full weight of his anger.

"She is important to me."

"You know what she is?" Colton growled. "She is death. Walking, talking death. Anyone who touches her will be killed. He will follow her to the ends of the universe to get her back."

"I don't care. This is what she wants, and if anyone has the resources to make it happen they do. Make the fucking call. You have to realize what they have with her on their side." I wasn't going to back down. Not after having her in my arms again.

"If she has ruined everything we've been building…" Colton turned his back. There were things he wasn't telling me.

"I'll ask, but there is no guarantee he'll want a high risk passenger. We don't even know how she got here, and if she was traced." He hissed the last. I knew he didn't understand, and probably never would.

"Colton, please find out?" I kept my temper in check, barely.

He pressed his eyes closed and shook his head. "I'll make a few calls, but this is stupid." He stepped outside closing the door behind him.

"We'll go together." I whispered as I pressed my lips below her ear.

She nodded looking up at me. "I can't be that person. Not after knowing you. My existence would be empty without you."

"Mine as well, look what I was volunteering for." I laid my forehead against hers.

"Where were you going?" She rested her chin on my chest, and I couldn't help but smile. She was here, and when we got away from this hellhole planet we could focus on each other, and the work of the Reds.

"The Reds have a base outside the rim planets where they house their research. I was going to live in the camp there." I took another kiss, not sure if I believed this to be real yet.

"Well it doesn't matter where it is—" She was cut off by Colton storming in. He was ranting, and it took me a few moments to process what he was saying.

"You stupid fucking girl. You think life is easy, and you're just handed everything on a silver platter along with those cuffs you wear. But there are rules and plans in place, in the real fucking world. People live and die for your whims. How fucking stupid do you have to be?"

I detangled myself from Jocelynn and slammed my fist into Colton's jaw.

He staggered back, his hand flying to his mouth. I stalked forward, and he removed his hand from his cheek putting his fists in a defensive position.

"You have no idea what she cost us." Colton turned his head and spat blood on the floor before dodging my second blow and throwing one of his own.

His fist glanced off my shoulder, and although Colton was thinner he knew how to fight better than I did. He ducked again, but it was a fake I realized too late as his fist landed in my gut. Colton didn't hesitate landing a few of his own in the aftermath. We traded blows until we both dropped our arms at the same time. I didn't want to fight him, and I knew he didn't want to fight me.

"What happened, Colton?" I asked rubbing my palm against where Colton had hit me hardest in the jaw.

"They know she's here. The Baron's fleet is en route. Our spies just gave word everything is hushed there, but half the fleet took off from the Gavin base." Colton shot J a look. "You ruined months and months of plans. Plans, you had no idea the plans we had." Anger dripped from him. I could see it in his rugged posture.

"What plans?" I didn't know what to make of his ranting now that we'd both cooled down.

He shook his head. "I have to go, but be ready. Both of you will need to be off planet by the end of the night."

I turned back to her, wrapping my arms tight around her much smaller frame.

"They are coming for me. It's safer if I leave. I can't put you at risk," she whispered.

"No, we have time. Don't say that. We'll escape together." I clung to her, trying to give her some sort of comfort. She'd chosen me over everything, and I wasn't letting her go anywhere. I didn't know what plans she'd ruined by coming here, but by Colton's reaction I could only guess. He was normally so calm and reserved. It scared me, but I couldn't tell her that.

She held onto me tighter and pressed her face into my shirt, muttering, "I'm sorry. I shouldn't have come."

She pushed away from me and turned her back.

"Come back here." I tried to grab her, but she tugged out of my grip.

Chapter Fifty-One

Jocelynn

"I should go. I'm putting you all in danger. I had no idea." Everything Colton said was right. I should have listened to Jacob and Phillip. I was playing adult games with childish whims. "I'm so stupid." It really sank home when Colton said it.

The Baron would kill Madden if he got his hands on him. I needed to let him escape and go back to my prison and hope Phillip forgave me.

"You're not going anywhere. If they want me, they'll figure out a way to get you away safely as well. You're more valuable anyway, if you agree to join their cause." He was rambling, and I wondered if he even knew how much trouble I'd caused. "It's too late to go back. We are all in now, and I will protect you."

I let him wrap his arms around me again. I wanted to talk to Jacob, but I didn't even know if I could trust him. I closed my eyes, willing myself to be calm. There was nothing we could do right now. When Colton came back we would discuss things.

Madden's comm vibrated. I bit my lip as I waited for the word.

"It's for you." He held it out.

Jacob: **You're a fucking idiot.**

Jacob: **Stay where you are. I have a head start on the fleet.**

Jocelynn: **What? How did you know where I went?**

But I knew. I hadn't deleted the messages. I'd led him and Phillip right to me.

Jacob: **I think the entire universe knows where you'd run to. You're shit at this. I'll contact you in a few hours when I'm on the ground. Trust Colton.**

I stared at the comm for a minute before I showed it to Madden.

"There is more going on here than we realize—" His eyes searched mine.

"But what?"

"I have a bad feeling we've been played with," he said tentatively.

"What do you mean?"

"I don't know, but I'm going to kick Colton's arse when he gets back." He sank into a seat on his cot. I took one next to him and folded my legs under me.

He leaned into me, and I looked into his eyes. "I have a bad feeling about all of this. How do Colton and Jacob even know each other?"

"I don't know. He seemed shocked when I told him anything about you."

"I feel like a pawn. I meant to tell you, Phillip and Jacob are in on something." I laid my head on his shoulder.

"We are missing a vital piece of the puzzle." He looked into my eyes.

"We need to have our own plan. I don't trust anyone." My mind reeled. I was grasping at anything that made sense, but nothing did.

"Do you trust me?" he asked.

I nodded.

"Then we will play it by ear, and if either of us wants to bail, we will."

"Okay." There was nothing else to do. I'd walked head first into a trap, and if he died it would be all my fault.

Chapter Fifty-Two

Madden

Colton burst back in the room. "We've got to run. They are closer than we thought. Fuck." He pushed his hands into his hair. I'd known and trusted Colton half my life, and I'd never seen him like this. I couldn't believe the mistrust in all of this. This would be my life from now on. I would be doubting everyone and everything. With lives and more importantly money at stake these people would only look out for their best interest.

"Run? How?" Jocelynn got to her feet.

I grabbed my pack and a spare helmet, tossing it to her. "They can't be."

"She put them all on the move. They will be on the ground any minute. This is your only chance, Madden, and I don't want to see you dead." He turned on his heel and walked out.

I made eye contact with her. "We don't have to follow him."

"Do you trust him?"

"Yes, I think so."

"What's clear is, they've all been keeping us in the dark, I think because they want to use us both." She blew out a breath. "We don't have many options right now, but he'd better explain, and Jacob, too."

"I agree."

She followed me out and climbed on my bike behind me. A rush of feelings hit me, but I had to ignore them all.

"Where are we going?" I asked Colton.

"Towards the mines. We are meeting the rest at the Raven One checkpoint. We need to split up so we aren't tracked." He took off without waiting for a reply.

I looked at J one more time before skidding off in the opposite direction. We raced through the thin roads between the mines, and she never flinched once. She had an iron will. I wasn't sure she was scared of anything. She squeezed me tighter as we neared the site. I smiled to myself until she yelled over the noise.

"We're being followed."

I glanced around, forcing myself to keep the bike steady. Colton was nowhere in sight, but there were at least three others closing in on us. All I could make out were clouds of dust coming our way.

"We're surrounded," I yelled taking another sharp turn cutting the corner too close. They were coming ever closer, boxing us in. I felt her face press in between my shoulder blades.

"Jocelynn." The strain showed in my voice. I took my hand off the throttle, letting the bike slow to a stop, only a kilometer from where Colton told us to meet him. There was nowhere to go.

I couldn't see them yet, but there was a dust cloud in every direction, signaling their impending approach.

"They'll kill you," she choked out.

"They couldn't have found us so fast." I swallowed past the lump in my throat. After all the times I considered death as freedom, it had now become something entirely different. I wanted to stay for her. Even put through hell I had to stay for her.

"Madden." Her hands fisted in my shirt. "I can't stand to watch them kill you."

"You don't have to watch." I pressed my face into the handlebars, and by the time I lifted it, it seemed they had closed the distance by half already. "Shit, J, get off the bike."

She picked her head up and then slid off. "Why?"

I kicked out the stand and then turned to face her. I had no words, so I collected her in my arms and held on.

"Madden, you're scaring me." Her voice hitched, and I gripped her tighter.

"Just let me hold you." I dug my nails into her skin, like somehow it would keep me there longer. But I knew they would drag me away from her.

"I don't want to live in a world without you. I'm sorry I came here."

I squeezed my eyes shut. "Don't say that. Please … you couldn't have known."

"I knew they'd come for me." She pulled out of my arms, and I didn't have the strength to keep her there.

She looked down at her wrists, and I knew what she was thinking. "I wish I could give these damn arm bands to anyone else." Her delicate fingers traced over the metal.

"No, you need to keep them." It hurt to say the words, but I believed it.

"How can you stand here and say that to me?" Her blue gaze showed the pain we both felt.

"Because you don't want the title or power, and that's why you're the only one who can do it. You can change things." I wrung my hands together to get them to stop shaking.

"You think by the time the Baron is through with me that there will be anything left? He fucking knows now."

The bikes approached, the hum of their engines like our death march. The first man pulled off his helmet, and my gut ignited in fiery anger. I wanted to kill the bastard. Phillip pushed his hair out of his eyes and stepped closer.

"Jocelynn, it's good to see you're all right," he called.

Jacob stood next to him, and the third was Colton.

I was going to die at the hands of my best friend out in the mines.

"What the fuck is this, Colton? You better start explaining." I reached for the knife I had.

Jocelynn set her hand on my arm stopping me from tugging it free.

"You can trust them. Fuck, when did you start doubting me?" Colton's voice was back to its deadly calm.

"You both are in on this?" I growled looking between my best friend and Jacob.

Jacob nodded. "We had to be sure."

I lifted a hand and pointed at Colton. "Fuck you." I sucked the hot air into my lungs. Jocelynn stepped closer to me and set her hand on my back, but I shrugged out of her grasp. "Him, I don't fucking know him, and he has to answer to J, but you, Colton, you were my best friend." I shoved both hands into my hair and turned around.

"We didn't know it would turn out like this." Colton stepped forward. "You two were great but…" He looked at Jacob.

"Who blocked my comm?" Jocelynn stomped toward her brother.

"No one." It seemed to click with Jacob. "That's why you used mine. Shit." He shook his head. "That's how they knew. That's how they traced you so fast. They had to have been watching both ours. We were behind from the start."

"Back the fuck off. You two planned this from the beginning." I was losing it. Did I even love her? Or was that part of the plan, too? I turned on Jocelynn stepping forward to get in her face. "Tell me what you knew about this." I saw Jacob take a step closer to me, but I ignored him.

"Jacob, let me." She held up a hand to him.

He reluctantly nodded but stayed near.

"Tell me." I growled, glaring down at her.

"I can't believe you would ask me that. It's both of us they want. Me for who I am, but they want you for your mind. I know as much, but do I assume you played me?"

It was all there. Her eyes told me everything. I was an idiot.

"Fuck." I dropped to my knees, pressing my face into her stomach. "I panicked. I didn't know what to think."

She pushed her fingers into my hair. "I know."

"Mad, this wasn't about you two until you were already together. Believe me. We were only reuniting you for your mind. We didn't know if you'd play ball unless she was involved. You were too hesitant. We would have gotten her out. Her brother and Phil had plans."

"Phillip?" She cut him off. "I still want to know what he has to do with this."

"He has been with them longer than I have. They wanted our house on board, but I wasn't enough." Jacob nodded. "It was why he was he was paying you special attention."

"You mean—" She wrinkled her nose then shrugged it off. "Not that I wanted his advances so it matters not."

"He would have married you regardless, but he did enjoy your company." Jacob dropped his gaze, and I thought there was something he was holding back.

"I am standing right here." Phillip crossed his arms over his chest.

A growl parted my lips, and I stood wrapping an arm around her waist. "No one gets her. I haven't come this far to watch her marry anyone, even you, Phillip."

"Had the match been made, our position would have been stronger. We had plans, and you two threw them all away." Phillip gritted his teeth.

"You could have told me, both of you." She looked between her brother and Phillip. "You led me to believe I'd never see him again."

"We need to get going." Colton gestured for us all to follow him to the supply shed.

"I want answers." Jocelynn pressed as we crowded into the lift. "Why did they help us if they wanted me with Phillip?"

Jacob sighed. "That was my bad. I thought you'd join easier if he brought you in. They were already looking at him, so it worked when you two got together on your own. I thought you were too much like the Baron, too fucking perfect. It wasn't until you were with him I had any idea you'd want to get in on this. So, I let you two build thinking with enough motivation you'd want out."

"So, you wanted me hooked so I would go along with your plans?" There was fire in her eyes, and I didn't blame her.

"You have to admit you went from perfect Baroness in waiting to rebel because of him. The Baron put the doubt in your mind himself sending Madden away. We didn't use you. We just helped it along." Jacob wasn't sorry. I could tell by the look on his face.

Jocelynn looked hurt and betrayed. I didn't blame her. Her own flesh and blood had done this to her. Colton was my best friend, but this was her twin.

"I cannot believe you, Jacob. I deserved the truth."

"This is not the time or place to discuss this," Colton said exchanging looks with Phillip. The lift stopped, and we stepped out into the first level of the mines. Colton went to the supply closet to grab gear, and I took a light pod from him.

"We are trapped down here unless either of you has a better plan, so I think it's the perfect time to discuss it." I return to her side and wrapped an arm around her. She leaned into me in turn.

"We are waiting for the Reds' backup. They should have been here by now." Jacob tapped his communicator and shifted.

"Why are we down here?" Jocelynn asked.

"Because if we are underground we have a better chance of getting close to the port unseen," Jacob shot back. He checked his comm again. "Let's get going."

Colton led the way through the dark passages.

"Why didn't you tell us, at least give us hope the last week?" I was struggling to keep my temper in check.

My words hung in the hot air. No one answered.

"Are you purposeful in avoiding Mad?" Jocelynn asked.

"J, not the time." Jacob locked his gaze with her. "There is more at stake here than you can imagine."

She held her ground. "I don't care."

"Because we didn't know if we could trust either of you. Like he said, she went from perfect to rebel for you, and you, you fuckin' know how you are. You just want a different life. You didn't care which one, that's why you went to Trenton instead of joining us in the first place. Like you said, you knew I was a member, but you abandoned me to change your status." Colton's voice was cold.

My lips twitched up at the corners. "We aren't doing this for either of you, or the Reds."

Colton opened his mouth, but I went on.

"We both support you, but we did this for each other. If we can help great, and obviously J will take her place when the time comes, but we will promise no more. Yes?" I turned to look at her.

"He's right. I will rule when the Baron dies as I am the only one with the cuffs, but I can't do it at Phillip's side."

Colton sighed. "We shouldn't be talking about this. Lincoln will explain better. Can we drop this?"

She nodded. "For now."

Another loud bang echoed through the chamber reminding us all of what was still on the other side.

"Where is the damn backup?" Jacob smacked his comm.

"The signal down here is shit." Colton turned a corner, and we came face to face with the city guard.

"Shit."

Colton turned around and started shoving us back the direction we came. There was shouting behind us. They were close. Colton ran past the group and punched a few keys to open a side door.

"In here." We all scrambled in, and he hit the button to close the door as the echo of our pursuer's boots radiated through the halls. He smashed the panel and then turned. "None of this will matter in about ten minutes when they get a crew down here to cut open that door."

"Since we can't rely on this so called backup, we need a plan." J pulled away from me and walked up to her brother. "Tell me you have more weapons?"

He handed her the duffel he grasped in one hand. She dug through it and pulled out a knife half as long as her arm. She attached it to her belt then knit her brow.

"There are no blasters in here?"

Jacob shook his head.

"Why the hell not?"

I took the bag from her and laughed. "The Ore. It would ignite it all."

Her eyes went wide for a moment, but then she nodded. "That's why they haven't cut the door apart yet."

"Yeah," I confirmed.

She pulled her knife out and checked the blade as I selected one for myself.

"We should go fight. Better than waiting in here like cowards." There was no waver in her voice. Further confirmation she was the leader her people needed. She walked up to the blast door and exhaled. "Get your weapons."

"J, give it time. We have backup coming."

"How long are we going to wait? The longer we wait here the more time they have to get reinforcements," she said.

Jacob pulled his knife and stepped up behind her. Colton, Phillip, and I followed.

"On the count of three," she said.

Chapter Fifty-Three

Jocelynn

I looked back at Madden as I counted. There had been several times over the last few days and months where I thought I would never see his face again, and I knew this was it. He met my eyes licking over his cracked lips.

"Three," I said and turned the handle, but I didn't take my gaze away from him. I mouthed, "I love you" before pulling open the door and charging out.

Knife in hand I expected to cut down at least a few opponents before they realized what was going on. But I ran into a dust cloud. There were bodies around my feet as I skidded to a halt. Jacob hit my back, and we both stumbled. It started to clear, and I could see no one left standing. The others flanked me, weapons raised, but nothing could be seen through the haze.

Boots clicked over the rock surface, but the figure wasn't visible yet. My heart raced as we waited. Three more steps and a man came into view. His face was masked in shadow.

"Looks like we are a little late to the party. Everyone okay?" he called out.

"Lincoln?" Relief showed in Colton's voice.

"Miss me?" An older man stepped into view. He had dark red hair that was tinged with gray at the temples. He looked younger than his hair suggested, but his eyes were old. He wore his pants on his hips with a holster sling at an angle across them. He stepped over bodies like they'd never been alive. Over all he had an heir of ownership that told me one thing: he was important, whoever he was.

Colton scoffed. "Good job, showing up when you're not needed." He resheathed his knife and stepped forward to grip the guy's hand. They pulled each other into a tight embrace.

Madden crossed the space between us setting his hand on my back.

"Madden, we meet again." He passed Colton and extended his hand, which Mad took. "Lincoln."

"You two know each other?" I directed my inquiry at Mad, but Lincoln answered.

"We do." He inclined his head in my direction. "It's a pleasure to finally meet you, m'lady."

"There is no need for all of that." I touched one of the red bands on my wrist absentmindedly. "I am no one but a traitor to the Baron now."

"There you are wrong, lady. Never give up your title, not with us, or anywhere else you may find yourself. You'll need it." He took one of my hands in his and traced over the metal. "This may be one of the most important things we have." His deep blue eyes locked on mine. "Not even the Grand Duke has such a guarantee of inheritance."

Phillip nodded. "Less now that I've blown things with you?"

My mouth fell open, and I thought I knew part of the reason they all wanted us together.

"Captain." A man called from behind Lincoln. He held my hand for a moment longer before turning. "What is it?"

A realization hit me. He was one of the Red Captains. There was no ruler of the Reds, but Jacob had told me "Captain" was reserved for the council of those in charge.

"The area is secure, but we better get them out of here before backup rears its head."

"Aye to that. Let's move out." Lincoln turned back to me catching me off guard. "Walk with me?" He extended his arm, and I detangled from Mad to take it.

The ground shook, and Lincoln had to grab me by the arm to shove me down to the ground. I threw my hands out in time to catch myself right before Lincoln landed over me. The air went out of my lungs in a rush, and another bang echoed off the cavern around us. It felt like the inside of my ears exploded and then everything went quiet. I pressed my hands to my ears squeezing my eyes shut.

The weight was off of me, and I was grabbed by the back of my shirt. I forced my eyes open stumbling forward. A hand was on my lower back, leading me. I assumed it was Lincoln, but I couldn't see through the haze well enough, nor did I have time to look back. Our group was scattered and running around us, but my ears rang, giving me none of their shouted words.

It came back slowly, and I was forced into another right elevator shaft as their voices started to become clear again. I scanned the lift, but he wasn't there.

"Where is Madden?" I knew I was screaming, but I could barely hear myself.

A few people looked at me and shook their heads. I couldn't see Colton either. They started to close the door to the lift. I pushed my way through the mass of bodies, but my arm was grabbed. I turned to look back and found Lincoln shaking his head at me. The lift door slammed, and I turned on him growling.

"We'll get him on the next one. We need to get you to the ship before they cut off our exit by the air."

I balled my hands into fists looking up. I took a steadying breath.

"He better be on the next lift and I want a report about the defense they've lined up in the atmosphere." It

was easier to flip into the leader mindset, as otherwise I'd
be in the corner shaking, and I was an Akillie. That
would never happen.

A smirk curled at his lips as I spoke. He turned to
the man beside him and said, "Make it so."

I stared them both down as he talked into his
comm. My heart pounded in my chest, but I crossed both
arms over it to hide the nerves. The man listened to his
comm for a moment then opened his mouth looking right
at Lincoln. The lift started to rumble taking us toward the
surface. Leaving Madden in danger.

"Not to me, to her." Lincoln told him.

"But…"

Lincoln lifted his lip, and the man nodded turning
to me.

"This planet is only equipped with ground defense
and not a standing fleet, as you know, there has never
been need to defend against an attack from the ground.
We will have more trouble switching phases of flight
outside the atmosphere than breaking away from the
surface of the planet."

I nodded. "All this I know. The Baron's fleet is in
the system. Where are they?"

"They are en route. We estimate two hours before
they arrive."

I looked at Lincoln. "How long before we can lift
off?"

"We have a fueled ship waiting at a gate already,
m'lady." The smirk broadened, like he wanted me to take
charge.

"Do we have a secure route to the dock?"

The lift quickened to its full speed forcing
everyone toward the ground. My stomach jumped to my
throat, but I didn't waver.

Lincoln nodded. "That was the only open space we had to cross. They shouldn't have found us, which means there is a leak."

I set my jaw. "I want to know who it is, and I want to know before we get on that ship."

"Ma'am?" Lincoln asked.

"If Madden has a scratch on him he will have the same inflicted on him tenfold before the interrogation starts."

The men in the lift fell silent at once, and all eyes were on me.

"I told you, boys."

I raised one brow at Lincoln.

"I told them we needed you. There was some doubt you'd be well, you. But I knew it was impossible for an Akillie to be weak."

Now I knew why he wore his smile.

"I also now know why Phillip is smitten."

I inclined my head, but before I could reply the doors of the lift slid open, and I found myself in a docking bay. "Trucks?"

Lincoln cracked a smile. "All full trucks go to the space port."

"Your plan is well executed." I pushed past the men, who were still staring. It was now. If my coronation hadn't pressed it upon me enough, this did. I wouldn't be anyone but the Baron in waiting from this moment forward. I had to act as much as the Baron did.

They followed me out, and we loaded ourselves in the trucks. One of the men pulled a cover all over his clothes, and he looked exactly like a driver. The lift had gone back down into the blackness of the mines, and I couldn't look away from it.

The truck started up, and still I waited. Lincoln paced the dock rubbing a hand over the back of his neck. His comm chirped, and he lifted it to his ear.

"Go ahead." He listened. "Fuck."

I resisted the urge to press my palm into my aching chest. I held my head high and watched Lincoln's every move.

"I need all the engineers back out here to get the lift moving again. They are trying to override it from below," Lincoln yelled.

Panic gripped my throat like a cold, dead hand. A few men jumped from the truck and went to work on the outdated controls. I listened for the rumbling of the car, but there was no sound, only tense silence. Minutes ticked by, and Lincoln kept his comm pressed to his ear.

"Who's our medic?" he asked looking up at the remaining men standing next to me.

A man stepped forward. "I am, sir."

"We have a few injured men who will be coming off this lift. Be quick about it. They all need attention."

I stared at Lincoln, but he wouldn't meet my eyes. It felt like I was stuck in the simulation again. Like I was going to lose Mad over and over until I somehow broke out of this hell. My chest heaved as my heart raced. The groans from the lift finally reached my ears, and I bit my tongue staring at the doors. I wanted him to run from the lift and scoop me up in his arms.

The doors slid back, and I searched every face. I didn't see him. The men poured out, and the medic started checking minor injuries as they ran from the lift. At the very back stood Colton supporting Mad under his arms. His shirt was soaked through, bright red. My voice caught in my throat, and I jumped out of the truck to run to him. I wrapped his other arm around my shoulders and took more weight off his feet.

"J," he hissed, in a hoarse voice.

"You're going to be okay," I said, not believing the words as they left my lips.

"Of course I am." His voice was a whisper, and he started to cough.

As we passed I grabbed the medic by the collar and jerked him around.

"He needs help," I shouted as we laid Mad down in the truck.

The medic looked into my eyes then quickly turned to Mad tearing away his shirt. He had a hole above his heart, right under his collarbone. Blood leaked from the edges of the blackened wound.

"It's hit him in the lung," the medic said pulling out a crude looking tool from his bag.

I grabbed his arm. "What are you doing to him?"

Colton tried to pry my hand off of him. "He knows what he's doing. I can vouch for him."

"I'm going to re-inflate his lung and patch the hole the best I can so he can get to the ship where we can give him blood."

I reluctantly let go. "Go on then."

"This is going to hurt," the medic said to Mad.

Madden nodded gritting his teeth. I took Mad's hand in mine, and he grunted as the medic pressed the tool to the hole in his chest. His back arched, and he gasped for breath. The medic flipped the tool around and pressed it into the hole again sealing it with artificial skin. He hadn't cleaned it or anything, but I knew he didn't have time. There were other men who needed treatment, and the truck was just pulling away.

"Thank you," I said as he moved away. I wrapped my arms around Mad, lightly, as to not cause him anymore pain. "Are you okay?"

"I will be." He tried to sit up, but both Colton and I kept a hand on him.

"Not 'til we have to get on the ship please."

He nodded laying his head back.

I looked over at Colton. "Tell me we won't have to fight our way to the ship."

He looked at me for a long moment, and my stomach dropped. "Let's hope they don't figure out where we're going. We didn't expect them to find us in the mines, and look how that turned out."

"Everyone," Lincoln yelled.

The truck fell silent.

"Give me your comms. We are radio silent until we get to our destination."

I breathed a little easier. I hoped this would prevent the leak from going any further.

Chapter Fifty-Four

Jocelynn

The loading bay was dark, and we seemed to be the only ones in the port this evening. It was after normal times for departure so I didn't think much of it as our small group made our way through the deserted halls. The thundering of boots hammered in my ears. We weren't going for stealth as time was more important. Every few moments I glanced back at Colton and Lincoln half carrying Madden. He kept trying to walk himself, but the pain was written all over his face. Two guards paced behind them, as we fell further and further behind the main group.

"Go with them," Lincoln said as they turned a corner.

I shook my head. He sighed and tried to urge Mad to move faster. The temporary skin covering his wound started to leak again. I wanted to stop, but I didn't ask, knowing at any moment we could find the Baron closing in.

"Where do we go from here?" I asked unable to take the silence or not knowing what was going to happen to Mad and me anymore.

My head had been spinning since the truck. We'd jumped in bed with the Reds knowing so little about them. I still wanted to know what I was being used for, which was exactly what this was. My brother and Phillip were fine, but I wore the red bands to the house of Akillie. I also suspected everyone knew the Emperor would live a lot longer than the Baron would.

"We go to our nearest base," Lincoln answered.

We limped forward in silence for another few minutes.

"You don't expect them to catch us."

Lincoln looked up at me wearing a sly grin. "We have something the Akillie doesn't."

It all clicked. If the Reds had grown to this size under the Emperor and Trenton's nose, they must under Akillie as well. "Time4?"

He nodded. "And that's not even the most of it. They have eight in the works, and at that speed Akillie will have amassed a huge advantage for exploration."

I blew out a breath. "That's why all this now?"

"We had a few years, but your movements spurred us into action."

Madden and I met eyes. He mouthed, "I love you." I returned it and smiled.

"And then what?"

"This is not the time for any of this, J," my brother, who was guarding the rear, added.

"She needs to understand what she's getting herself into. You had years, this, I'm sure, is a bit of a shock to her," Lincoln said.

"So, you are uniting the Akillie, and the Emperor's house, under a rebel flag to persuade more to your cause?"

"She's quick," Colton said.

Jacob chuckled. "Told you both."

"We are, that and a few minor houses."

"What of the Jok?"

"We have none of them. Between the Emperor's army, if Phillip can't win them over, and the Jok, we have our work cut out for us." Lincoln's comm went off, and he moved Mad's weight around so he could bring it to his lips. "Go ahead."

"We are holding off the Baron's forces and our window for escape is closing. What is your ETA?"

"Shit." Lincoln looked around as if trying to pull a magical answer from the surrounding area. "Jacob, take her to the ship."

"Don't any of you dare touch me." I put my hand on the blaster I'd been given on the truck.

Jacob shook his head. "She won't go without him, and she certainly won't aid you after you've forced her to leave him behind."

"Colton and I will stay back and keep him safe." Lincoln had an edge to his voice.

"But I know you're replaceable, there are other faction leaders. He's not." Jacob put both hands on the blasters on his hips.

Lincoln growled. "We need to move or all of us are dying, not just him."

We jogged off and on to the mouth of the hangar. Jacob moved in front of us to scout. The area was silent. Lincoln whispered into his comm.

Seconds ticked by, and Jacob came back shaking his head. "They seem to have fallen back to regroup. This might be our window."

"My crew has taken refuge in the ship."

They all looked at me. My fingers touched the band on the opposite wrist. "Let's go." I looked at the men standing with us. "Jacob, take the lead with me. You." I pointed to the other who held the rear. "Keep your position and provide cover."

"I can walk. Let me, the rest of you need your hands free for guns." Madden was pale, but he was standing on his own.

"Are you sure?"

His nostrils flared.

"Okay, let's go."

We ran out, and the Baron's forces ducked out from behind the opposite hall.

Chapter Fifty-Five

Madden

I growled when she offered to run off. I struggled against those still trying to help me.

"Let me go. You're not letting her take the heat of this."

They held up their hands and backed up. I took my blaster out of my holster. Holding it up I nodded that I was ready to proceed. As soon as Jacob peeked out from behind the corner we took fire. Jocelynn positioned herself. I growled deep in my chest pushing one foot in front of the other to drag her back.

Phillip grabbed my shoulder and squeezed, sending shooting pain down my arm. "Those two are a unique pair. Let them work."

"You're not giving me much choice," I snarled.

Phillip half shrugged in his condescending way. Had I not had a large hole in my chest I would have hit him, not only for holding me back, but for all the times he touched her. They could claim what they wanted, but Phillip had feelings for her. I could see it in his eyes and in the way he watched her.

We both watched her. She picked off the shooters with her brother one by one. It was a sight.

"We are clear," Jacob called over his shoulder offering his hand to J to help her off from where she had lain on her belly shooting.

Lincoln, blaster raised, stalked out into the bay. No one else shot at him. "Get a damn move on. We need to get 'er off the ground now."

Jocelynn took my arm, and I let her help me. We crossed the short space to the ship. I was going to have to fight for her. The battle wasn't over just because I'd won this fight with Phillip. She had power, and even among rebels it was going to be a fight to protect her. She was like a hurricane. She would tear even the strongest walls down, but even if you gripped her with both hands she would slip through your fingers like air. I had to ride a fine line with keeping Phillip away from her and not holding on too tight.

"You'll never be able to go home, Jocelynn."

Jacob turned at the top of the gangplank and looked at her. "Oh, if they catch 'er she'll go home, in iron cuffs I reckon. Won't be pretty."

"Madden, whatever that puts in our path it will be worth it at your side. This is the right thing to do."

I took her hand in mine and kissed her fingers. "Let's go then."

We turned our backs on them and inhaled. I took a step, then another walking up the gangplank of the starship.

Boots pounded on metal, and I felt her warm hand on mine. I laced our fingers together. "Whatever we have to face, it'll be together."

We ducked into the cramped interior, and the entryway was lined with hard faces all staring at us. "Together," I whispered.

Epilogue

Madden

I lived and breathed pain, and not the good kind. I was torn apart from the inside out, and my body didn't want to heal. Bullets had ravaged me. For the first time in my life, I'd fought to stay alive. Sure, I'd been in some tight scrapes, but I'd never cared if I'd lived through them.

The pain became a turning point. I lived on purpose. I wasn't some joke the cosmos played anymore.

"You're awake."

"I am." The words felt like fire leaving my mouth. "Water?"

She already had a cup in hand and pressed the straw between my lips. The water went down a little easier than the words came out.

"We're good?" I asked.

"Well on our way." She pushed her fingers into my hair.

"You came for me. You threw away everything."

"Not everything." She held up her wrist so I could see the band there. "But I couldn't get rid of these if I tried."

"No, I suppose not." I closed my eyes. "It's us against the world now?"

"I like the sound of us."

"Me too," I said.

She stretched out beside me, trying not to touch me, but I wanted it. I wanted to feel her, even if it caused more pain. "Come here."

"I don't want to hurt you."

"Feeling you is being alive. I'm glad I'm alive."

"Even with this shit show we've walked into?" She tentatively got closer, until she was pressed up against my side and her head leading against mine.

"Like I said, us against the world." I opened my eyes again. "What about your brother?"

"I don't know." She looked into my eyes, and there was all love there.

"You haven't talked to him yet."

"No, I've been here. You're more important." She stroked her fingers over my cheek.

"Can't get enough of touching me?"

"I thought I'd never get to again," she said.

"Me too." I exhaled too fast and winced. "Don't write your brother off. He's a good ally to have."

"How can you say that? He tried to keep us apart."

"We are here, and I suspect he had his reasons. Jacob always has a reason. I've learned that much about him." I turned my head and pressed my lips to her temple. "I'm alive and I love you, which he's partly responsible for. We'll figure the rest out together."

"I love you, too."

"Don't avoid him forever."

****

Jocelynn

I stood at the window, watching Harden getting further and further away. I'd only been there a short time, and I was ready to never see the planet again. But probably not as happy as Madden was to see it fading in the distance. I heard the footsteps long before my brother approached me. I knew it was him before he placed his hand on my shoulder.

"Can we talk." It wasn't so much a question as a statement.

I looked over at him. The weight on his shoulders had multiplied overnight. There were bags under his eyes, and I wasn't sure I recognized him anymore.

"I guess."

"Are you ever going to forgive me?" Even his voice was hollow.

"I'm not sure I can." I broke the eye contact opting to stare back into the blackness of space.

"I was trying to do the right thing."

"The right thing would have been to trust me."

He lent out a breath he'd probably been holding for years. "You were—are—the heir to the House Akillie. You lived and breathed it. It was easier to let you believe me the fuck up than for you have to choose between me and what you'd been raised for."

"And when I was wavering? When my heart was being ripped from my chest you let me believe it all."

He opened his mouth to speak, but I cut him off.

"Not only that, you tried to keep me from him."

"It wasn't like that."

I turned on him, standing at my full height. "Then what was it like?"

"You had to go through with the coronation."

I took a slow breath, calming myself instinctively, from the years of training I'd had in dealing with these types of situations. I didn't even realize what I was doing until the words were on my lips. I was still exactly who they'd raised me to be, and it was going to take a lot of soul searching to find myself, and then even more work to break the habits. It wasn't entirely Jacob's fault, but I hated him a little bit for it.

"I should have been free to make my own choices."

"You have always been free to make your own choices, Jocelynn."

"No, you withheld information from me. You treated me like a pawn. It was us against everyone else, at least I thought it was, but you joined a different side and left me to rot." My chest tightened. He was blood. He was the only family I'd ever claimed. "I don't think I'll ever understand."

"I wanted to tell you."

I searched his face, and I thought there was truth there, but I didn't trust myself when it came to reading him anymore. "There is no explanation you could give now."

"I love him."

I froze. The world stopped. "Phillip?"

He nodded.

My mouth went dry, but I forced myself to speak. "I was wondering how he played into all of this."

I'd been too wrapped up in myself to see it. Phillip spending so much time on Trenton. Them whispering together. The scenes flashed before my eyes, and I finally saw the story. I could even see Jacob dabbling on the fringes of the Red Stars and meeting the Emperor to be.

"Does he love you?"

"I hope so." Jacob looked away.

"So, you two came up with the idea for him and me to be together, and then you'd have an excuse to be together." It clicked into place, one by one. The puzzle I'd been looking at for months, suddenly changed by adding one piece.

"Basically."

"Then why did he spend so much time with me? He had me convinced he wanted me…" I wasn't sure what was real anymore.

"If you weren't convinced, do you think the Baron would have been? We couldn't let anyone see through this. It was too dangerous."

"Why didn't you tell me?"

"I was going to tell you everything, but you wouldn't listen. There was just no getting through to you."

"So, you blocked my comm?" It was impossible not to let my anger color every reaction with him.

"I didn't, but I know who probably did to get you through coronation and the engagement with as few problems as possible."

"You risked me losing Madden. He would have been gone." I pressed my eyes closed. The fear of losing him was still to close like an open wound. It festered.

"I didn't know until after he did it. We were trying to do what was best." The conviction showed in his tone. "It was a clear one hand not speaking to the other. They didn't know this had all been arranged. It's a large organization, with so many working parts."

"You don't get to decide what's best for me."

"I see that now. I'm sorry. If anyone understands what love does to the mind you do." He dropped his head, and it hung between his shoulders like a weight.

"Then why let me see him at all? Why share the tech?" I wanted to know everything. I wanted to see the entire picture for myself.

"It wasn't my idea. I didn't know they'd shared it with him until it was too late."

"Why'd they share it with him? If they already had him on the hook?"

"It was decided above my head that who controls him, controls you. Clearly they wanted him on his own merit, but controlling you is a bonus."

I felt sick. Bile rose in my throat. "And I walked right into their arms."

"You both did."

"And you followed?" The realization hit me like a ton of bricks.

"What did you expect me to do? I couldn't sit back and watch them take control of you. I might agree with their cause, but you weren't ever something I planned on handing them."

"And why did Phillip follow?"

"His absence is easier to explain than mine. He has a history of going off the grid, but I assume he followed me for similar reasons as you following Madden to that hellhole of a planet." He stared back at me with my own eyes.

"You don't get to keep things from me."

"I know."

He held out his hand, and when I took it he pulled me into his embrace. "We need each other. The four of us do."

"What now?" I asked.

He tightened the embrace and brought his lips to my ear. "We take control."

The End

www.jrgraybooks.com

EVERNIGHT PUBLISHING ®

www.evernightpublishing.com